tHe
LoON

By

MiChaelbRENt
CoLLingS

DEDICATION

To...

My buds from Paraguay, who provided me with many
of my names...

and to Laura, FTAAE.

PROLOGUE:
PARTING

This is how the man lost his child.

They were together in the park. The sun shone brightly around them, falling lightly down from the sky to kiss them both with soft golden touches. The grass was green, greener than grass had a right to be in the middle of winter, just as the sky was bluer than skies usually were. It was a perfect day, and the man marveled at the sheer beauty of it all.

How could some people say there is no God? he wondered.

The rain had come two days before, and though it was gone – rain rarely stayed long in southern California, when it came at all – it had left behind the sparkling crispness peculiar to rain: a sharpness that hummed with barely restrained electrical energy and heightened one's ability to smell the beautiful odors of nature that usually hid beneath a tough blanket of smog, a rough quilt of hydrocarbons and methane emissions.

The man breathed in deeply, and the air that filled his lungs was reminiscent of the rainy days of his childhood. He could almost feel his mother draping a warm flannel blanket over his shoulders as he walked in from school. He could smell her – Mother always smelled like peppermint and vanilla – and could feel the soft tousle of the fabric as she used it to dry his wet hair after a walk through the rain, whispering softly, "So wet, my baby, where did you go? What did you do, my son?"

He smiled at the thought, and looked at his own son, who waited expectantly some twenty feet away.

So beautiful, my baby, he thought. So lovely, my son.

The boy was five today. He was five, he was beautiful, with a perfect smile of wonderfully crooked baby teeth: a grin that pulled mischievously to one side, as though he were constantly being tugged by pixies who were urging him to run, play, be merry in the Neverland of imagination. His hair was brown. Thick and lustrous, ever windswept in appearance, for the boy was like the wind: never at rest, always on the move, always searching for a place to go next, for something to do. Restless, but not anxious.

No, the man thought, not anxious. He is merely too full of life to stop for even an instant. Like the wind, perhaps if he stopped moving, he would die and that would be the end.

But no chance of that. Even now, when the boy was waiting, his hands were dancing through the air, weaving tiny patterns, conducting silly symphonies of childhood impatience. A touch to his pants, a scratch to his ear, a rub at his cheek. The music his son led was too quiet for the man to hear, but he knew it must be beautiful, for his son was beautiful.

The boy's eyes were blue, like his mother's. They were always moving as well, peering intently into bushes to try and find a lizard, watching the trees for signs of a squirrel, then skipping with a smile across the man's face.

"C'mon, daddy!" shouted the boy, and clapped his hands in excitement. He was five, he was beautiful.

So beautiful, my baby, the man thought again. So lovely, my son. Out loud he laughed, and kicked the soccer ball he held over to his boy. The ball overshot his son slightly, and the child ran after it, small legs pumping with ever-greater speed as he sprinted after the new toy. He laughed, a light merry laugh that warmed the man. The boy was happy, and that was more than enough cause for him to be happy as well.

The mother stood nearby, and the man tore his gaze from his son long enough to look at her for a moment. She stood straight and tall, like a Good Queen from a fairy land. Her hair was black and straight and lustrous. It seemed to pull light in, deep and darker than blackest night. Her skin was as fair as her hair was dark, almost translucent in its purity and perfection. Her lips were thick and full, and always held a cool kiss on one side, and though the whole world could see that the kiss was there, only *he* was allowed to come and steal it from her.

This the man did often, for he knew that kisses, when stolen by the right person, will only grow back stronger and more fair than before. He had stolen such kisses so many times now that the kisses that remained with her were almost too perfect to bear.

The woman saw him looking at her, and smiled. Her smile was cool, like her kisses. It did not warm the man, but rather refreshed him like a draught of ice water on a hot day. His son threw off heat, his wife touched with cool touches, and the man found himself somewhere in the middle: somewhere perfect.

"You going to stare, or help?" said his wife, and laughed her tinkling laugh, a laugh like a merry bell over a doorway in a small bookstore. Come in, said the laugh, come in and make yourself at home and find my treasures, if you wish.

The man laughed as well. He laughed harder than she, for that was his way, to laugh hard and laugh often. God was easily visible, his son was beautiful, and his wife loved him, so he found it hard to contain what happiness he had. And therefore, when he laughed, it all came rushing out of him in a torrent of mirth. Laughing Paul, some of his friends called him, and he did not mind that because it was true.

3

He felt something brush his foot. The ball. His son's new soccer ball, given to him this morning, on a day when he was supposed to be in school. But it was his birthday, so the man had taken him out of his kindergarten class at eleven thirty that morning, and brought him here, to the park.

"C'mon, Daddy!" urged his son again.

The man grinned and laughed once more. "I have to help Mommy."

"Then kick one more, 'kay?"

"'Kay, kiddo."

The man booted the soccer ball, and it flew high, over and beyond the boy's head, bouncing softly over grass that was greener than grass had a right to be, and finally settling near the tiny brook that trickled through the park. The boy hooted and whooped, and ran toward the ball.

The man trotted to his lovely wife. She opened her mouth to speak, but before she could, he stole her kiss. It was short and sweet, the way stolen kisses must be, but as quick as he was, as fast as the kiss, by the time it was over he could see that another kiss had already grown to replace the one she had lost. And sure enough, it was lovelier than the one he had stolen.

He would have stolen yet another kiss, but she held a hand against his chest and said, "Later, Casanova. Help me with the cake."

She put a shiny party hat on his head, a cardboard cone with glitter and tinsel that said "Happy Birthday" against a background of bright balloons. A thin elastic cord snapped around his chin, holding the party favor tight against his hair. The man knew he must look silly, but did not care. He could afford to be silly, for his family loved him that way.

He took the knife his wife had offered, and moved to cut the cake. It was a small, simple cake, just as their family was small and simple. But like the family, the cake was sweet, and it was enough for anyone. The boy had already blown his candles out, before insisting that the man play ball with him *now*, and then leaving chocolate behind without a thought in favor of playing with his daddy.

A bear, the small stuffed guardian that had watched over his son since his first birthday, sat next to the cake. It was the boy's favorite toy. It slumped next to the cake as though exhausted; as though resting from its guard duties.

The man removed the burnt-out candles from the cake, like five steadfast wax soldiers that stood more upright than the Queen's guards at Buckingham Palace, and then sliced the cake in neat, even slices. The last cut went through his son's name.

As he made the incision, the man's neck prickled. The knife cut across his son's name, and an icy chill cut him to the bone. Cool tendrils of fear wrapped themselves around his spine, his hands trembled. Why, he could not say, but the man felt something awful in the wind.

"What is it?" asked his wife.

The man did not answer. He did not know the answer. He only knew that he was suddenly afraid. The day, so bright and crisp only a moment ago, now seemed dark and muffled as by a black cotton sheet. The sun had lost its winter warmth and now hid behind a cloud that had not been in the sky only seconds ago. Gloom descended in the man's heart, and the sky darkened with it.

He realized that the bear was the boy's guardian. It should be with the boy. Without it, the boy was alone. Alone and not safe.

He looked around frantically. It had been less than twenty seconds since he kicked the ball, but he could not see his son near the brook. Where could he be?

The grass was no longer greener than grass had a right to be. It was dark, and the fey sky snatched its brightness and replaced it with a somber tone more appropriate to the season and more frightening to the eye.

The man looked to the sandbox. His boy was not there. The jungle gym stood vacant, a boxy skeleton whose cold bones had been stained to a deep gray by thousands of hands pulling children through its ribcage, gripping its fleshless frame and jumping from rib to rib before sliding down its spine. The teeter totter listed to one side, its wooden plank equally devoid of human touch. The swings drifted slowly back and forth, pushed by the wind or by the phantom touch of ghostly children who wished to play but could not quite find the tangible strength to move the swing to its intended heights. Slowly back and forth, the swings were hypnotic and frightening. But the man pulled his gaze away from their mesmerizing drift.

The man looked to his left, and the tendrils of fear sprouted into full-grown horror. His boy had followed his new ball into the street.

"Sammy!" screamed the man, but the boy did not hear him, or perhaps heard but was too intent upon following his toy to heed the man's call.

The man dropped the knife. It fell to the cake, its tip piercing the spongy softness before the handle also fell down, landing in the perfectly-spread frosting without a sound, but marring the cake with grim hostility. The knife handle lay across the frosting balloons, and its weight had levered up the point of the knife while it was still imbedded in the cake, tearing up a great chunk of the "Happy Birthday" and shredding it beyond repair. The boy's name remained as it had been, with a perfect slice down its center, a single deep incision that the man had made himself.

The man ran to his son, screaming his name. Hundred Pines was not a bustling metropolis, it was a small city near the sea. It was not a heavily congested area, and remained

6

blissfully untouched by the thick traffic jams that congested nearby Los Angeles. There was no car in the street where the boy now ran, but the man knew that something horrible was in the air. Fear powered his legs and his screams.

His boy picked up the ball, and now he apparently heard his father, for he faced the man and waved. He smiled his perfect, crooked-tooth smile, and the man could almost see the fairies pulling at the boy's cheek.

He remembered in that instant that fairies were actually monsters, who would lure children to their deaths in a forest; that fairy tales were horror stories told by parents who wished to frighten their sons and daughters into good behavior. The man knew his life was a fairy tale, and like all fairy tales it had to end in death.

"Son!" he screamed, and his voice came out in burning gasps, choking him even as he yelled. He was one hundred feet away, and there was nothing. His boy was alone, his boy was safe. The grass flattened below his heavy footfalls, bending down moistly with each running step. The man did not know if the grass would rise up again after he passed, such was the force of his speed as he pushed himself to go ever faster.

Horror still draped its vines over him, adding its weight to his own, dragging him down, holding him back.

He was fifty feet away, and there was nothing. His boy was alone, his boy was safe. The sky darkened still further, becoming almost a storm-sky, driving away the light and draping everything in a gray funeral shroud. A chill wind swept along the ground, touching the man's forehead with its icy breath, drying the sweat that had beaded upon his brow. It cooled, but did not invigorate. Rather, it cut him with icy razors, pruning the terror that rode him, making it stronger, pushing him down into the ground. The grass blades flattened beneath him, and did not rise after he passed.

He was thirty feet away, and still there was nothing. His boy was alone, his boy was safe. The child was looking at him with something strange in his eyes, something the man had never seen in them before: fear. And the boy was not moving, he was not moving an inch. He had come to rest, and the man pushed his legs even faster, for his boy was like the summer breeze, and could not safely stay at rest.

"Move, son!" screamed the man. He was twenty feet away, and now there was something. His boy was no longer alone, his son was no longer safe.

A pickup truck came screeching around the bend of the street, oversized wheels screaming with banshee wails as they grasped for traction on a turn taken too fast for safety. The cries of the tires assaulted the man, and time slowed down as he heard the thick gun of the engine. Each turn of the wheels could be clearly discerned by the man in this slow-time where everything moved through the thick syrup that had suddenly drowned the world in its cloying grasp. Only terror sped along at its normal speed, the vines wrapped around the man's neck pulling tighter, choking him with fear.

The man could see each turn of the wheels, each revolution of the tires as the machine hurtled down the street. The truck was a custom job. In bright light it was probably cherry red, bright and cheerful, but in this murky light it looked like blood, dark and arterial. Its tires stood well over three feet high. A lift kit had been installed, jacking the chassis of the truck up even higher. The top of the vehicle was adorned with a roll cage and powerful lights that stood easily ten feet above the ground.

The man's son was not ten feet tall, he was only three feet from toe to crown. He was barely as tall as the tires, and the truck's driver would not be able to see the child.

The man was ten feet away, and his boy was not alone, his son was not safe.

8

He could dimly hear his wife screaming behind him, the cool kisses fled from her lips, the translucent perfection of her brow undoubtedly marred by horror. He was screaming, too, or thought he was. He could not be sure, for the air, so thick and dim, tried to steal his breath as it pushed against him, trying to keep him from his son. The man heard a noise, a high-pitched whine: brakes being engaged, but too late. The fairies had pulled his boy into the street, urging him to follow his little ball. Now they laughed as the truck driver saw, not the boy standing motionless before the truck, but the man hurtling at his vehicle from the side. The brake's screams increased in pitch and intensity as the truck laid down black tracks of molten rubber, darker swaths on the dark concrete behind.

Time continued its awkward dilation, slowing down even further as the man ran through air that felt thick as mud, clawed through an atmosphere suddenly hostile and unyielding to reach his son. Every detail of the boy's shocked face imprinted itself on the man's mind, an overexposed photograph etched into his cerebrum. Each hair, each pore, each feature and aspect of the boy hung before him with preternatural detail.

The man's fingers stretched forth, stiff and unyielding, only inches away from the boy, only inches away from the oncoming truck. Only inches away, and his boy was not alone, his son was not safe.

The man knew he could not grab his child and run; knew there was no time to pick him up and move him to safety. So he didn't try. His hand twisted up, palm to the child, and he shoved forward with all his strength. He felt his son's soft, unyielding form as his hands contacted shoulder and chest. He pushed with every ounce of his power, using his own forward momentum to add force and speed to the movement.

Centimeters away from the still-onrushing truck, he saw his boy's mouth open in a wide "O" of shock and pain, and then the boy's face was turned away as he spun out of the truck's path, as he flew to safety, propelled not by fairy wings but by his own father's own strong hands. The truck was millimeters away, but his boy was safe.

Time returned to normal speed, then, and the man did not have the opportunity to do more than half-twist as the truck struck him. It smashed into his hip, and the man felt his pelvis disintegrate, fragment into a thousand pieces in his body. Then the truck moved forward still more, an unstoppable juggernaut powered by the irresistible laws of physics and momentum, and the man's spine was wracked by the thrust of the chrome bumper, twisted and bent. His body flew up, but the truck was so high that he never got higher than the grill, his head smashing into the decorative logo, his ear scorched by the hot metal.

Then downward again, the man's trunk was propelled forward and down as the truck finally came to a halt behind him. *He* did not stop, however, but continued his trajectory with mind-numbing force, hitting the cool concrete before him, bouncing, flipping over, bouncing again, and then all was black.

And then all was pain. His eyes opened, and the man knew he was in a hospital. He could not move, his body utterly unresponsive, as though frozen in ice, or encased in steel. He could only move his eyes, and the miniscule effort required to use the tiny muscles surrounding those orbs was almost too much for him to bear.

His wife was there. Thank God, he thought, for he knew that no matter what happened, he could bear it with his family's help.

But then he saw something that chilled his heart.

The kiss. That cool, refreshing kiss that waited to be stolen from her lips was gone. It was gone, and in its place was only ice and barrenness. His wife's blue eyes flashed, crackled with electricity.

"You killed my son," she said, and then was gone.

She left, and the man was alone in the room, and the lights in the room were dim, and did not kiss him with golden touches like the sun in the park, and his only sky was a white tile ceiling. The man had lost his child, though he did not know how. He had lost his wife, for her kisses were gone. He was alone, and could not even weep, for his eyes were too tired for tears.

He closed his eyes, and wished for death, and knew that God was dead, and that his wish would not be granted.

Part One: The Calm Before

Dreams brought me to this catacomb
Dank necropolis breathing heavy rot
Through sable soil moldering with age.

Dreams unspeakable - drawn from ancient tomes,
Dark whisperings - brought me here. I wait, caught
Between sleep and madness - in this close cage.

- *...Is Death*

Cold beyond white fields it stands,
Empty, lone, outlined
With grey, landscape winter-bland,
Blind façade unlined
By twisted, dead ivy strands.

- *In the House Beyond the Field*

COLD

Paul Wiseman stared out between the bars on his window, and shivered.

It was cold outside the Crane Institute. Freezing, in fact. Snow draped the ground in a thick blanket that not only stole all warmth from his view, but somehow added yet another layer of frost to his heart.

A storm was coming.

Sammy was gone.

He momentarily saw his boy's beautiful eyes, his son's crooked smile. Then the vision disappeared, as though the snow outside had the ability to not only blind the eyes, but to cloud the mind. Paul believed that was entirely possible, so thick was the white blanket of frozen water.

This part of the world was far from the temperate zones of southern California, and winter here was more than just a date on the calendar. Unlike the "seasons" of Hundred Pines near the Pacific Ocean, the seasons in Dayton County, Montana, were real things, beautiful, ever-changing, potentially deadly. Snow was not something made by machines on a mountain, it was a constant companion from as early as August, and could remain on the ground as late as April or even May. It could soothe the soul with its spare beauty, or could kill the body with its biting touch.

Once, a few days before Paul had come to this place, he had found a deer on the side of the road. It was dead, but no marks, either from gunshots or from impact with a passing car, were visible on its coat. When Paul had put forth his hand

13

to touch the animal, he felt only an unyielding shape, rather than the soft, pliant form of death. The deer had frozen to death, and lay as a block of ice beside the country highway.

The snow was a constant companion, but not necessarily a friend.

Paul sat down on his small chair. The room he spent most of his time in was as small and Spartan as any other cell in this massive penitentiary: only a few items were personal in nature. The rest had been given him upon his entering this institution, and would be taken from him if and when he left.

He did not know when that would be. Some days he longed to walk out of this place. Others days he knew it was the only comfort he had left, to know that at least he belonged somewhere. Those were the dark days, the black days, the days when he felt bitterness rising up within him like a bilious, hideous beast. Those were the days he missed Sammy, and missed the life he had once led.

A picture of his boy sat nearby. A picture from a happier time, the boy clutching at his bear, the bear that had protected him for so many years until a day when it rested for just a moment...and the moment was just a moment too long.

Paul took the picture in trembling hands, and ran his fingers slowly over the glass protecting the photo from the elements. The glass was smudged and smeared, for he often touched it in this manner, as though the frame were a talisman, a magic lamp that could grant wishes if properly rubbed.

It was not, of course, and Paul knew it. Because if it *had* been possessed of such powers, he would long ago have been returned to the company of his son.

He put the frame down and stared out the window. The sky was gray, thick, roiling. Pregnant storm clouds hung low, and he knew it was only a matter of time before the threatened storm began. When it did, life would get very dangerous around this place. It always did during a storm. The inmates of any prison could be goaded into violence by the electricity of a severe storm, but in this place it was worse than that.

The Crane Institute was a prison, but its inmates were far from being run-of-the-mill thugs or robbers. Severe weather of any kind always urged the inhabitants of this singular fortress into worse-than-usual activity levels. And considering that most of them were people the Menendez brothers would have felt uncomfortable around, that was saying a lot.

Still, for Paul the storm and its attendant dangers were of only secondary importance. As much as he dreaded the possible threats to life and limb that were coming, he dreaded the conversation he was about to have still more.

Marsha. He was going to have to call her, he knew. Neither he nor she wanted the call to happen, but both knew it would. He was aware of her deep hatred of him, and his own self-revulsion reared up powerfully whenever he spoke to her. Sometimes, he could almost forget what had happened. His son was gone, but occasionally he could forget that fact as he buried himself in work and study and survival. He could never forget when he was speaking to Marsha, though. She reminded him without speaking of what had happened, of what he had done.

Of the fact that he had killed their son.

Paul hitched in his breath, drawing the cold air of this frigid room deep into his lungs, feeling the chill seep deeply into his bones before he exhaled. His fingers tingled in the cold, but were not – unfortunately – too numb to make the call.

He picked up the telephone that sat on his desk and dialed the number. The dial tone went through immediately, which was something of a surprise and a disappointment:

Paul had been hoping that phone communications would be knocked out by now. It would have been a good excuse. But no, the dial tone was strong and clear. One, two, three, four rings and then Marsha's answering machine picked up.

"Leave . . . a . . . message," said the machine, its sexless tones as perfectly straight and cheerless as his ex-wife's smiles. Marsha never recorded her own messages. Normally the phone message would have bothered Paul, would have made him feel strangely uncomfortable with its lack of humanity. Today, however, the voice was sweet to him. Marsha wasn't home, so the discomfort he felt on this day would not be sharpened even more by her silent remonstrances.

The machine beeped. "Hi, Marsha, it's me," he said. It had been almost five years, but he continued to announce himself that way every time he spoke to her. She would not – could not – ever forget his voice, any more than he would ever forget hers. "It's Sammy's birthday," he continued. "You're probably at the cemetery, but I . . . I just wanted to call and see how you are. It's been awhile."

That last sentence sounded lame, even to his own ears. It had indeed been awhile. Exactly one year, in fact. Since Sammy's last birthday. He strove to think of something that would make up for his feeble speech, but all he could think to say was, "The storm might keep me here for a day or two, but I'll call again when I get back home if I don't hear from you before then."

Paul's mouth hung open for another moment, as though trying to push out a few more words, but nothing came. At last he closed his mouth and then hung up the phone. He missed the cradle, pinching his finger between the receiver and the base. The cold air made the contact more painful, and he cried out slightly, slipping his finger into his mouth and sucking it for a moment before hopping up onto his desk.

He stood and unlatched the large vent on the ceiling. The heating vent was almost two feet across, designed to deliver massive amounts of heat to counteract the Arctic temperatures outside. Currently, however, it was doing nothing, a gawking hole in his ceiling that served no purpose except to provide plenty of comfortable space for rats to breed.

The vent's removal exposed a dark void. Paul knew from experience that the hole led to a large duct which wound throughout the staff compound, making its way gradually to the basement, where a gas heater was supposed to work around the clock to keep everyone from freezing to death.

"Hey," he shouted into dark maw above him. "How about some heat? I'm getting hypothermia!"

He waited a moment, then repeated, "It's too damn cold, I'm freezing! You hear me?"

A moment later, a voice responded to his cries: "Don't get your panties in a knot!"

The voice belonged to Vincent, who was supposed to be in the basement fixing the heater. Apparently that was what he was doing, because the heating ducts carried sound from the basement like Dixie cups and string. Paul thought about asking how long it was going to be before the prison had heat again, but realized that Vincent's repairs would not be hurried along by such needless verbiage. The guard who doubled as a general maintenance technician was operating under the same pressure they all felt: heat would mean the difference between life and death over the next few days.

So Paul stepped down off his desk. He looked at the nameplate that sat on the table: "Dr. Paul Wiseman, chief of staff." Paul almost laughed when he saw that. Such a fancy title, he thought, considering that I'm little more than an inmate myself. Don't want to stay, but can't leave. Chief of staff indeed.

17

He actually did chuckle a bit, but the sound was cheerless. Laughter was not a thing that would come easy on a day like today. The storm was too close, and the past was all-too present.

He looked again at the picture of his son.

"Happy birthday, kiddo," he said. "I love you, you know?"

His son's eyes peered back at him from behind the glass. As always, though, there was no reply to Paul's words. He stared for a long moment at the photo, then turned it face-down next to his overturned nameplate.

He pulled a post-it note from under a pile of papers on his desk. "No reply from Hales, call again," it said.

Paul had never met Jack Hales in person. The actual hiring of guards was not something he was generally involved in, but Paul did have to train them when they arrived, so he knew that Hales was scheduled to start work today. Normally that would be a good thing, but today that was bad news.

The prison was a dangerous, even deadly place. And the level of danger went up exponentially during severe storms, so now would not be a good time to break in new help. Paul had left several messages for the man over the last few days, telling him not to come in until further notice, but had not received any return calls to acknowledge his instructions.

He quickly dialed the new employee's number again. As before, the machine picked up after only two rings. "Hi," said a pleasant young baritone. "This is Jack. Leave a message or I'll kill you."

Paul smiled tightly. "Mr. Hales," he said after the beep, "This is Dr. Wiseman, the chief of staff and head psychiatrist at the Crane Institute. I hope you've gotten my preceding messages, but haven't yet heard back from you. We'll probably lose communications here in the next few hours, so someone from the Institute will call you to reschedule your orientation as soon as the weather permits. Maybe late tomorrow or the next day. I probably won't be able to call again before the white-out hits, so I'll have to assume you've gotten my messages."

As if to reinforce his guess that communications with the outside world would soon be lost, a sudden gust hit his window. The double-paned glass shook and rattled slightly, and when the quivering died down the low ghost-whistle of the wind could still be heard clearly.

A "white-out" was what the prison staff called a storm that knocked power and phone capability. This one coming up looked like it would also probably keep them from having CB capability, either. Cell-phones were also not an option, as apparently Ma Bell had decided a population that averaged one eighth of a person per square mile wasn't enough to make providing coverage cost-effective. The prison was about to be effectively cut off from the rest of the world, and Paul didn't need some new guy coming in and getting himself or anyone else killed.

He continued the message. "So like I say, hopefully you've gotten my messages. Just settle down and enjoy a last day off, and we'll be in contact soon. Bye." Paul hung up the receiver, this time managing not to smash his fingers in the process, and once again looked out the window. The bars were still there, but somehow he felt less safe than he usually did; more exposed. It was the storm, he knew. Hard to feel safe when you were so completely and utterly at the mercy of mother nature. The banshee wind moaned slightly, a deep song of ice and terror.

The storm was coming.

TIO

Rachel de los Santos Taylor lay on the bed and looked up at her husband.

Tommy Taylor was a big man, thick and powerful from years working on construction crews, operating heavy rigs and digging ditches. His wrists were almost thicker than her upper arms, and he could easily wrap one hand around her neck. He had done that often when they were dating, and she had thrilled at the warmth of his touch, and at the time his strength had provided her with a sense of security and protection she had not felt since she was a young child.

Rachel's parents were immigrants. They came to the United States illegally when she was only four years old, leaving their small town in Mexico on foot and gradually traveling to the border and crossing over with her and her brother Jorge in tow. They had eked a bare existence for several years, her father taking whatever jobs he could and her mother doing the same. In Mexico they had been fairly educated people: both were teachers at the local school. In the United States, however, they were little more than animals, forced to do the demeaning work that no employer could convince a white person to do.

Still, neither of them complained, not even on the day when her father broke his back. He was picking oranges in one of the fields outside San Diego, standing on a rickety ladder that had probably been carved out of balsa wood by some miserly ladder-maker in the mid eighteen hundreds.

The ladder snapped beneath him, cracking to pieces under his weight and sending him plummeting to the ground below. He landed on a root, fracturing three vertebrae.

Suddenly the family had even less income, and hospital bills they had no hope of paying. Rachel – only she was not Rachel then, but Raquel – had vivid memories of her mother going to the bathroom, the only semi-private place in the studio apartment where the family stayed. Mother would spend hours in that room, flushing the toilet over and over again in an effort to cover up the sound of her weeping. But of course in that room in the *barrio*, where the walls were so thin that they cracked under the weight of the roaches that crawled on them, mere flushing of a toilet could not hope to hide the devastating sound of a mother's tears.

Soon it looked though the family would have to flee again, but this time they would be running back to Mexico. The bills were coming faster and faster, and finally there was no more money, no job, no hope.

That was why *Tío* had seemed like such a blessing to the family. Miguel was Raquel's uncle, her mother's youngest brother. He was living in Los Angeles, and had made money running a Xeroxing business, servicing lawyers and architects, people who needed massive amounts of documentation copied and processed. Enough money, in fact, that he offered to pay off their hospital bills and move them out to Los Angeles to live with him.

Of course, Raquel's parents accepted his generous offer, and the family moved to the City of Angels to start over yet again. Her father helped Miguel in the office however he could, Mother worked at a fast food establishment, and all was perfect. For a while, at least.

When things changed, it was very gradual. Raquel would be playing with Jorge, and Miguel would come into her room and watch them. It made her feel safe and protected, to have her big strong uncle watching over them – watching over *her* – so very closely. Soon, he came into the room to play, too. And after they were finished playing, he would sweep them into his arms, hold them tight, and whisper that he loved them. "*Les quiero,*" he would say, and kiss them.

One day, Raquel was playing alone. Jorge was at the office with her father, and she was playing with her dolls, dressing them, and gradually became aware that Miguel was watching her.

"Hello, *tío,*" she said.

"*Hola, linda,*" he replied. Hello beautiful.

He sat by her as always, and played with her as she made believe that her dolls were famous movie stars come to spend the day with her. Before long, however, Miguel stopped playing. He stared at her, then said he was tired, and sat back against her bed, the bed he had purchased for her when they moved in.

He pulled her to him, and held her, and said, "*Te quiero,*" as he had always done. But this time, the words left her cold inside. His touch was different, too. His hands and arms were sweaty, and his breath, usually smelling pleasantly of mint and coffee, was foul.

He kissed her then, not on the cheek, but on the lips. "*Te quiero,*" he whispered again. It meant "I love you." Then he said, "*Te amo,*" which also meant "I love you." But it was strange to hear those words. The richly emotive language of Spanish had many different words for love, and the ones he had chosen were generally reserved for lovers, for passionate moments that a girl Raquel's age could not yet really comprehend.

"I love you, my lover," was the feel of his words.

But it wasn't love. He was different now, and from that day forth Raquel noticed him more and more, standing in her doorway, watching her play. His kisses were more frequent, his touches more hesitant and yet somehow more intrusive. The pattern continued until she was eight, and at last he came to her room on a night no one else was home. He came to her, and held her, and then hurt her in a way she had never dreamed possible, proclaiming his love all the while, and then telling her that if she told anyone of what had happened, she would burn forever *en el infierno*, in hell, and her parents and she would be sent back to Mexico, and Jorge sold as a slave to rich Americans.

She told no one. Her father died when she was ten, and she told no one. She turned twelve, and took Holy Communion at the church, and felt the burning shame of impurity before God, but told no one. Finally, when she was sixteen, and had been raped and molested repeatedly for almost a decade, Miguel was killed with her mother in a car crash. She wept, for her mother was gone, but she also laughed on the night of the funeral, for she could sleep at last without fear that he would come to her bed before the night was over.

Soon after that, she petitioned for adult status, got Jorge put under her legal guardianship, and used the money she received as a beneficiary under Miguel's life insurance policy to move them as far as she could from the house that she had suffered in for most of her life. She moved to Montana, for no other reason than that it was far away from Los Angeles. She no longer believed in angels, and so could not live in a city named for them.

She came with Jorge, who went through high school and college and eventually got a job working as a security guard at the Crane Institute, a prison for crazies thirty miles away from the small town of Stonetree, where she lived. She changed her name to Rachel, and vowed she would have a new life, a good life.

She met Tommy, who could wrap his hand around her neck and make her feel safe. She married him, because he was good and kind, and promised to love her forever.

And then one day she came home and found that he had lost his job. He was drunk, and swaying, and his breath stank, and his hands were sweaty as he clumsily tried to take off her clothes, and when she resisted, he hit her.

Both of them were surprised, and his eyes filled with tears. He sank to his knees and begged her forgiveness and promised it would never happen again. But it did. More and more often, and now she looked up at him, looming over her as she lay on the bed, and wondered if this would be the time that he finally killed her.

One of his fingers, short and thick, powerful appendages that were as heavy and hard as hammerheads, pointed at her. He weaved a bit as he prepared to speak, and when he did, it was in that slurred voice that she now knew so well.

"You never, *ever* touch my wallet," he said. His eyes shone dully, like lights covered in Vaseline.

"I'm sorry," Rachel whispered. "So sorry, I didn't mean anything. Just the landlord came and you were asleep and I didn't have the mon -"

Tommy lifted his hand. Rachel cringed as best she could, a small cry escaping her lips. She wanted to stand up to him, to fight back. But every time she tried, she thought she could hear her uncle, standing behind her, whispering, "*Te quiero, te amo,*" and her knees would go weak. She was powerless against men like this, men who would hurt you for their pleasure, who would use you and throw you away at a whim. And so she was powerless against all men. She hated it, but all she could do was cry.

"Shut up," said Tommy. His voice was thick, he was even more drunk than usual, it seemed. Rachel closed her eyes, and would have prayed if she thought it would do any good. But the saints and the virgin were long dead, and God no longer listened to prayers, if ever he had. So instead she tried to think of nothing, of a darkness so perfect and absolute that she could hide in it and never be found.

"What're you lookin' at?" said Tommy.

That made no sense to Rachel, but then she realized who Tommy was talking to. Her eyes snapped open, no longer merely frightened now but panicked as she realized that Becky was watching them from the doorway.

Her daughter was dark of hair and skin, like her mother. She was strong and beautiful, too, with eyes so large and luminous that they engendered instant affection in nearly everyone who met her. She was only eight years old, but her eyes were wise.

Now, however, Rachel could see that her daughter's lovely eyes were clouded with fear as she watched Tommy beating her: as she watched her father hurting her mother.

"You hear me?" said Tommy, his voice growing in volume and raising in pitch. His drunken anger was quickly becoming rage. "What are you lookin' at?"

Becky did not answer, but instead ran out of the room, no doubt trying to get away from the nightmare that she lived in daily.

Just like me, thought Rachel. Becky is just like her mother, living in hell with no one to protect her.

She looked back at Tommy. His nostrils were flaring and his hands tightened into thick fists. He stepped away from Rachel, swiveling to face the doorway their daughter had run through.

"Wh . . . what are you doing?" asked Rachel.

Tommy glanced back at her. He smiled at her, and the smile was almost tender. That frightened Rachel more than

25

anything: he was growing so cruel that he no longer felt guilt at his abuses, merely pleasure and satisfaction.

"Shut your face, woman," he said dreamily. He swayed again, then took a step toward the door.

"Where are you going?" she said.

Tommy continued smiling as he turned back to her. He flipped her over, and she felt his belt smash against her back. She cried out, bit her lip to keep from screaming, and felt blood run across her tongue.

Three hard whips with his belt, and she felt skin ripping off her back. She cried, and the salt of her tears mingled with the salty blood on her lip.

"When I tell you to shut your face, you do it," he said.

She rolled over agonizingly, turning back to face him, her fear at what would come next overcoming the terror she felt at seeing his face. She did not speak, but he chose to answer her earlier question.

"Where am I going?" he said. His smile grew even wider, his eyes grew dreamy, (and she could hear Miguel in her mind, saying, "*Te amo*") as Tommy said, "I'm going to teach our daughter a lesson in manners."

HEATER

Paul walked down the stairs, clanking heavily on the metal plates beneath his feet, and entered the basement. He had taken no particular pains to mask his entry, walking heavily the entire way, but in spite of his lack of stealth, the basement's two other occupants were apparently unaware of him.

Vincent Marcuzzi was laying on the floor, the upper half of his body inside the ventilation shaft that opened into the basement at floor level. Donald Hicks stood nearby, his back to the other guard, tightening a gauge on the huge gas heater that took up nearly one quarter of the basement space.

Before Paul could speak and announce his presence to the two men, Vincent's voice, high and whining, emerged from the shaft where he had ensconced himself. "Mr. Smartypants should try working for a change. That'd warm Wiseman up without us having to be stuck in this hole."

Without turning around, Donald mumbled, "He's working, Vince."

"Right. One day, Don, Mr. Ph.D. is gonna need us for something more important than fixing the heater. And on that day I'm gonna enjoy laughing in his face and then walking out on him."

There was a moment of silence, and then Paul heard a high-pitched shriek and Vincent threw himself backward out of the vent shaft, flopping like a trout on the concrete floor. His contortions would have been funny had not they been so obviously the product of terror. Even so, his coworker obviously found them hysterical, for Donald doubled over in silent laughter.

Donald was a short man, this around the middle, seeming almost as wide as he was tall, with a black mustache that didn't match the auburn tones of his hair. Paul remembered asking him about it once, inquiring whether it was dyed that color. Donald had laughed and said slowly, "My gramps was Irish, go figure," leaving Paul without a solid answer.

That was not an atypical response for Donald, as Paul came to learn. If two words could describe Donald, they would be round and slow. Round of body, slow to speak. Donald spoke so slowly and so little, in fact, that Paul had thought for a time that Donald had a developmental disability, finally dismissing the theory for the simple reason that no one with such a challenge could have remained as long at The Loon as Donald – over a decade; only Hip-Hop and Dr. Crane had been here longer – and survived. Finally, only last year, Paul had discovered something that explained three things about Donald: his almost painfully retiring manner, his slow speech, and his thick black mustache.

While doing a routine check on some old paperwork, Paul had discovered that Donald had been born with both a cleft lip *and* a cleft palate. Either defect alone was not medically strange: just around one in seven hundred people had some degree of cleft lip or cleft palate. But the degree to which the roof of Donald's mouth had been unfinished and deformed had been unusually severe. Whereas most people with the condition had a slight notch in their lips, or the roofs of their mouths had a small gap, Donald had been born with a lip that was split in completely in half, only coming together at his nose. The soft roof of his mouth had also had a fissure that ran its length, a potentially dangerous physical condition that often led to death in less-developed countries.

According to the medical papers that were a part of his personnel file, Donald had had to undergo over a dozen major and minor surgeries: sewing the lips and mouth together properly, skin grafts, even a rhinoplasty to repair the parts of Donald's nose that were affected by the condition. As a result, Donald had not spoken at all until he was six, and only after a decade of speech therapy had he managed to speak well.

With a condition such as his, one that was visible, audible, and – to many people – highly disturbing, Paul imagined that Donald had likely been the brunt of many unkind words at school and perhaps even in his home. Small surprise, then, that he had grown a mustache to cover the scars, and that he was still reticent to speak.

At least Donald *would* speak to him, however. Not so Vincent, who obviously resented Paul for reasons he had never been able to discern. Vincent was in his late twenties, a clean-cut Italian who tried to exude Mob-boss toughness. However, that tough projection ultimately petered out into the false bravado of a coward. Paul didn't like Vincent, and the feeling was mutual. In spades.

Now, however, Vincent's wrath was not focused on Paul, but on Donald, who still laughed his near-silent laugh as Vincent got to his feet and dusted off his uniform.

"Shut up," hissed Vincent. He beat at his trousers, sending clouds of dust into the air. The dust motes hung suspended in the dim light of the basement, then slowly floated downward to the floor. "Goddam rats hibernating in the vents. Scared shit out of me."

Donald slowly stopped laughing, and said the longest sentence Paul had ever heard him utter: "Can't blame 'em, Vince: the air shafts are the warmest place around."

Donald turned back to the heater, chuckling again as he put the wrench back to the valve he had been working on before Vincent began his frantic wormcrawl across the floor. Paul, still unobserved by the two men, saw Vincent open his mouth – no doubt to say something singularly nasty. But instead of speaking, he shocked Paul by screaming semi-hysterically and launching himself physically at Donald. Vincent body-checked the older man, and the two went down in a thrashing pile.

Paul felt himself travel the distance between the two men in an instant. He had semi-consciously expected Vincent to snap at some point, but had *not* expected that he would choose Donald – the only person who seemed to genuinely like the Mafia wannabe – as his object of attack when it happened.

Paul reached down and yanked Vincent upward by the collar of his jacket. He expected to get dragged down into the fight, but Vincent came up without resistance, surprisingly light under Paul's pull.

"Shitforbrains!" yelled Vincent.

"Sorry, sorry, sorry," Donald was mumbling, still laying on the ground with a stunned look on his face.

"Hey!" shouted Paul. Vincent didn't seem to hear him.

"Stupid sonofa –" said Vincent.

"HEY!" Paul cut him off with what was almost a shriek. He felt himself grow enraged. In the back of his mind he knew that thinking about Donald as a child had made him think of Sammy again, of his own son who would have been strong and bright and good and who would never have made fun of a child like Donald. In the *back* of his mind he knew that he was not nearly as angry at Vincent as he was at the universe; at God. But he couldn't grab God, couldn't pull God up by His shirt collar and throttle Him a bit, couldn't shout at His face and see shock in His eyes.

He *could* do those things to Vincent though.

"What the *hell* are you doing, Marcuzzi?" Paul hollered, quietly reveling at the hint of fear he saw in the man's eyes. Paul normally didn't even raise his voice, let alone scream like this. It had to be a surprise to Vincent Marcuzzi that there was someone else at The Loon who could match his vocal ferocity. "You want me to kick your ass out into the snow?"

Vincent blinked, and Paul thought he looked unsure: as though he couldn't comprehend why Paul could possibly be yelling at him.

Just like any other bully, thought Paul. The universe revolves around *you*, Vincent, doesn't it? At least in your head.

Then Paul's own universe tilted as comprehension came into Vincent's eyes and the younger man screamed back at him, "Fine, you jackass! Next time I'll just let dumb Donald blow us up!"

Paul felt his grip loosen of its own accord. "What?" he said.

Vincent pulled his jacket out of Paul's slack fingers with a too-violent jerk. Paul felt one of his fingers twist, and grunted. It felt like Vincent's explosive movement had probably just sprained one of Paul's fingers.

But Paul didn't have a chance to say anything. Vincent glared down at Donald, who was still cringing on the basement floor. Then Vincent murmured, "Idiot," before turning to a large red valve on the side of the heater that Donald had been about to start working on. Marcuzzi turned the valve a quarter turn. "You turn off the gas *before* you work on the pipe, Don," he said in a quietly angry voice.

"Sorry," mumbled Donald, clearly cowed by his friend's anger.

"More sorry if a spark flew down here," answered Vincent. Then the young man turned to Paul. "Or didn't you know that, Mr. Ph.D.?"

"Know *what*?" snapped Paul.

Vincent pointed at the red lever. "I'll say it in Smartypants language so you can understand: gas main. Gas main plus spark on main heater equals ka-boom."

Paul glared back at Vincent for a moment, but his heart was no longer in it. The sudden rage that had gripped him had passed as quickly as it came. Leaving behind only...

(*Grief. Sadness. Pain. Sammy is dead. I killed my son.*)

...a sense of exhaustion. He didn't want to deal with Vincent. Not now. Especially not when the man had just stopped Donald from potentially blowing them all to pieces. Vincent-as-hero was not an image that Paul wanted to contemplate.

Paul turned away from the two men.

"What, leaving so soon?" snapped Vincent. "Why don't you stick around for a while? Maybe you and dumb Donald here can find some new and interesting way to kill everyone. Whaddya say?"

Paul sighed. "Not today, Vincent," he said.

"'Not today' *what*?" retorted the other man. Without waiting for a response, he turned to Donald and pulled the man to his feet. "Get up, Don," he hissed. Then turned back to Paul again, demanding a reply with an impudent, "Well?"

"Just not today," said Paul again.

He walked away from the two men, ignoring Vincent's whisper of "Thanks for the visit, Dr. Smartypants" and Donald's too-quiet-to-hear reply.

The men went back to their work as Paul tramped back up the metal stairs to the main level. Warm air suddenly began blasting out of the nearest vent as he reached the hallway. But Paul didn't feel warmed by it. A chill crept through his bones, as real and as cold as the collected snow outside.

    I killed Sammy.

LATE

Jacky Hales cursed as his tires lost traction for the umpteenth time. The wheel spun beneath his hands and the car lurched sickeningly to one side before he was able to tighten his grip and regain a modicum of control. Not for the first time, he wished he could afford a big four-wheel-drive sport utility vehicle. Maybe a Lincoln Navigator or a Ford Expedition. Instead, however, he was stuck in his 1995 Toyota Corolla, which weighed about seven pounds when wet and provided almost enough traction to stay on the road. Almost.

It wasn't snowing, not yet, but in spite of that fact, snow was all the Jacky could see. The featureless terrain stretched endlessly from horizon to horizon, nothing apparent on this wasteland but single shroud of snow, which coated everything and left all hidden and mysterious.

Jacky checked the tiny clock built into his dash. It said ten twenty a.m.

"Perfect," he muttered to himself. "Wonderful way to make a first impression."

Things had been going from bad to worse over the last few days. He had arrived in Stonetree a few days before to discover that his apartment was without water: the pipes had not been properly blown out in preparation for the winter season. That meant that water had remained in the pipes, and as the temperature had dropped it had frozen and expanded, leading to a system of destroyed water lines throughout the neighborhood.

Then Jacky discovered that one of his suitcases had gotten lost on his flight in. It was a small one, and in the crush and press of getting out of the airport, he hadn't even realized it until he got to his (waterless) apartment. And of course, the bag had been the one to hold his most important possessions: his journal and his scriptures. He had called the airline, and the person on the other end of the line had assured him that everything possible would be done to recover his luggage, but under the polite words, Jacky heard "Get used to loss, kid." He had little hope of ever seeing his journal or his own personalized copy of the word of God ever again.

But he tried to take it all in stride. Even tried to shrug off disappointment when he discovered that the movers had nicked his only semi-expensive piece of furniture, a two-piece hutch that his grandmother had left him when she died. He had had dreams of using it one day as a China cabinet or something like that, perhaps after he got married, assuming he could ever find someone who could stand him enough to marry him.

Now, with the nicks, the hutch probably couldn't serve as a China display, but would no doubt be relegated to a back room somewhere, holding dog-eared paperbacks or old phonebooks on its dilapidated shelves.

The final straw came this morning. It wasn't enough that he hadn't been able to contact his new place of employment. It wasn't enough that he wasn't sure how he should dress on his first day. It wasn't enough that he hadn't had a bath in three days.

No, none of that was enough. So on top of it all he discovered that morning that the reason he hadn't gotten any calls was because his answering machine was erasing messages before he got them. His mother had called from Idaho that very morning, asking how he was and wanting to know why he hadn't called her back. He told her he hadn't gotten any messages on his machine, and after she insisted she had left several, he investigated and found that the device was malfunctioning. It would answer the phone all right, and callers could leave their messages after a beep, but as soon as they hung up the machine deleted them.

That was why he was wearing the Crane Institute uniform that had been sent to him, but also had packed blue jeans and a T-shirt, because he didn't even know what he was supposed to wear to work on his first day. He figured a uniform would probably be provided to him, but didn't have any idea if he was expected to bring anything with him. There was a storm brewing, too, a pretty serious one if you believed the weather reports, and so Jacky had never been able to get through the switchboard to call the prison.

Or rather, to call the Crane Institute. It wasn't, technically, a prison. But as his mother liked to say, "If it looks like a turd and smells like a turd, it's a turd no matter how many idiots call it a rose." And the Crane Institute certainly looked like a prison, to judge from the information packet he had been sent.

As if to confirm his thoughts, he saw something on the horizon: a small gray dot that slowly grew in his field of vision until at last he was able to confirm his suspicions: it was the Crane Institute, and it was most definitely a prison.

FIGHT

Rachel stared in horror at the doorway that Tommy had just gone through.

She smelled *Tío*'s breath.

She might have stayed there forever, in a paralytic state of fear and memory, had she not heard the noise.

Thump. A cry.

Rachel bolted upright and was through the doorway without her feet touching the floor more than once. In the small "living room" in the hovel they called home, she could not help but see everything: her daughter, cowering against the front door, clawing at the lock, trying to get out. Tommy, swinging his belt loosely in his hands, drunken eyes feverish and too-bright, his pants starting to fall down.

Rachel ran, but she was too late.

Tommy reached their daughter. Reached Becky, and in a move far too fast for a drunken man he reached out and slapped her.

But no. Not *slapped*. At the last second Rachel saw her husband's thick hand curl into a tight knot of a fist. Becky was knocked into the wall, the breath whooshing out of her as Tommy's fist hit her square in the chest.

"Don't look at me!" screamed Tommy.

Becky was trying to cry, Rachel could see, but the little girl couldn't draw in even enough breath to do that.

"Don't . . . *look* . . . *at* . . . *me!*" Tommy shrieked once more. Madness crawled over his face like a centipede, one hundred different ugly emotions playing across what had once been handsome, good. Strong.

His hand raised again.

It turned into a fist.

Rachel wasn't sure how what happened next occurred. She only saw the fist, its slow crawl upward, hanging over their daughter – over *Becky!* – like a wrecking ball.

He was going to kill her.

The fist.

Hanging.

Becky – somewhere, she couldn't see her, could only see the fist – screaming and crying.

And then more screaming. And blood. Too much blood.

"What . . . what . . . ?" said Tommy.

He turned to Rachel. To his wife. She felt the knife she had just plunged into his back rip from her fingers, remaining stuck in his body. He tried to pull it out. Couldn't reach it.

Becky was not trying to cry any more. Just looking at her mother with a shattered gaze that was so much worse than crying.

Something broke in Rachel. A thin, brittle veneer of civilization cracked and fell away. "You never touch my daughter!" she shrieked.

If she could have found another knife, she would have stabbed Tommy again. But she had no knife. Indeed, now things were worse than before, as Tommy somehow managed to reach around his thick chest and yank the blade out of his own back.

A gout of blood splashed across the walls and floor.

I'll have to clean that, thought Rachel crazily. He'll kill me if I don't clean that.

Then Tommy rushed her. His large body bore down on her like a jumbo jet, his arms spread wide, the knife in his hand as he collided with her. They went down in a heap, Rachel kicking instinctively as she fell, trying to free herself from the horror that her husband had become.

She was only partially successful, pulling all but one leg free of him. But he grabbed that leg and slashed it with the knife. The cut was long, but superficial. Still, the pain acted like a cleaning agent, clarifying her thoughts and focusing her mind.

This is it, she thought. This is the day he kills me.

She almost succumbed to the idea. It was *Tío* all over again. She was a little girl, helpless. Good for nothing.

Worthless.

Then a small cry jolted out of her near-suicidal self pity.

Becky!

Rachel was not a little girl. The *real* little girl was looking at her with terror, clutching at her hands the way she had done more and more as Tommy had slowly turned from a good man and good father into . . . whatever it was he had become.

Tommy had flipped Rachel over. He was fumbling with his pants with one hand, the other holding the knife loosely, almost as an afterthought.

"Shoulda done this years ago," he mumbled. His breath was fetid.

Tío.

Rachel almost froze again. But she shook herself free of the pain of the now, and the worse pain of the past. She reached behind her blindly, wildly feeling about for anything that might serve to stop her husband.

He was on top of her now.

She felt something. A heavy vase that had been a present from Tommy's mother.

Tommy saw her reaching. "No way, kid," he sneered, and yanked her backward. Then, as though to reassure himself, he repeated, "Shoulda done this years ago."

He reached for Rachel's pants.

Then he stiffened. Blood ran over his face in a sudden torrent, bits of crystal in his hair. She had managed to grab the vase and had crashed it over his head with all her strength: the strength of a lifetime of abuse and horrific pain.

He coughed, a blood bubble popping on his lips, his eyes suddenly somewhere very far away.

"I shoulda . . . I shoulda . . . ," he said, his voice strangled. His head turned, and she saw that part of it was caved in, a convex angle where before it had been a perfect sphere.

"No," said Rachel. She kicked Tommy off her with hysterical strength, her voice quivering with rage, disgust, horror. "*I* shoulda done *that* years ago."

But her words were a lie. Because the rage, the disgust, the horror . . . they were not directed at Tommy. Not even at *Tío*. They were directed at herself.

I deserve this, she thought. I've killed someone, and I will burn forever *en el infierno*.

Murderess, her mind whispered at her. And she had no answer for it.

Her daughter saved her again, though.

"Mommy," said the little girl.

Rachel almost cried. She's safe, she thought. Becky is safe.

"Mommy," said the girl again. "What are we going to do?"

Becky was looking at her father. At her father's body. And Rachel could tell in a glance that her daughter knew exactly what had just happened.

Murderess.

GONE

Ten minutes later Rachel had packed a pair of bags: one for her and a smaller one for Becky. She had thought it would take longer to pack, but was quickly surprised at how little she needed, and how much less she *wanted*. She was not a part of this house. Not now, perhaps not ever. So the things she packed were few.

She buckled Becky into the backseat of their small car, a VW bug that had been broken down and rebuilt so many times that its age was a question of open and loud debate between Tommy and his friends.

Or, at any rate, it *had* been. Tommy would not be debating any more.

"Where are we going?" asked Becky. The girl's voice was small, smaller than her tiny frame demanded. It was as though a shadow spoke from within her: a piece of what she should have been – *could* have been – if only she had been born to a better place.

To a better mother.

Rachel shook off the thought. She glanced behind her. Thick clouds were gathering, a storm that hung over the flatlands beyond the small town like a shroud. They didn't have much time. And even if they had had all the time in the world, it wouldn't have mattered. There was only one place Rachel could go, only one person in the world she still trusted.

"We're going to visit Uncle Jorge," Rachel said to her daughter.

"At his work?"

Rachel nodded.

"That's a bad place," said Becky, her voice even quieter.

Rachel hesitated.   Then nodded again.   "I know, sweetie." She looked at the house that she was about to leave forever. "But it's better than here."

She kissed her daughter on the forehead, then flipped the front car seat forward and climbed in. Started the car. Pulled out of the driveway.

And headed into the storm.

INTERLOPER

Jacky Hales pulled off the highway, noting with satisfaction that he had managed to slide only minimally this time, and turned onto the mile-long path that led to his new place of employ.

The Crane Institute.

Even a mile away, it was an imposing structure, a patch of impenetrable gray hunched in a field of forever white. And the closer Jacky got, the more ponderous and somehow . . . *serious* . . . the place became.

It was a prison. That was clear. A fortress. Gothic, huge. A world apart from a place that was already so desolate that it was almost alien. A high-voltage chain link fence surrounded the entire facility, razor wire wrapped in loose, ugly curls atop the fence.

Jacky could see several vehicles within the fence.

Staff's cars, he thought. He noted that snow was piled up as high as the windows against several, and wondered how long the shifts were at this place.

Just beyond the cars was a thick poured-concrete wall that Jacky guessed was forty feet high if it was an inch. A gate in the chain-link fence sat directly across from a matching gate in the concrete wall, reminding Jacky of nothing so much as a fortress from some King Arthur movie. Except that medieval fortresses didn't usually have a thick steel door built into the concrete. The purpose of the smaller door was clear: quick and secure entrances and exits, closely monitored and easily halted if need be.

Jacky had found out something of the inhabitants of the Crane Institute in the process of getting his job, but even so, he had to wonder looking at this place, just what kind of people the building held.

If they even *are* people, he thought.

He pulled up to the first gate – the one in the chain link fence that marked the outer limits of the Crane Institute. And the last edges of the sanity and safety of the outside world.

A noise sounded. Tinny, whispering, like an alien broadcasting its interstellar message of menace into Jacky's fillings. Jacky looked around for a few seconds in bewilderment before he realized where the sound was coming from. He rolled down the window and faced a closed-circuit camera that was pointing directly at him.

"Sorry?" he said into the speaker below the camera.

"You should be," said the voice, a deep bass that sounded as though its owner liked to chew rocks as a hobby. "Who are you?"

"Uhhh, Jackson Hales. I was supposed to report at ten this morning for primary orientation." He looked at the clock on his dashboard again, closing his eyes as though if he couldn't see the numbers they wouldn't say what they did. "I'm a little late," he said lamely.

Jacky was braced for an angry retort, perhaps even a summary dismissal for his tardiness. But he was not prepared for the next words: "Your *orientation*? Didn't you get Dr. Wiseman's message?"

"Uhhh . . . what message?"

"Dammit. Hold on." The intercom turned off with an audible click, leaving only the whine of the wind and the feel of the first snowfall on Jacky's left arm. He shivered, not sure what to do. Was he fired? Should he just leave? Wait?

"Park next to the other cars," said the intercom voice suddenly. Jacky almost jumped out of his skin as a loud claxon sounded and the chain-link gate started to slide to one side on oiled rollers. "Walk down the path to the steel door in the wall," continued the voice, adding with audible wryness, "I hope you brought a change of underwear."

"Huh?" Jacky felt totally lost. Forget the rabbit hole, he thought. That sucker's been nuked and I'm falling into the center of the earth. "Leave my car out here?"

The voice either misunderstood him or intentionally ignored Jacky's confusion. "It's okay. The cars are on the sheltered side of The Loon, so you won't have to dig yours out when you leave."

"Dig it out?" Jacky began, but the intercom clicked off again. "Hey!" he shouted.

No response.

Sighing, Jacky pulled through the fully-open gate, almost jumping again when another klaxon sounded the instant he was through. The gate slid closed behind him.

Curiouser and curiouser, he thought.

He pulled up next to the other cars parked on the inside of the chain-link fence. Most of them *were* cars, not much more snow-ready than his, though there was one exception: a tricked-out four-by-four that Jacky suspected could probably haul a load of Sherpas up Mount Everest without so much as a single slide.

He got out of his car, the frigid Montana wind cutting through his uniform with impunity. He hurried to the steel door in the side of the concrete wall, breath pluming in front of him like a white razor slicing his way through the arctic environment.

The second before he reached the door, it opened. A woman dressed in a thick parka and holding what looked like some kind of modified rifle stepped out. She had a large pin on her jacket that said "Leann." It was the kind of thing that Jacky would imagine a waitress in a diner would wear. But he suspected that if he made that observation to Leann, she would probably break him in two. She wasn't particularly large, but her face was rough and weathered, the kind of face that bespoke of decades of work and the strength to not only survive, but thrive.

"In," said Leann, beckoning with the rifle.

Jacky entered the door.

Through the looking glass, he thought as he stepped through and left the real world behind.

INSIDE

The door clanged shut behind him, and Jacky was finally in.

And immediately wondered if he hadn't been better off half-marooned in the snow on the trip over.

To his left was a small building, wires running off what looked like some kind of transformer on the top of it.

"Generator," said Leann, though he hadn't asked. "Don't want to lose power in The Loon. Ever."

"Huh," was all Jacky could manage before his gaze was arrested by another sight: the guard tower above the entrance where two figures stood, looking down at Jacky and Leann, rifles like hers covering both of them.

What are they protecting us from? wondered Jacky. But only for a moment, because almost immediately he saw another security guard ("Jeff" said his name tag, and again Jacky had to stifle the urge to ask for some waffles and a refill on his coffee) nervously standing watch over fifteen men in orange jump suits. The men – clearly inmates – were shackled together, hands and arms chained behind them. Most of them were obviously drugged, some of them actually drooling in the frigid air, the spittle sticking to their chins and freezing like repugnant icicles.

Jeff, unlike the tough-as-exceptionally-tough-nails Leann and the two guards on the watchtower, did not hold a rifle. Rather, he held a drawn gun of some kind, pointed directly at one of the inmates. Unlike the others, this inmate did not appear drugged. Rather he looked strangely . . . *normal.* A pleasant-faced man in his forties, he nodded cordially at Jacky, who nodded back automatically.

"Don't, Steiger" said Jeff, gesturing with his strange gun. The kind-faced man just grinned, and continued looking at Jacky in spite of the weapon being pointed at him.

It's a trank, Jacky finally realized. They're all using tranquilizer guns.

Somehow the thought that people would be shot by drug-filled syringes rather than good old-fashioned bullets and ball bearings made Jacky feel about two hundred percent less safe than he had already been feeling.

"Through sight-seeing?" asked Leann, the question almost a bark that snapped Jacky out of his half-stupor of amazement. He nodded. "Good," said Leann, and began trudging through the thick snow to the closest part of the large building that stood like an angry cement troll before them. "C'mon, you're screwing up their play time."

Jacky hurried after her, catching up just as she arrived at another steel door, a carbon copy of the one in the massive outer gate. She buzzed an intercom, and Jacky looked around.

The inmates were still standing in a row under the watchful gaze of Jeff and the two watchtower guards. Beyond them was the generator shack, and then the large building that Jacky now stood before. It was huge, the size of a large inner-city high school. It consisted of two buildings, connected in the middle by a thick, windowless concrete tunnel, like some strange umbilical cord between concrete parent and child. The building that Jacky stood before was the smaller of the two, a two-story building with barred windows on the second floor.

The other, larger building was at least three stories tall. No windows.

It was ominous. An eyeless monster that would eat anything that came close enough to it.

"Wow," Jacky mumbled inadvertently.

"What?" snapped Leann. Her voice was sharp. Not a joker, Jacky decided. Then again, he wondered how many people *could* be jokers and work at a place like this.

"Nothing," he said.

Then the intercom that Leann had pressed buzzed and the same gravelly voice Jacky had heard on the intercom at the chain-link gate said, "Well?"

"Sending him in," said Leann. The door buzzed, and Jacky went in.

DIS-ORIENTATION

The room Jacky stepped into was small, much smaller than he had expected. Just big enough for a monitor station with myriad closed circuit television screens, a line of heavy parkas with "CRANE INSTITUTE" written on their backs in heavy yellow stitching, and two doors behind the monitor station, the other sides of which Jacky could only guess at.

Two men sat at the monitor station. Like everyone else in this place, they wore name plates. One, a baby-faced man with arms that Jacky figured could probably tie telephone poles into pretzel knots, was "Darryl." The other one, a grizzled black man who looked to be in his early fifties, had a tag that said merely "H.H."

The man must have noticed Jacky's look of confusion, because he laughed and said, "Hip-Hop." It was the same voice that had been speaking to Jacky on the intercom. He laughed again, holding out a hand for Jacky to shake. Then, growing almost too-quickly serious, he repeated the words he had already said to Jacky outside: "Didn't you get the message?"

ANGELS

As soon as the door closed behind the newbie, Leann turned and marched back to Jeff, who was still nervously covering the fifteen orange-suited men. And even though only one of them was worth being nervous around, Leann didn't blame Jeff in the least. She looked up at the guard tower before walking to close to the group, assuring herself that two extra rifles were covering the situation before she stepped into the range of any of the deeply disturbed and very deadly men.

As soon as she was next to Jeff, the younger man said, "All right, you know the drill." The inmates looked at each other stupidly, the drugs in their systems acting as a filter that kept them from fully understanding what was going on.

All except for Steiger. Always Steiger. The middle-aged man sighed good-naturedly, then lay face-down in the snow. His action pulled the next man down as well, shackled together as they were, and soon all the men were on their stomachs on the frozen, snowy ground, hands still behind them.

Leann approached slowly. Carefully. Careful was the watchword at the Crane Institute. At The Loon. Careful meant you went home at the end of the shift.

One by one, she unlocked the men's shackles and cuffs.

As always, she saved Steiger for last. He watched her with eyes so gray they were almost silver, the barest trace of a smile playing across his face.

She moved very, *very* slowly when unchaining him. And when he was free, he didn't move. Just continued to look at her. "You look very pretty today," he said. "The new earrings suit you."

Leann didn't answer. Indeed, she wasn't sure she *could* have answered had she wanted to. Then she jumped as Steiger suddenly flipped over, stifling a cry that wanted to explode out of her mouth as the demon in human form moved.

She hadn't made a sound, but Steiger's smile grew larger. He knew how much he scared her, she could tell.

But then, Steiger scared everyone.

Leann stepped away with the chains as the inmates moved around the area, groggily walking about and making the most of their short exercise period.

All except one. Steiger didn't rise. He just smiled at Leann once more, then – at last – freed her from the binding effect of his gaze as he looked up at the darkening sky and started to make snow angels on the white ground.

WELCOME

"As you can see," Hip-Hop said to Jacky, "this here is Darryl. You need any bars bent or grizzly bears punched out, this is the guy to call."

"Pleasure," said the tree-trunk of a man, enveloping Jacky's right hand in his huge paw. But he did it without looking at Jacky, his gaze never wavering from the bank of television monitors that Jacky could see covered dozens of locations both inside and outside of the Crane Institute.

Hip-Hop moved to one of the two doors behind the monitor station – the one on the right. He pulled what looked like a credit card from an inside pocket and swiped it through a card reader on the side of the door, then entered a long code on the ten-digit keypad attached to the reader. A green light blinked, and the door opened.

"Hold down the fort for a sec?" Hip-Hop asked Darryl. The big man nodded, eyes still never straying from the monitors. Jacky had to respect the man's intensity. "Come on," said Hip-Hop, gesturing for Jacky to step through the open door.

Jacky did so, Hip-Hop close behind. As Jacky expected, the door shut quickly and automatically behind them, clicking shut with a sort of finality that made Jacky want to shudder.

Hip-Hop led him down a short hall and then turned into a doorway. Unlike all the others, this door had no keypad, no card reader. Just a simple door that opened into something that looked like any of the million other employee break rooms Jacky had seen in his life: Mr. Coffee, vending machine, cheap plastic seats, cheaper plastic floors. The only thing that distinguished this particular break room was the line of tranquilizer pistols on a rack near the door, and a much-larger-than-average first aid kit that Jacky suspected probably had enough supplies to perform any medical action this side of open heart surgery.

Jacky's thoughts were halted by the sound of Hip-Hop pouring himself a mug of coffee. The black man gestured with his mug, offering Jacky some. Jacky shook his head.

Hip-Hop took a deep drink of the coffee, then grimaced as though he'd just made a serious mistake. Finally, he looked up at Jacky and said, "All right, Newbie, welcome to The Loon."

"The Loon?" Jacky felt confusion once again threatening to overwhelm him. "What's The Loon? And are you the one who's supposed to show me around?"

"Nah," said Hip-Hop, apparently ignoring the first part of Jacky's question. Another painful sip of his coffee, and then he said, "I don't do the tours. That's Wiseman's job."

TOUR

Paul was stapling reports together and trying to concentrate on the show playing on the TV in the corner of his office. It was playing a documentary about Eskimos. Anything to avoid thinking about Sammy.

" . . . enabling the Eskimo to survive, even in the harsh, sub-freezing weather of -"

The picture suddenly flickered, then disappeared completely, obscured by the snowy static of lost reception. Paul whacked the television a few times, but he knew it was hopeless. He'd seen this before: when a white-out was on its way, the first thing to go was always the television.

"Lucky Eskimos," he said to himself, continuing to staple his reports and hoping against hope that he would be able to get through this day without thinking too much about his dead son. "Don't have to live in Montana." Then he shouted as he carelessly slipped his thumb into the stapler before slamming it shut. A blood blister erupted immediately on his thumb and he popped it in his mouth, sucking it and staring at the still-white television as though it was the Eskimos' fault that he had just pinched himself.

"I should move to Hawaii," he said. Then grew immediately silent. It had been a stupid thing to say, a stupid thing to even *think*. He and Marsha had gone to Hawaii on their honeymoon, and had planned to take Sammy when he was old enough.

He's never going to be old enough now.

The phone rang at that instant, the noise jarring him away from his thoughts. He picked it up eagerly, knowing he was hiding from himself in his work, and knowing just as well that he was fine with that.

"Wiseman speaking," he said. Then, a moment later: "You're kidding."

He slammed the phone down on its cradle, grabbed the papers he had been stapling, and bolted out of his office. He stepped into the hall, and quickly stomped over to the stairwell that was one of the most distinctive and – to Paul's eyes – disconcerting features of the staff building. It was a clanky, winding steel staircase that looked like it had been made by a psychotic seven-year old with an Erector set. The stairs dumped out into the downstairs hall, and then continued to the basement. Paul got off on the first floor and hustled past several doors, heading for the staff lounge.

Before he got to the door, Hip-Hop popped his head out and grinned a wide, insincere grin. "Oh, hey, great, you're here." The chief of security motioned with his head. "The newbie's in the lounge."

"Didn't he get my message?" asked Paul. Then, without waiting for an answer, he continued, "Okay, fine. Here." He handed the papers he had been working on to Hip-Hop. "Give these to God for me."

For the first time in quite some time, Paul saw Hip-Hop look visibly disconcerted. That wasn't surprising. The mention of God could do that to people. But Hip-Hop finally nodded and headed down the hall, swiping his card and entering his code to get back into the lobby where Darryl was no doubt watching the goings-on of the Institute with the single-minded intensity that Paul so admired about the huge man.

As soon as Hip-Hop was gone, Paul stepped into the lounge, immediately seeing Jack Hales, dressed in his guard's uniform as though he was actually *supposed to be here.*

Geez, thought Paul. He looks like he's twelve.

"Jack Hales?" said Paul, even though he knew the answer.

"Jacky," said the other man, sticking out his hand.

Paul took it. Good handshake, he thought. "Dr. Paul Wiseman," he said. "I'm -"

"Chief of staff, right?" finished Jacky for him.

"You got it. Didn't you get my message?"

Paul saw a flicker of irritation pass over Jacky's eyes, but the man quickly masked it. "What message?" said the new guard. "Everyone keeps asking that, and I don't have the foggiest idea what anyone's saying, and no one seems real eager to explain it to me, either."

Paul pursed his lips. "There's a big storm coming in," he said to Jacky. "It's expected to snow over all the roads around here. That's why we're so minimally staffed right now. Anyone here is here for the next day or two, I'm afraid."

"You mean -" began Jacky.

Paul nodded, silencing him. "'Fraid so. The storm should blow over by tomorrow afternoon, but I sent you a message – several, actually – asking you to come in after the storm broke."

Jacky's expression fell into what Paul thought looked like that of an embarrassed five-year-old. "Oh," said Jacky. Paul half-expected him to put his hands in his pockets and start rubbing his toe on the ground. "My machine's been on the fritz." He paused for a moment, clearly trying to think of something to say that would make him sound less incompetent, finally settling on a simple, "Sorry."

"Yeah, me too," said Paul. He sighed, putting his hands behind his head as though stretching would turn this situation into anything other than a hassle-at-best-nightmare-at-worst sort of thing. Finally he blew out his cheeks and said, "Well, might as well make the best of it while you're here. We can assign you a bunk in the sleeping quarters tonight."

Paul looked at his watch. "I have half an hour before I start rounds. Time enough for the Grand Tour."

He stepped to the door to the hall, then stopped and turned back to Jacky. "You meet God yet?"

"Who?" said Jacky, his face growing confused.

Paul almost laughed in relief. "Good," he said, and went out the door.

GOD

Dr. Whitman Crane knew that the others called him God behind his back. And didn't mind one bit. If anything, he felt that God should be rather pleased to be compared to someone like Whitman Crane.

Crane turned in his seat to look at the mirror behind his desk. Long, patrician features accentuated laser-blue eyes and a gaze that could cook a filet mignon. Just the way Crane pictured God actually looking. But not the pansy God of the New Testament. No, Crane was the spitting image of the God of the Old Testament. The one who had destroyed the Pharaoh's armies without a second thought, the God who had conjured armies of angels to strike down his enemies.

The God who created life.

Crane smiled at the thought, as he always did.

He turned to survey his domain. His office took up over one-quarter of the floor space on the first floor of the staff building. Research papers and scientific journals were stacked neatly in wall sconces, packed tightly among the many diplomas and awards Crane had received in his illustrious career.

And I'm just getting started, he thought.

A radio blared in the corner. Normally, Crane disdained listening to such things. He preferred to get his news from the internet. But with the storm coming, the internet connections had been lost some hours ago. The radio was going, too, the voice crackly and at times indistinct.

" . . . the big one is still moving toward Cherry County. Residents are advised to stay indoors, as temperatures are expected with wind-chill to drop to eighty-below tonight . . . ."

Crane smiled. He didn't like the cold, particularly. But he did like the isolation it brought.

PROTECTION

"Mommy, are we gonna get caught in the storm?" asked Becky.

Rachel had no real answer. Not one that she could back up with any hard evidence. Finally she settled on the best alternative to a lie: "Better the storm than your father."

Then she added, "*Dios not protegerá.*"

God will protect us.

She hoped it was true.

PREPARATIONS

Crane turned away from the mirror where he had been examining his face once again when the knock sounded at the door. He turned irritably toward the door, which led out to the "lobby," as the staff sardonically called the monitoring center which was the eyes of the Institute.

"In," Crane snapped.

Hip-Hop entered, setting a sheaf of papers on Crane's desk, and without preamble said, "Wiseman sent these for you."

Crane stifled the urge to fire the man. It wasn't bad enough that he insisted on being called Hip-Hop, as though Nowhere, Montana, was the black recording capital of the world. But he acted as though he were . . . *important*.

Crane would disavow him of that notion soon enough. For now, though, he needed the man. In fact . . .

"How is everything proceeding outside? With Steiger?" Crane's lips curled inadvertently at the last word. Of all the inmates that had come through the Crane Institute over the years, Steiger was the one who most disconcerted, even – Crane had to admit it – frightened him.

"Nothing yet," Hip-Hop was saying. "But soon, I'm sure."

"He has a code card."

"Yes, sir," said Hip-Hop, and Crane was pleased to see the man look uncomfortable at the thought. Which was fine by Crane. Not merely because it validated his own fears of the lunatic, but because it made him happy to see others tremble. Best if they trembled at Crane himself, but still . . . any port in a storm, as the saying went.

Hip-Hop apparently took Crane's silence as a dismissal, for he turned to go.

"Lock the door on your way out. And hang a sign or something," said Crane.

Hip-Hop turned. "Sir?" he asked.

"I don't wish to be disturbed. For any reason."

"What about when -"

"For *any* reason."

"Yes, sir."

Hip-Hop waited for a moment, and Crane could see that there was something else. "Yes?" he almost barked. He was anxious to see Hip-Hop go. So he could go and *play* with his current toy.

"What about the new employee?" asked Hip-Hop.

That surprised Crane. "He's *here*?" he asked. He knew that Wiseman – a do-gooder and sometimes a royal pain, but someone who was very detail-oriented – had been sending the new man messages for days, warning him to stay away until after the storm.

"Yes, sir," said Hip-Hop. "Do you want to meet him?"

"Later," said Crane. He waved Hip-Hop away, turning back to his mirror. "Don't forget the sign," said Crane as the man left.

As soon as the door clicked shut, and Crane heard the hum of the electromagnetic locks that were standard throughout the Institute engaging, he stood from his chair. Waiting for a moment to make sure that Hip-Hop would not return with some item he had forgotten to mention – the man's mind could be like a sieve on occasion – Crane went to another corner of the room. There was a refrigerator there, as well as a bed and a television. Crane didn't like to leave his office unless he had to. Or unless he was going – as he was now – to his other office. The more electrifying – the more *world-changing* – one.

There were flashlights placed in a semi-circle around his bed. He knew that Hip-Hop and Wiseman – the only two men who regularly intruded on him here – had looked askance at the dozen or so high-powered LED flashlights on more than one occasion. But then, neither of them knew what Crane did.

The scientist picked one of the lights. He checked it to make sure it was in good working order – force of habit that he had developed over the last several years of staying alive – and then went to the refrigerator. He pulled it away from the wall. It was on rollers, so slid fairly easily back. Not far, just enough for Crane to reach back and slip his hand onto a panel on the wall.

He pressed it.

The panel slid back with an almost inaudible sigh, exposing a dark stairwell.

Crane flicked on his light.

He squeezed behind the refrigerator, taking a few steps downward before reaching out and pulling the appliance back into position.

The panel slid closed.

And Crane was gone.

QUALITY

The long dark corridor that wended its way through the staff building of the Crane Institute was dim and dreary. Like the wintry landscape outside, it seemed isolated somehow, and Jacky couldn't help but think of *Alice in Wonderland* again. Or *The Wizard of Oz*. Only those books had at least started out pleasantly enough before turning into nightmares.

Wiseman was talking to Jacky, who pulled his thoughts away from the darkness of the area, which was lit only dimly by recessed fluorescents, to listen:

"The Crane Institute is the largest privately-funded facility for the criminally insane in the country," Wiseman droned, clearly repeating something memorized from an employment guide or a sales brochure. Although what this place could offer to sell was completely beyond Jacky. "Dr. Whitman Crane," continued Wiseman, "won a Nobel prize in the early seventies for his work on cellular structure and diversity. He also invested in several of what are now two or three of the biggest pharmaceutical suppliers in the country. He's worth approximately seven hundred million dollars, and a substantial portion of that is invested here, at the Crane Institute."

"The Loon," Jacky said, guessing that this was what all the staff called it.

"Yes," said Wiseman, but his features darkened. "Just don't let Dr. Crane hear you refer to it that way. At any rate,

The Loon," and here he cracked the barest hint of a grin, "was a federal pen in the twenties. It was closed for . . . ." Dr. Wiseman paused, and Jacky could see that he was struggling to find the words that would sound least horrifying. "Well, it was closed because the wardens' choice of behavioral modification wasn't what you'd call exemplary."

"Whoa!" said Jacky, stopping in mid-step. "You mean the guy tortured the inmates?" Jacky knew that such practices had occurred in the Prohibition era, but this was the first time he heard of a specific place *where* they had occurred.

Wiseman paused again, then shook his head. That relieved Jacky until he said, "I don't think what they did would give the word 'torture' a very good name, Mr. Hales." Wiseman continued walking, and Jacky had no choice but to follow. "At any rate, Dr. Crane purchased the place in the nineties, when government cutbacks required that many institutions be either destroyed or taken over by private parties. Since then it has housed over seven *hundred* of the country's most deeply screwed-up people."

Jacky couldn't help but offer up a grin. "'Deeply screwed-up.' That a fancy medical term?"

Wiseman didn't grin back. "For most of these people, Mr. Hales, there *are* no 'fancy medical terms.' At least, not until we name one after them."

"Why is Crane –" began Jacky, but a semi-harsh look from Wiseman corrected his wording. "– I mean, *Dr.* Crane – interested in psychos?"

They had reached the end of the hall. A steel door identical to the one Hip-Hop had brought Jacky through from the monitoring station stood before them. Wiseman swiped an ID card through the magnetic reader and typed a code into the keypad as he continued his orientation speech.

"The Loon holds up to one hundred eighty-five prisoners at a time, Mr. Hales. Currently, due to the storm conditions, we only have one hundred twenty-seven in the prison area. But they are quality."

"Quality?" asked Hales.

The door unsealed. Wiseman put a hand on the door, but didn't push it open. He looked at Jacky earnestly. "Quality means that of the one hundred twenty-seven men at the other end of this corridor, one hundred twenty-six of them would be more than happy to pull your eyes out with their fingers and eat them."

"What about the last one?"

"Steiger?" Wiseman finally *did* crack a smile. But it was a cold smile, the kind of smile Jacky associated with kids who want to stay in a movie theater even though the monster is about to pop out of the screen and they know they're going to have nightmares. "Steiger isn't quality. If the others are evil, Steiger's the Devil."

"Happy thought."

"The Loon is not a happy place, Mr. Hales."

Wiseman swung the door open.

COFFIN

The long dark corridor that connected the staff building to what Dr. Wiseman had called "the prison area" was no more inviting on the inside than it had appeared from the outside. Long and dark, no windows, absolutely lifeless.

Even before he stepped in, Jacky felt like he was looking into his own coffin.

Wiseman fumbled next to the door and a red light switched on, illuminating the corridor in blood-glows that were if anything less comforting than the darkness had been. "Make no mistake," said Wiseman as he began to walk the tunnel, Jacky staying as close as he could, trying not to let the fear he felt creeping up on him show in his face, "I'd rather have you wash out now than when – and I say *when*, not *if* – an emergency occurs."

Emergency? thought Jacky. This whole place already seems like an emergency in progress.

As though sensing his thoughts, Wiseman continued, "And by emergency I mean this: since The Loon opened, there have been forty-six breakout attempts. Twenty-four successful. Of the forty-six, fourteen resulted in inmate fatalities." Wiseman stopped for a moment, gripping Jacky's arm, clearly wanting to emphasize what came next. He needn't have bothered: Jacky already felt like he had been hit by a hammer. "And *forty-three* resulted in staff fatalities."

"God."

"That's what we're paying you the big bucks for, Mr. Hales. Or didn't you wonder why the average security guard here makes six figures a year?"

"I don't know if I need to be that rich."

"Scared?"

"Shitless."

"Good." They had reached the inner door – the door to the "prison area." Wiseman stared at Jacky again. "Scared is the right frame of mind here. Scared and careful. You stay that way, you live through the day. No second chances at The Loon."

Paul again swiped his card through this door's card-reader. "I'll give you a quick run-through of security protocols," he said, "and a manual. The manual has procedures for every possible contingency. Study it, and you'll always know what to do in any emergency. Don't study, and the only thing you'll know how to do is get killed." Wiseman began typing his key code, still talking as he pushed the buttons: the actions of someone who had done this a thousand times and could run on automatic pilot, though Jacky was also growing aware of the fact that no matter how off-hand Wiseman seemed at first, in reality he was tense. His whole body was alert, his eyes darting into shadows, left, right, left, right.

It feels like *we're* the ones in prison, thought Jacky.

"You'll notice," said Wiseman as he keyed in the last numbers, "that this tunnel is sealed from both ends. It's the only way in or out of The Loon prison. Electromagnetic locks hold the doors in place, and those seals will only disengage with the use of the correct card and its accompanying code." Paul flashed his card at Jacky before putting it in an inner pocket in his coat. "You'll get a card and a code of your own. Don't lose either. The card identifies you to the security system, and the code is in case one of the inmates escapes and takes the card off your body."

"*Body?*" Jacky said. He was dismayed to hear his voice crack on the second syllable. Six figures a year was seeming like a lot less money than it had when the recruiter had contacted him in Idaho a few months ago, where he'd been working at a state correctional facility for less than a quarter what the recruiter had offered.

No such thing as a free ride, Jacky thought.

Wiseman smiled tightly, but didn't say "It's a joke" as Jacky secretly hoped he would. Rather, he continued his orientation lecture. "The card can't break the electromagnetic seal without the matching code. So don't tell it to *anybody*, understand?" Jacky nodded. Who would he tell the code *to*? "Good," said Wiseman. "Any questions."

"No – yeah. You said the doors are electromagnetically sealed. What happens if there's a power failure?"

Wiseman nodded as though Jacky had just passed his first test. Jacky's fear didn't dissipate, but it was suddenly tinged with a bit of pride, as though he'd gotten the first right answer on the first day of school. He suddenly realized that Wiseman, in spite of his stoic demeanor, was a good guy. Jacky didn't know exactly how he knew that, but he did. Wiseman could be believed. Could be trusted.

"Did you notice the shack out in the yard?" asked Wiseman by way of response. "The one with all the wiring coming off it?" Jacky nodded, and again Wiseman gave him what Jacky thought to be an approving look. "It's an onsite generator, good for up to two weeks of constant use. The building is *highly* reinforced, and only Dr. Crane has the key."

Wiseman paused for a moment, as though he might say something more, but the door hummed and clicked, and he simply pulled it open instead. "First floor," he said in a pretty good imitation of an old-fashioned elevator operator, gesturing for Jacky to precede him. "Lingerie, dirty magazines, FBI's most wanted."

FOOD

It slithers back and forth, back and forth, back and forth.

Not far to move. Too far is pain. Too far is light, and that is also pain.

Now it doesn't slither. It has feet now. Walking. Back and forth, back and forth, back and forth.

Not too far.

Sound comes from nearby. Clip-clop, clip-clop.

The monster is coming, it thinks. The monster is bringing pain.

It moves to the back of its cell.

Don't touch the bars.

Not far to move. Too far is pain. But the monster is also pain. Always. Never goodness. Sometimes food, but always pain.

Its feet retract, disappearing within its mass as it tries to stay away. From the monster that is coming down the stairs.

Someday, somehow, it will escape.

And it will kill the monster.

It's hungry. The walking made it hungry. Everything makes it hungry.

It must eat.

Clip-clop, clip-clop. Monster at the stairs. Food. It needs food.

It will die without food.

Food.

It moves forward again, even though the monster is coming.

Food.

It needs food.
Food.
Food, food.
Food, food, food, food, food, food, food, food, food, food....

MONSTER

Dr. Crane walked down the steps that led into his favorite part of the building.

No, not his favorite. The entire *reason* for the building. The *only* reason for the *entirety* of the Crane Institute. He stood at the bottom of the stairs, as he always did, taking a moment to admire the space, to worship at the feet of what he had wrought.

The front half of the room – which took up nearly half the basement space in the staff facility – gleamed brightly under sets of precisely-aimed high-intensity halogen track lights. They illuminated the lab area of the room.

Two supercomputers and their memory storage and processing units, each about the size of a refrigerator, hummed and clicked, making computations that would have flummoxed a NASA scientist. Next to them was an ultra-modern lab. Elaborate bio-testing machinery sat on a long table: centrifuges, DNA testers, sampling trays, refrigerant units.

Everything he needed. There was even a refrigerator with some candy bars in it. Crane loved candy bars. Especially with caramel. He opened the refrigerator now and took out one of the candy bars, opening it and taking a bite.

A low growl sounded. The sound made Crane smile.

"Hungry?" he asked, as he looked at the other side – the *dark side* – of the lab. The track lights' precise aim resulted in a sharp demarcation right down the middle of the lab. On

Crane's side, all was bright and neat. But at the line a curtain of darkness fell over everything, as though a black hole rested just beyond, with its event horizon ending at the light. Beyond that line, everything – even the brightness – was sucked into the black hole and disappeared.

Of course, Crane knew there was no black hole in the darkness. What *was* there was something far more amazing. And far more deadly.

The growl came again. Lower than any animal's voice, it thrummed through the room at an almost cellular level. Crane sometimes felt like checking his fillings when the thing growled like that. "Definitely hungry," he said.

He looked into the darkness, only barely able to make out the cage. It was a perfect square, twelve feet to a side, with close set bars that you could barely fit a hand through.

It was in the back. Still growling, an amorphous mass whose details could not be made out. Not in the darkness. Perhaps not ever.

Crane flipped a switch on one of the computers. It hummed as myriad sensors that were hidden both inside and out of the cage came online, ready to measure everything about the beast, from its temperature to its brain functions to its body mass fluctuations.

The beast heard the sensors come on. It whimpered.

Crane smiled. His creation feared him. And that was as it should be. Creations should always fear their God.

"Let's begin," said Crane. He took another bite of his candy bar, and then quickly flicked his flashlight upward, so that the sharp LED beam glanced off the beast's undulating skin.

It was only a fraction of a second, but the reaction was instantaneous. The whimper was replaced by an enraged roar of pain. The thing shot forward, and Crane got the barest glimpse. A misshapen body – if *body* was even the right word any more – hitting the bars. A sense of the inhuman. A flash of sparks. Another howl of fury, so loud that if the room had not been utterly soundproofed Crane knew it could have been heard for a mile.

The thing hurled itself at the bars again, its mass shifting and pulsating as it tried to reach through the bars. Sparks once more as the highly electrified bars reacted to the thing's presence. Another howl.

"Ah, ah, ah," said Crane.

The howl quieted. The thing moved back into the darkness, and it seemed almost reptilian now, reminding Crane of a snake in the reptile house of a zoo.

It whimpered.

Crane smiled.

"Good boy."

TOWER

Being one of the two guards on tower duty was a shitty detail at the best of times. And now was definitely not the best of times. With the storm coming, and the wind chill factor, temperatures were rapidly dropping. Sandra Dickerson shivered and pulled the heavy parka closer to her, but it didn't do any good. The wind still blew, her nose was still on the verge of falling off, and worst of all...Wade Shickler was up here with her.

As if reading her thoughts, the fat fifty-year old said, "Sucks being us."

Sandy glared at him. She agreed with him on this particular point, but there was no way she was going to let Wade *know* she agreed. The man was a pig. Foul-mouthed, misogynist – the man still thought "Princess" was a valid way to address any female younger and more attractive than he was. Which was nearly everyone.

Again, Wade exercised his new mind-reading skill. "Sucks being us, Princess."

Sandy sighed. Sometimes she wanted to haul off and start screaming at the man, asking him in her shrillest voice what decade he thought he was living in and pointing out that speaking like a *film noir* detective from the nineteen thirties was no longer considered cool or even appropriate. And this time she seriously considered it: getting into a fight with Wade was never fun, but at least it tended to raise her body temp, which would be a welcome relief out here.

But no. Not worth it. So she settled for her usual: "Shut up, Wade."

"Screw you," he replied.

"Your dreams and my nightmares," she said back. She glanced down into the inner courtyard. Leann and Jeff were making rounds, so only Jeff could be seen right now, but that was fine. She did a quick count of the inmates who were walking around aimlessly in the snow. Fourteen. And there was Steiger, still making snow angels.

Fifteen, she thought. Then, on top of that thought: *How can he lay in the snow like that?* Steiger continued to amaze her...with a large dose of freaking her out added in for good measure. She shivered, and it wasn't the cold.

She looked down at the checkerboard. Wade, she had discovered to her delight a few months ago, made considerably less noise when occupied by a board game. Ever since then, she had made it a point never to do tower detail without a pocket checker board shoved in her jacket. Never knew when she'd be marooned up here with Wade. If it had been *Darryl* up here...she sighed, thinking of the guard's large biceps and solid, sincere face. No need for checkers, then.

But now...

She jumped two of Wade's three remaining checkers. "King me," she said smugly.

Wade glared at her. But he didn't call her "Princess." Success.

He kinged her checker.

A hot thermos of coffee sat on the small stool they were using as a table for the checkerboard. They had placed it next to the stairwell exit which doubled as the supply closet and bunker on top of the tower – this small floating island above the prison – in order to shelter the board from the wind as much as possible. The coffee and the checkers were the only things that made this job bearable.

Wade glanced over into the courtyard, and she saw
him making the same calculations she had done: two guards,
Leann and Jeff; fourteen crazies, all of them sedated; and
Steiger, who was also crazy and sedated but who rarely
showed any signs the sedation had any more effect on him
than a piece of Pez candy.

Wade looked back at the board, then moved his last
piece haltingly.

Sandy grinned widely. She hopped one of her kings
over the last checker.

"Shit," muttered Wade. He glanced into the courtyard
again, showing an unusual level of dedication to his job.
Usually she didn't see him look at the courtyard more than
once every half hour when they were on guard duty together.
Maybe it was because they were sitting down, so he couldn't
ogle her behind as easily as he enjoyed when they weren't
playing.

Thank you, God, for sending us checkers, she thought.

Then Wade did something that genuinely surprised
Sandy. Just when she had completely written him off as an
utter cad, he smiled at her and said, without a trace of irony or
sarcasm, "Good game." Her surprise meter red-lined then,
when he followed it up with, "Coffee?" and held out the
thermos in a way that bordered on gentlemanly. She had an
urge to grab his face and see if she could pull it off to reveal
Darryl underneath, since this gallantry was more the
wrestler's style. But there was no way Darryl could cram his
six foot-plus frame into Wade's chubby body.

She held out her coffee mug. Maybe Wade was just
doing some really late New Year's resolution thing. If so, best
to encourage it. "Thanks," she said.

The next moment, she was on her feet, screaming as
hot coffee soaked her crotch. "Sorry," said Wade. "Princess,"
he added after a moment. Sandy cursed herself for a fool. Of

course he wasn't being nice. Wade being nice would be like a frog learning how to tap-dance. He was pissed about the game, and so had reacted in his typical juvenile fashion and poured coffee over her.

"Asshole," she muttered. She didn't like to curse as a rule, but sometimes Wade brought out the absolute worst in her.

"Only in my dreams," Wade leered. Sandy wanted to gag.

She quashed the urge, though, and stomped to the stairwell door. There was a small microwave inside, a tiny refrigerator, and some paper towels. She grabbed a handful of the towels and blotted herself dry as best she could. But her lap was still damp five minutes later, and she had a feeling she was going to end up going inside to change because the wet clothing would probably freeze stiff in this weather. Going inside was – like everything else – a pain when you were on tower duty. Call inside to get a temp guard up top. Wait for the guard. Double check him in. Fill out a form explaining why the shift change. Use *her* card to get through the stairs. Call the guards in the courtyard to alert them she was coming down so they didn't accidentally shoot her with a trank dart. Go to the inner door. Call the lobby guard to alert *him* so *he* didn't shoot her. Go inside. More forms. Then reverse the process to come back up.

"Crap," she muttered, chucking the wadded up paper towels into a small trash can. "Crap, crap, crap."

She was still muttering under her breath when she walked back out. Too angry to even look at Wade, she glanced down into the courtyard again. Jeff and Leann. Fourteen sedated crazies. And...

Her brow furrowed. It was forty feet down, another seventy or eighty feet away at ground level, so it was hard to see. She could make out the jumpsuit easily in the snow:

bright orange showed up like a flare against the perfect white of the frozen prison courtyard. But Steiger didn't seem to be moving. Just laying there.

That wasn't like him. Steiger did a lot of weird things, but she could never recall him simply laying there. She counted to ten to herself, waiting silently to see if the man would move.

"Whatcha lookin' at, Princess?" asked Wade. "*Darryl* down there?"

She could hear the smirk in his voice but ignored him. "Hey, Steiger," she shouted. She was dismayed at how fast the wind stole her voice, whipping it away from her like some tangible object, a paper doll blown away in the storm. But still, Steiger should have heard it.

She felt rather than saw Wade stand up, lugging his ponderous body off his chair, then walking over to stand next to her.

"What're you hawkin' about now?" he said. He leaned over and looked into the courtyard. Sandy glanced at him. Wade was a turd, but he was turd with excellent vision. His eyes narrowed as he tried to see what was below. Then his face changed. "Kee-rist," he muttered.

"What?" asked Sandy.

Wade was already turning. Fast. He knocked over the still-open coffee, and Sandy had a split second to see the spilled liquid freeze over almost instantly on the frozen floor of the tower. Then Wade spoke, and all thoughts of coffee fled.

"Steiger," he said.

"Why's he laying there?" asked Sandy. "What did you see?"

"He's *not* laying there."

"What?"

She hustled after Wade, who was already through the door into the stairwell and punching in his code on the stairwell door.

"He's *not* laying there," Wade repeated, throwing the door open, hustling down the stairs. His voice floated over his shoulder. "Steiger's *gone*."

PRISON

Paul watched Jacky Hales' face as they entered the prison – The Loon's most awesome and frightening feature. It was always the same with new guards: shock, awe, discomfort. Sometimes Paul tried to remember what it had felt like when *he* was the new guy, walking in for the first time.

Two guards greeted them. Always two. The "companion" model that Hip-Hop had based the security system around. One of them, Marty Furtak, was tall and thin and about as happy-looking as an enema administered through a sharp stick. He constituted the third member of what Paul sometimes thought of as Vincent Marcuzzi's "gang of three." Marty, along with Vincent and Donald, could usually be found together in off-hours, sharing a Playboy back and forth and talking about their "big plans" for life.

The other guard, Jorge de los Santos, was a gleefully sarcastic type with a whip-fast wit that Paul usually enjoyed. Jorge was one of his favorite guards, in fact, and along with Darryl was one of the few guards who actually made an attempt to befriend Paul when he had arrived.

"How's things?" Paul asked the guards.

"Could be worse, could be better," said Marty morosely.

"The Montana motto," chimed in Jorge. Then he nodded at Hales. "Newbie?" he asked Paul.

Paul nodded, then turned to look at Hales. The man was looking around slowly, trying to drink it all in. Paul knew it was impossible to take in *everything* – there was simply too much to take in all at once – but he also knew it was equally impossible not to try. Like her inmates, The Loon demanded attention and more than a small dose of fear.

The prison facility was three stories of cells and iron catwalks. Each cell was in reality *two* cells in one: a set of bars on the outside, with another cell set inside it. The inner cell was standard-looking for any asylum: white, with a slot on the bottom, another in the middle, and a porthole on top.

Flashes of movement could be seen through several of the portholes as the occupants flitted by, always just out of the corner of one's eye, giving visitors and newcomers the disturbing sensation of being in a prison that held only ghosts and phantoms.

But the strangest and most discomfiting thing about The Loon's prison was her silence. The inner prison cells were all soundproofed, so the inmates couldn't goad each other into beyond-usual levels of insanity. It resulted in an even greater sense of detachment and strangeness. Prisons, Paul knew, were supposed to be noisy and almost garish, visitors surrounded on all sides by catcalls and derisive comments.

Not here, though. Not in The Loon. All was silent, here. All was deep and silent and alone. Alone in a full prison: if anything could describe The Loon in a single phrase, that was it.

An unaccustomed sound broke through the silence, shattering it with its suddenness and making Paul, Marty, Jorge, and (especially) Hales jump.

Storm's getting worse, thought Paul.

The sound had been the wind, wailing its banshee call through the walls. Banshees, Paul knew, were harbingers of death in the tales where they appeared. Paul prayed that would not be the case here. Not here, not today.

"Wind," Paul reassured Hales. Or rather, he tried to reassure the new man. But Hales still looked a bit freaked.

Jorge must have seen Hales' look as well, because he laughed in an obviously reassuring way. "Welcome to the Twilight Zone, Newbie," he said graciously, and Paul again thanked Jorge in his mind for being one of the few people whose time at The Loon hadn't turned them cynical and/or morose. Jorge was a genuinely good guy. Good enough that Paul had even told him...

(about Sammy...)

...about his past.

Paul pursed his lips. That had been an unbidden and unwelcome thought, reminding him again what today was: the anniversary of the day he had killed his own son.

Again, Jorge came to the rescue. He was talking to Hales, but Paul grabbed the words as well, holding onto Jorge's voice like a rescue ring in a choppy ocean. "Hey, Newbie, c'mere and check this out," said the chirpy guard. Paul knew more than a little about Jorge, too, about how he and his sister Raquel had been abused as children by their uncle before coming to Montana, and for the millionth time he marveled at the man's happiness. If anyone had as difficult a past as Paul did, it was Jorge de los Santos. But still the man remained happy.

Paul didn't know how he did it.

"What's your name, Newbie?" asked Jorge as Hales walked over to where the other guard was standing: a bank of monitors similar to the one in the lobby.

"Jackson – Jacky – Hales," said the new guard.

"Nice to meet you Jackson-Jacky-Hales," said Jorge. "Me Jorge. That," he said, pointing to Marty, "Tarzan. Together we make big love."

"Jorge," said Marty in a warning tone.

Jorge laughed. "Just yankin' your chain, man." He turned back to Hales. "Nice to meetcha, Jacky. I'm Jorge and this ball of fun is Marty. And I guess you already know The Chief."

Now it was Paul's turn to put on his warning tone. "Jorge," he repeated, and was dismayed at how much he sounded like Marty.

Is that what I've become? thought Paul to himself. I hope not.

Jorge put up his hands. "Kidding, *jefe*." And then Jorge focused on Hales again. "Check this out, Jacky." He pulled Hales over to his station, pointing at the monitors and their controls. "Cool, huh? Each monitor can show any of the cells." Jorge let go of Hales so he could fiddle with the controls, flipping rapidly through about a dozen different viewpoints in as many seconds.

In most of the cells, the inmates slept. Several of them shuffled quietly back and forth in their cells. The one he stopped on, though, did neither.

"Check *this* guy out," said Jorge.

"Who is he?" asked Hales.

"Name's Ronny Reagan, if you can believe that," said Jorge. "But we call him Bloodhound."

Bloodhound was in a straightjacket. Paul frowned when he saw that the vicious-looking inmate – covered in scars and tattoos, the most prominent one being a large dog tattooed on the front of his neck – was ramming himself against the walls with manic ferocity.

"Why didn't he get his meds today?" asked Paul, pulling out a notepad from his pockets. The notepad contained a single half-page set of notes on every inmate present at The Loon and served as his Cliff's Notes for what was occurring daily in these very troubled waters.

"He did," responded Marty. Paul thought for a moment that the man sounded like Eeyore from the Disney cartoon; half expected the man to add "Thanks for noticing" in a long, low voice. But that, like so many other things today, brought up thoughts of Sammy.

Paul quickly looked at his book. Bloodhound was on a potent combination of anti-psychotics and tranquilizers. Indeed, of everyone in The Loon, only Steiger was more heavily medicated. And yet, here was Bloodhound, who should have been fairly quiet, running forcibly into wall after wall.

"How long's this been going on?" asked Paul.

"Five minutes," said Jorge. "We woulda paged you, but we knew that the Newbie was here and figured you'd be along shortly."

"Well, let's increase his dos –" Paul began, then changed his voice in mid-stream to shout "DON'T TOUCH THAT!"

Hales, the object of his shout, jumped backward in surprise, tripping into Marty, the two men falling into Marty's chair, Hales on top and looking like some ridiculously huge kid getting ready to tell Marty what he wanted for Christmas.

Marty straightened up quickly, almost dumping Hales. Paul reached out and caught him. Helped him to his feet. "Sorry," said Paul to the confused young man. He showed Hales a blue button on the control unit in front of the monitor display. The button was covered with a semi-transparent flip-top, so Paul could see Hales was confused.

"You probably couldn't have triggered it accidentally," said Paul. He glanced at Marty and Jorge and saw that both the guards had, like him, erupted in sudden sweat. "But you would *not* have wanted to touch that button."

"Why?" asked Hales. "What does it do?"

EMPTY

Sandy was helping Jeff and Leann push the fourteen inmates against the wall. All of them were in chains already, Jeff and Leann reacting with lightning speed when Wade had burst out of the stairwell into the courtyard area.

Now, Sandy glanced over her shoulder. Wade was approaching Steiger – *was* it Steiger? – slowly and carefully, his trank drawn. He was about twenty feet away from the bright orange splotch in the snow.

Then ten.

Moving more slowly now. Carefully.

"The hell's going on?" asked Jeff.

Sandy shrugged. Wade hadn't said anything on the way down. Just huffed and puffed like a locomotive with a burst gasket as he ran down the stairs from the tower, taking some of them three or four at a time.

She saw Wade close in.

Five feet.

Two.

Then....

"SHIT!" screamed Wade.

"What is it?" hollered Sandy and Leann in unison.

"It's empty! It's friggin' empty!" yelled Wade. Sandy turned around again in time to see Wade waving the uniform around in the air.

Steiger was gone.

CODE

"Well?" Jacky repeated. He didn't feel like Alice falling down the rabbit hole anymore. Instead he felt like the rabbit hole had been nuked and he was traveling through a mutated Wonderland...a Wonderland much more strange and dangerous than Mr. Carroll's invention had ever been. "What does the button do?"

He saw Dr. Wiseman glance at the two guards – Jorge and Marty, he repeated to himself, trying even now to make a good impression on his first day by learning everyone's names. Then the chief of staff leaned over and pointed again at the blue button that Jacky had apparently almost touched.

"The doors to the prison are on a separate circuit, so even if the power *and* the backup generator somehow blow out at the same time, we still have control over the cell doors. But it's minimal, just meant to get them out in an emergency." Jacky saw Dr. Wiseman swallow, his Adam's apple bobbing up and down, before he continued: "Touch that button once, the circuit activates. Touch it twice, the inner doors open but the outer cells stay closed. Touch it three times, and *every* door in here opens."

Jacky looked around.

Three floors of cells. Over one hundred wackos waiting inside them...waiting to come out and play. Now Jacky gulped, and his mouth was dry.

"Sorry," he managed to get out through his suddenly parched lips.

"'S cool, bro," said Jorge after a moment. "I shouldn't have let you get so close to the panel without telling you not to touch anything."

Jacky was about to apologize again, Jorge's reassurances notwithstanding, when suddenly the walkie-talkies that were strapped to Jorge's and Marty's belts both crackled as. "All units, Code Three alert," said a voice that Jacky didn't recognize. "Repeat, Code Three alert."

Jacky felt the hairs on the back of his neck stand on end as the atmosphere in the cavernous prison charged as though an electric storm had moved in with the words.

"What's a Code Three?" asked Jacky.

Marty ignored him, picking up his walkie-talkie and saying, "Where, Wade? Inside or outside?"

At the same time, Paul spoke to Jacky, and Jacky noted with dismay that the calm-seeming doctor now wore a shocked expression on a face that looked white and strained as a sheet on a tightly made bed. "Inmate escape attempt," said Paul, pulling a matching walkie-talkie from one of his voluminous coat pockets.

"Not sure yet," said the voice – Wade, Marty had said it was – and there was a short pause before Wade continued: "We think out. Definitely outside the prison facility. Not sure about the staff facility yet."

"Who was it?" barked Paul into his walkie-talkie.

"Steiger," came Wade's voice.

The air charged again, but this time Jacky understood why as he recalled Paul's words: "*Steiger isn't quality, he's* really *mean.*"

SEARCH

Not what I needed today, thought Paul. Not what I needed.

Then he thought, What *did* you need today? Other than Sammy? before slamming through the front door of the staff facility, Jacky Hales hot on his heels. Paul had quickly debated the idea of leaving Hales in the prison facility where he likely couldn't get into any trouble, but realized that since no one knew where Steiger was yet, he'd just as soon have the new guy where he could keep an eye on him.

The cold outside hit Paul like a knife that easily sliced through the thin fabric of his coat and shirt. The storm was getting much worse, flurries thrown up and about in front of his eyes, snowflakes the size of pennies dropping all around them.

It was getting dark.

Not too dark to see yet. Thank goodness. Paul instantly spotted the fourteen inmates, being walked toward him, herded along by Jeff. He could also see beyond them to where three more guards stood, all looking nervous: Vincent, Donald, and the largest member of the staff – a guy named Mitchell who looked like he could pick up the bear-sized Darryl by the scruff of the neck as easily as Paul would a kitten.

Paul led Jacky around the inmates, giving them plenty of room as they re-entered The Loon. As soon as he and Jacky got past the inmates, he could see Wade and Sandy kneeling down beside what looked like a wadded-up uniform. Both had their tranks drawn, and Wade wore the unhappy expression of a man who has committed some mortal sin.

"We have a lockdown?" asked Paul as soon as he was close enough to Wade and Sandy to be heard.

"The security perimeter's unbreached," said Sandy. "We ran a gate diagnostic and the main entrance hasn't been opened or closed at any time."

That was good news, at least. The Loon's walls were forty feet high and utterly smooth on the inside, so climbing them was physically impossible. The main entrance was the only way in or out of The Loon, and the gate computer registered every single time it opened or closed.

So Steiger's in here with us, thought Paul. "When did it happen?" he said, and was now close enough to see that the orange cloth was in fact a uniform. An empty uniform.

"Just a minute ago," said Wade. "I called it in right away. He was here, playing in the snow, then he wasn't."

Paul looked around, glancing at the enormous form of Mitchell, then moving to Vincent and Donald, finally settling on Wade and Sandy. "Who was watching the courtyard from the tower?"

He saw Wade and Sandy exchange guilty looks and felt his eyes narrow. "You two," he said. "In my office when this is over."

He widened his gaze to take in all five of the seasoned guards at once. "All right, spread out and check the courtyard."

"Where's he gonna hide out here?" asked Wade, clearly seeking to hide his guilt by attacking Paul.

"I don't know," Paul snapped. "But the perimeter's intact, which means he hasn't gotten out, which means he's still inside. We check the courtyard and work our way in until we find him and that includes looking *under the snow* if you have to!"

Sandy, Vincent, Donald, and Mitchell split up, two of them heading in each direction, a circuit that would eventually take them all the way around The Loon. Wade didn't move for a moment, staying behind to start a short staring contest with Paul.

Paul felt himself get genuinely angry for the first time. This was clearly Wade's fault, and the guy was dense enough to think now was a good time to try passive-aggressive blame-shifting tactics. "I'm going to notify God that there's a problem," he almost hissed. "And you're going to be out here fixing that problem while I do so, right?"

Wade moved off without replying, following after Vincent and Donald. Paul watched him go for a few steps, then turned toward the staff facility, knocking into Hales as he did. He had forgotten in the heat of the moment that the new guard was still with him. He felt himself slip on the deep snow beneath them, but Hales caught him and kept him from going down completely.

"Anything I can do to help?" asked Hales.

"Yeah," said Paul, hurrying toward the front door of the staff facility. "Follow me. When we get to the lobby, sit and stay."

"That's it?" asked Hales, still close on Paul's feet as they reached the front door.

Paul keyed in his code, swiped his card, then opened the door. "If a naked guy comes in, scream," he replied, then stepped through into the lobby area.

Hip-Hop and Leann, The Loon's longest-working female employee, were manning the security monitors now; apparently they had assigned Darryl some other duty while Paul and Jacky had been outside.

Both Hip-Hop and Leann jumped to their feet as Paul slammed open the door, twitchy hands holding their already-drawn trank guns.

Paul raised his hands quickly.

Stupid, he thought, cursing himself for forgetting to announce himself before entering. That was a good way to take an unscheduled nap.

"Whoa, whoa!" he hollered, waving his hands in the air. "Just the good guys."

Hip-Hop and Leann holstered their weapons and returned their gazes to the monitor screens. Paul pulled Jacky around to where the two older guards sat. He glanced at the monitors for a moment but knew without looking that Steiger would show up on none of them. The man was too smart for Paul's liking. Insane, but calculating. Careful in spite of his shredded grip on sanity.

"Okay, guys," said Paul, "we're in serious crap. Hip-Hop, you man the monitors. Leann, I want your trank drawn and aimed at that door," he motioned at the door that led outside, "and you shoot anything that comes in there without notice."

"You woulda been downed if that's how we were playing it," said Hip-Hop, but Leann did as Paul had said.

Paul nodded. "True." He pulled his walkie-talkie out and put out a call on the general frequency. "All outside units, front is covered. Warn before entering. Repeat, you don't want a trank guard in the face, you warn before entering."

A chorus of "confirmed" came through on the walkie-talkies. But they sounded thin. Too few.

"What's the staffing situation today?" Paul asked.

His stomach felt like it was dropping another foot or two closer to the floor when Hip-Hop answered: "Sent Darryl in to cover the prison with Jorge and Marty. So that's three in the prison, five outside, two here. Ten total. Eleven with the newbie."

"What?" Paul almost shouted. "Where *is* everyone?"

"Called in sick," replied Hip-Hop, his hands moving rapidly across the monitor control bank as he scanned the prison for traces of Steiger. "No one wanted to get caught in the storm."

"Geez, Hip-Hop, you're supposed to tell me these things. Ten is barely enough to maintain a skeleton shift, much less a harsh-weather situation with a Code Three lockdown thrown in for good measure."

Hip-Hop ignored him, glancing at Jacky and saying, "How you likin' your first day?" to Hales.

"Uhhh…" began the younger man.

Paul cut him off. "Cute, Hip-Hop. Watch Jacky and don't let him get in the way."

"Where *you* goin'?" demanded Hip-Hop.

"To tell God," answered Paul, heading toward the door that led into Crane's private office and quarters.

"He said he didn't want nobody disturbing him," said Hip-Hop, moving to block Paul from reaching the prison owner's door.

Paul gently but firmly pushed Hip-Hop out of the way. "What?" he said, entering his code and swiping his card through the reader on Crane's door. "He wants to be the only undisturbed person in this place?"

Paul stepped opened the door and threw it open.

And gaped at what he saw.

OFFICE

Paul stepped further into the office to verify what he was seeing. Or rather, what he *wasn't* seeing.

A radio was playing in the corner, static eradicating the voice every couple of words. "National Weather Service...already closed roads...Clay and Jackson Counties due...preliminary storm danger –"

Paul snapped off the radio. Silence, broken only by the mournful howl of the wind.

The room was empty. Which it shouldn't have been: Crane was *always* in his office. Always.

Paul stepped to the door that led to his boss's private living quarters. He knocked, saying, "Dr. Crane?" in a hushed voice before knocking harder. "Dr. Crane!" he said again.

No answer.

Paul again swiped his card, entered his code, and went through the door. He was treading on thin ice here, he knew: Crane despised being bothered, and had made it very clear early on that his room was off-limits. Still, Paul *had* been there once or twice, and he also thought that if anything merited an uninvited trip to his boss's room, the prospect of Steiger escaping would be it.

He opened the door.

And faced another empty room.

Where was Crane?

HUNGER

It hurts. It slides and slithers and tries to get away from the pain, but it cannot. It cannot do it.

The monster won't let it get away.

Never.

Always pain.

Never escape.

Just pain.

Then hunger. It feels itself grow hungry, then famished, then starving in a matter of seconds. The hunger becomes a new kind of pain, and the thing can hear the sizzle of its own flesh dissolving within itself as it feeds. If there is no other food, it will eat itself.

Because the hunger must end. The pain will go on, the monster will never leave it in peace, but hunger...

Hunger cannot be borne.

LETTERS

Crane sat at the edge of his stool and watched and listened as his creation started to make strange noises. Like the sound of acid etching across metal, and Crane started as he realized he could actually *see* the thing in the cage shrinking.

Losing mass, thought Crane. He checked his watch, noting the time on the lab computer, and thought, Its metabolism is speeding up.

Crane pressed a button then and a new sound entered the lab: the sound of metal on metal as a small door in the side of the beast's cage opened. A huge dog charged out, flinging itself madly about inside the larger cage it had been allowed to "escape" into. A flurry of sparks bit at the dog each time he hit the bars, but the animal continued to ram into them, as though sensing what he was with, as though suspecting what was about to happen.

It didn't have long to wait.

Crane watched as the beast waited for a moment. Then it moved. Lightning fast, so fast Crane almost couldn't see it in the darkness of that side of the lab. It hit the dog, and the dog made a sound Crane had never heard before. It sounded like a child's scream, high-pitched and horrified.

Then the same acidic sizzling noise returned as the beast...*engulfed* the dog. The dogs screams disappeared, replaced by a pant/whisper/whine that was even more horrifying to hear. And then that sound, too, disappeared, leaving behind only that awful sizzle and a sound like a toddler sucking at the last bits of strawberry milkshake.

The sounds ended.

The beast moved away.

The dog was gone. The cage floor steamed where it had been, the acid scorches visible even from behind the wall of light where Crane sat.

"Very good," he murmured with approval. He checked the computer, which had sensors throughout the cage, and saw that the monster's eating speed was increasing as well.

An inhuman cry of rage made Crane turn back to look at the beast. It threw itself at the iron bars which separated it from its master and maker. As they had before, the bars sparked, and the beast's cries were loud and long. But still it tried to push against the bars.

Crane smiled. "Now, now," he said in the same tone of voice one might hear a mother speaking to a wayward child. He grabbed the nearest flashlight. "You know the rules."

At this the beast immediately began to whine and moved as far back as the rear bars on its cage would permit.

Crane's smile grew even wider.

He turned on the flashlight.

The dog's screams of pain and fear were as nothing compared to those that emerged from the beast's cage. The thing jittered around the cage, trying to avoid the beam from Crane's LED flashlight, but the light followed it mercilessly. It was almost like watching a strobe light, the beam moved so fast. And where it hit the beast, the skin of Crane's creation seemed to flow like mercury.

Finally, after a few minutes of fun, Crane turned the flashlight off. He could hear panting and realized after a moment that it was him, and that he had been aroused by the sounds of pain that came from the beast.

No time to think on that fact, though, for movement drew his eye back to the cage.

The beast had moved to the front again. Meekly, though, no fight left in it. It paused, and then a wet tendril-like appendage emerged from its side, dripping. The liquid it spilled spattered against the floor, again leaving etch-marks behind.

The tendril touched the ground. Sizzling. It lifted, then dropped again. More noise. Crane couldn't fathom what he was looking at for a moment, then realized:

Letters.

The beast was writing.

Crane wanted to look at the words, to see what the thing was writing. But he didn't want to use the flashlight until the thing was done, for fear of dissuading it. He made furious notations on his computer log until he heard the noise stop.

At the same time as Crane swiveled back to face it, the beast made a noise that Crane had never heard before. A weird, undulating sound that ground into Crane's mind like a spike. Frightening.

It was laughing. The thing *was laughing.*

Now Crane looked at the letters:

i wiLL Kil U ForEVer

Crane frowned. He felt suddenly unsure and unsafe, as though the bars and the light could not hold the beast back, or as though they might suddenly disappear and leave him as defenseless as the dog had been.

As much to reassure himself as for the pleasure – no, *science* – of it, Crane turned on the flashlight.

The weird, dancing laughter disappeared.

And the screaming began once more.

JOBS

Paul walked back out into the lobby, confused and more than a little worried about Crane's absence.

Hip-Hop was still watching the monitors, Leann still aimed her trank at the front door. The new Mr. Hales sat behind Hip-Hop, clearly trying to help look and just as clearly unable to figure out what he should be looking *for*.

"Anything?" said Paul as re-entered the lobby.

Hip-Hop shook his head. "Almost done with the exterior sweep." He flipped through a few more camera angles, then said, "What did God say?"

"He wasn't there," said Paul.

"Had to be," said Hip-Hop. "I been sitting here since he went in. He's in there."

"Then he was being invisible when I looked," growled Paul. He wasn't in the mood to deal with Hip-Hop's minor attitude problems.

Hip-Hop opened his mouth – no doubt to keep their little argument going – when the walkie-talkies everyone wore crackled to life. It was Mitchell, the huge man's voice oddly comforting. "Sweep done. Five coming in."

Hip-Hop unclipped his walkie-talkie and spoke into it. "Cleared. Come on in."

The door clicked and then buzzed as Wade, Sandy, Donald, Vincent, and Mitchell entered the room. Hip-Hop kept watching the monitors, flipping through them uselessly. Leann kept her gun out and pointed into the storm until after the door closed, and then she resumed aiming at the door, the five guards who had just entered quickly moving out of her way.

Paul looked at Sandy. As the member of the sweep crew with the most seniority he should have spoken to Wade, but he wasn't about to deal with the older man's particular brand of guilt/assholeness, so he spoke to the other member of the tower team that should have kept this situation from happening. "You didn't find anything?" he asked.

"No," said Sandy. "Zip."

"All right." Hip-Hop stood up and stretched quickly, then sat on the terminal in front of the monitors. Paul heard a metallic click and turned around in time to see Hales holding a lighter to a cigarette. It was against the rules to smoke while on The Loon premises, but Paul didn't have time to nit-pick that kind of thing right now. Hip-Hop was still speaking: "...we'll start a sweep of the staff facility before moving to the prison area. Me and Leann will stay on watch detail." He looked at the older woman, who had glanced at him when her name was spoken. "You keep on the front, Leann. All our people are inside, so anything opening the door is unfriendly. Shoot it if it moves. You got enough darts?"

"Racked and stacked," replied Leann in a cold tone that Paul had to admire. Of all of them, she seemed the least agitated.

"Good." Hip-Hop turned to Hales. "You stay here, Newbie. Watch the monitors with me, stay out of the way, and don't get dead."

"I get overtime for this, right?" Hales asked weakly, blowing smoke nervously.

Nobody laughed at his attempt to lighten the mood.

"Anyone else in the facility?" asked Paul.

"Nope," said Hip-Hop.

"Nobody upstairs taking a nap?" he asked. He already knew the answer, but couldn't help but ask, as though five or ten or a hundred more guards might materialize if he just inquired long enough.

Hip-Hop crossed his arms, clearly irritated with Paul. "Now   didn't   I   just   say   no?"

MOVEMENT

Nobody noticed the monitor behind Hip-Hop: a shot of the courtyard, showing only snow.

And then movement.

NAKED

Steiger was very cold. Very very cold. Perhaps even hypothermic.

But he waited.

Footsteps sounded nearby.

And he waited.

Finally, when there had been no sound but the wind for a very long time, and when the only vibrations he felt were those of the falling snow, he sat up.

The layer of snow that had covered him in the courtyard fell away. Steiger immediately started shivering as the cold air hit his naked body. He forced himself to his feet, standing up from the shallow, grave-like pit he had quickly dug and then hidden himself in while the guards weren't watching.

He had been patient. He had waited. But now it was not time to wait. It was time to run.

He flitted over the snow, thankful he had thought to keep his shoes and socks on, the cold wind biting at his face and genitals as he ran.

He got to the door inset in wall: the door that he knew led to the outer courtyard and freedom.

He pulled a keycard from where he had hidden it: between his buttocks, where he knew that the homophobic guards would not check him carefully. They were all homophobic, he knew. Except for the two ladies on staff, Leann and Sandy. Leann was, he felt fairly certain, bisexual.

That was as unacceptable as homophobia. And Sandy, he suspected, was gay, for she rebuffed his advances at every turn. Also unacceptable.

He had not been surprised to find the keycard in his cell that morning. Nor had he been surprised to turn it over and find, written in pen that smudged when he touched it, a long string of numbers that he intuited was the code that belonged to this particular card. He had not been surprised, for he knew that he was watched. Protected. Invincible. No person could hurt him, no cell could hold him forever.

Eventually, all servants of chaos found a way to break free. That was the nature of chaos, and it could not be contained. The universe tended toward entropy; toward the broken. Happiness was hollow, love fleeting. The only contentment that could be found was in surrendering oneself to the moment, to the chaos of a world hurtling through space at a thousand miles a minute.

So few people understood that. So few of them understood that what he was doing was not to harm them, but to allow them the only true joy that could be found: the joy of *feeling*. Of feeling pain, of feeling abuse, of feeling themselves ripped open and exposed to the light of chaos.

He was a servant of chaos.

He was protected.

He ran to the outer door of the courtyard. Slid the code-card that had been given him through the card reader by the small metal door inset in the huge metal gate of the wall. He began punching in the code. It was no longer written on the card – he had taken great joy in rubbing the code off with his thumb, rubbing it so hard the ink broke down and disintegrated into a smudge – but he had memorized it soon after receiving the gift.

He had only punched in two numbers when the alarm sounded.

OUTSIDE

Hip-Hop was still parked on the desk in front of the monitors, giving out assignments. Paul didn't mind that: Hip-Hop *was* chief of security, so the job of assigning search teams and setting up a perimeter that would – hopefully – collapse in upon itself until someone found Steiger was his. The only thing that bothered Paul was the fact that any of this had happened in the first place.

"...and Wade, I want you and Sandy back out on the wall," finished Hip-Hop.

That irritated Paul a bit. *That* was how this mess had started in the first place. He couldn't resist saying something. "And try to actually *watch* this time."

Wade glared daggers at him, Sandy looked dejected and downcast. And Hip-Hop looked clearly irritated that Paul had butted in on his domain. But the chief of security didn't say anything, just motioned for the guards to split up into their assigned details.

They started to move, and Hip-Hop finally stood from his perch on the edge of the monitor control table. That was when Paul saw it.

"Oh, crap."

"What is it?"

Paul wasn't sure who had said that; he was too focused on what he was watching: the small door that led to the outer courtyard, slowly opening.

Steiger.

"He's outside!" he screamed. "About to go through the inner door!"

CHASE

Sandy could barely stand to look at what was happening. Steiger was a killer. A mass murderer, a child molester, a serial rapist. If you could think of something awful, then Steiger had probably done it…as a warm-up.

Now he was escaping. And it was her fault. Her and Wade's fault. If he hadn't spilled the coffee on her….

The thought was pulled from her when Paul shouted, "He's outside! About to go through the inner door!"

Sandy felt herself turn and start running instinctively. Wade was right behind her, she knew: she could hear him huffing along. She swiped her card through the door that led from the lobby to the courtyard, then punched in her code so hard and fast she felt like she had probably bruised her fingers.

The door clicked open, and Sandy felt Wade's elbow dig into her ribs as he shoved past her. Apparently he was feeling even more guilty than she was. He already had his trank out, and was moving faster than Sandy had ever seen.

She followed him out, pulling her own gun, wanting to hit Steiger, wanting to be the one who brought him back, but knowing it was too far for the trank: the dart would never fly straight in this wind. They had to get closer. Besides, Wade's fat form was blocking any kind of shot she might have had.

Then Wade did something that surprised her: he stopped in his tracks.

Steiger was pulling open the door.

In a moment he'd be outside the prison proper.

At the cars, she thought. Please, God, don't let him get to the cars.

She didn't have time to think more than that, because she tried to veer around Wade. But instead of turning, her right foot slipped out from under her as it hit an icy patch, and she knocked into him. He cursed and she heard the sharp "Pptht" of a trank being fired. Then he cursed again as they both went down on the snow in a pile of arms and legs.

Wade was first to his feet and – true to form – didn't bother to help her up. Just went barreling toward the door to the outer courtyard.

The *open* door to the outer courtyard.

The open, *empty* door.

"Shit," she muttered. "Shitshitshitshitshitshitshit." Steiger was out.

She got to her feet and ran after Wade. She could hear others right behind her, but somehow she and Wade were still in the lead. Adrenaline must have leant them greater speed than usual. Especially Wade, who was dashing at the open door. Sandy would have stared in shock had she not been so terrified of losing Steiger. The idea of Wade running *anywhere*, much less into the arms of danger, was almost impossible to contemplate.

Yet it was most certainly happening.

Wade was at the outer door.

He stepped through.

Then fell out of sight with a shout of terror.

Steiger, thought Sandy.

She put on an extra burst of speed, fearing for Wade. He was a pig, but he didn't deserve whatever Steiger might choose to do to him.

She ran for the door...and fell with a shout similar to Wade's.

Unlike Wade, though, who lay sprawled in front of her, Sandy managed to keep her feet under her. She looked at him.

Then looked at Steiger, who was asleep under Wade, a bright red plume sticking out of his naked buttock and steam rising from his nude body.

She stifled a laugh that was half comical, half relieved hysteria. Wade had *hit* Steiger. At *that range*, in *that wind*, he had managed to take the madman down with a trank.

She uttered a silent prayer of thanks to whatever cadre of guardian angels must have been watching over them, then looked back at Wade. He was still struggling to get up, but each time he posted his hands in the snow they would slip out from under him, landing him on top of Steiger again and again.

"Maybe I should let you two be alone," she chortled.

"Shut up," said Wade. "Help me up."

"You sure?" she asked, laughter finally escaping her. "I mean, looks like you and Steiger are getting awful *frisky*." She made a cat "mrow" and hissed in mock sexiness.

"Shut *up*," insisted Wade. "Just get me the hell off him."

Sandy did, but couldn't help laughing.

She kept on laughing, too, until she heard the stomp of footsteps behind her.

It was Dr. Wiseman, who looked quickly at her and Wade before going to Steiger.

He pried something out of Steiger's grasp. A code card.

"How did he get this?" asked Paul.

How indeed? thought Sandy.

A chill that had nothing to do with the wind bit through her.

How   indeed?

HOW?

Jacky watched as Wade and Sandy dragged the unconscious man through the lobby area, past Hip-Hop, Leann, and Dr. Wiseman. He noted that no one had bothered to put the man's clothing back on, but they *had* shackled him from head to toe with no fewer than six sets of handcuffs and leg irons.

"*That's* the mean one?" he said.

He couldn't help but ask. The man being dragged in appeared even less imposing now than he had when Jacky first saw him in the courtyard earlier that day...and he hadn't seemed very imposing then.

"Yeah," said Dr. Wiseman. "He's the mean one, all right."

Wade, the guard who was now getting accolades from the other guards for downing Steiger when the man literally had one foot out the front door, swiped his card through the reader that led to the staff area and then, beyond that, to the prison. Jacky thought for a moment that the setup for entering the prison was odd, since it meant inmates would be tramping through within feet of the staff quarters every day, but then he realized that the layout was just one more line of defense: putting the guards in harm's way by putting them between the prisoners and any chance of escape meant that breakouts would be more difficult and the guard staff were more likely to be extremely careful with security protocols.

So how had this Steiger guy gotten out?

HACKER

Dr. Wiseman turned to Wade as he and Sandy dragged Steiger through the hall. "Put him in his cell and then go to my office." The chief of staff turned to Hip-Hop. "You, too. Five minutes." Jacky saw expressions darken all around. Some serious ass-chewing was apparently in the making. "Where's everybody at right now?" continued Dr. Wiseman.

Hip-Hop checked the monitor screens, but he was already reciting positions before he even looked. "Marty and Jorge are still in the prison. I put Jeff, Vincent, and Donald on the tower. Mitchell's upstairs with Darryl getting the cots ready for tonight, and Wade and Sandy are in the tunnel with Steiger. Leann's here with us. So's the newbie."

"All right," said Paul. "Let me know if anything else happens. And don't forget to come to my office in five." Paul motioned to Jacky to follow him through the still-open door to the staff area. He stopped suddenly, though, almost causing Jacky to run into him. "And have Darryl and Mitchell start looking for God. The cots can wait."

"He's probably just in his office and you just missed seeing him," insisted Hip-Hop.

Dr. Wiseman waved him off. "If they don't find him in fifteen minutes, we have a problem." Then he turned and motioned again for Jacky to follow him. "You come with me," he said, and tramped through the open door.

Jacky followed him into the hall, and finally blurted, "*That* was the 'really mean' guy?"

113

Dr. Wiseman nodded. "Maurice J. Steiger. Also known as The Hacker. He killed his mother and father when he was twelve. Then went on a spree and took out half his little hometown before they caught him. Spent twenty-two years undergoing psychiatric treatment, was finally released, and killed six people that same week. That's when we got him." Dr. Wiseman stopped walking for a moment, then whispered, almost as though he were speaking to himself instead of to Jacky, "Four of the six were little girls." Paul started walking as he spoke, his voice cold and emotionless as a machine. Jacky realized that he must be witnessing a defense mechanism: something about what Steiger did so unnerved The Loon's chief of staff and head psychiatrist that he could only speak about it in a clinical, detached manner. "And he didn't hurt them right away. He kept them with him for several days, was apparently very nice to them...then he raped and murdered them."

Jacky felt queasy. He had been in corrections for over seven right now, but he'd never before heard of such a person, such an embodiment of evil. "He seemed so...normal," he finally managed.

Dr. Wiseman reached the metal staircase that led both up to the second level and down to the basement; started climbing. Darryl, the wrestler; and Mitchell, the man big enough to eat entire horses whole and come back for seconds, were both coming down the ladder at that moment. Jacky had to squeeze as far over as he could to let the two bear-like men pass, and suddenly knew what a pro quarterback probably felt like when getting blitzed by the entire opposing team.

"Yeah, *seems* is right," Dr. Wiseman finally said when the two juggernauts passed. "It's just an act. He'll keep it up until he's pronounced sane." The psychiatrist kept walking for a long moment, then finished, "And then he'll kill again."

They reached the upstairs hall and started walking toward Dr. Wiseman's office.

"How does he test?" asked Jacky, his professional curiosity piqued.

"Normal," said Dr. Wiseman. They reached the door to his office, and the psychiatrist swiped his card through and entered his code so they could enter. Dr. Wiseman sat behind his desk, motioning for Jacky to sit as well before he began rummaging through some papers in one of the desk drawers.

"How can you keep him here, then?" asked Jacky. "I mean, if he tests out, and he's been here a while…"

"He tests *too* normal," responded Dr. Wiseman. "He's been through the system enough that he knows all the right answers to give."

"Still –" began Jacky before Dr. Wiseman cut him off.

"Besides, while the psych profiles show us a nice, extremely misjudged man, there are physiological abnormalities severe enough to get him a place in medical history under the 'Real Sick-os' category and an Academy Award for Best Actor in a Psychopathic Role." Paul pulled something out of his desk. Looked like a thick booklet or manual of some kind. "Don't ever make the mistake of speaking to him," Dr. Wiseman said. "You do that, you start thinking of him as your pal. He's very likable. One guard smuggled cigarettes to him, and Steiger killed him in an escape attempt a few weeks later." The psychiatrist paused again, and once more his voice took on that chillingly clinical demeanor. "Actually, that's not quite right. Steiger broke the guy's skull, all his ribs, and both legs. But the man didn't actually *die* until three very painful days later."

FOUND

Rachel pulled on the wheel, trying to keep a modicum of control over the car that seemed to slither like a snake over the white road. Like an unbroken horse, the car refused to go where she wanted it to without her practically forcing it. At least she no longer had to worry about ice on the road, which was the good news. The bad news was that the ice was gone because it had been buried under several inches of new powder. Snow was still falling, not hard enough to clog her wipers, but hard enough to make seeing difficult and headlights next to useless in the pre-night gloom.

Becky sat behind her, looking out the window at the formless white. Rachel had tried to talk to her a few times, but the little girl wasn't responding to her at all. And right now, Rachel couldn't spare the brain space necessary to talk: all her attention had to be on her driving, or they risked a wreck of huge proportions.

Flip-flop, flip-flop. The wipers went back and forth with numbing force, slamming snow out of the way with such power that the end of each arc was punctuated by a little slam as they changed direction. It was almost mesmerizing, and Rachel felt herself being lulled by the hypnotic sameness of the movement.

Flip-flop.

She felt her eyes droop. Just for a second; a second during which her body momentarily surrendered to the serenity of the snow, to the fatigue that her final battle with her husband had caused.

Then she snapped them back open, but it was too late.

The storm had come, and it had found them in the worst possible way.

Part Two: The Storm

Where ash-streams clash with frozen stones;
Where melancholy dwells;
Where time-lost souls proceed with groans
To hidden, nightmare-ringed cells,
To endure prodigious hells.

- *"Night's Plutonian Shore"*

Cold seeped through my clothes, touched my skin and gripped
With all the fierceness of a winter moan.
Behind the darkness, stretched across bleak hills,
The graveyard waited. I could not see dim stones.

-                               *Christmas   in   Elba*

MEAN

Paul swiveled around in his chair, looking out the barred window. The weather was literally deteriorating in front of his eyes. Snow dropped in a sudden sheet, and darkness seemed to fall over the landscape in an instant. The guard tower and the wall beyond were barely visible through the weather and the darkness.

"Here's the deal," said Paul, still looking out the window. "We have plenty of food in the facility for the staff and inmates for the next few days. So there's no danger of us starving out here. But it looks like we are going to be cut off until tomorrow, at least, and you're stuck here, too. I'll have Hip-Hop show you where you can bunk down, and we'll probably assign you to food detail. It's the least dangerous option right now." He swiveled back to face Jacky, who nodded.

A knock sounded at the door. Paul shouted, "In!" A moment later the door buzzed and unlocked, admitting Hip-Hop, Wade, and Sandy, the latter two looking downcast and bedraggled as puppies that had been hit with a rolled-up newspaper. Paul grimaced internally: he hadn't even started to reprimand them and they were already feeling sorry for themselves.

He spoke before any of the newcomers could. Hip-Hop tended to get territorial when Paul intruded on what the chief of security thought of as his exclusive domain, which included the guards, the prisoners, and just about everything else at The Loon. Paul also knew that Hip-Hop resented him for being his boss. Though just as with Wade and with Vincent Marcuzzi, Paul did not know what he had ever done to earn Hip-Hop's ire. So Paul didn't give the man a chance to take control of the conversation. "Hip-Hip," he said, "can you assign Jacky to one of the food details? And show him the ropes?"

"Sure," said Hip-Hop, and Paul could see the man was fuming.

"All right, Mr. Hales, why don't you wait outside the office until I'm done talking to Hip-Hop," said Paul. He made no mention of Wade and Sandy because, even though they were due for a serious chastising, he saw no need to humiliate them in front of one of their new co-workers.

"You want us to wait, too?" said Wade, the man sounding almost hopeful. Paul sighed. After purposefully avoiding this in front of Mr. Hales, here was Wade making it impossible for Paul to avoid confronting him. "No, he said, "I want to talk to you, too."

He fell silent then, waiting as Hip-Hop opened the door for Jacky and then shut it behind the new guard. Then he unleashed on Wade. He focused on Wade because Sandy, though not perfect, was a far better guard than Wade was, and he suspected that the whole Steiger fiasco would end up being Wade's fault when all the facts were known. "What the *hell* were you doing on the tower? Did watching the courtyard have anything to do with it?"

"We were watching," said Sandy in a sullen half-whisper.

"And you didn't notice Steiger stripping bare-butt naked and digging a cave the size of the Grand Canyon in the snow?" said Paul incredulously.

"It was cold. We were...uh, pouring coffee," said Wade.

"Pouring coffee?" Paul repeated. "Well, that's okay then. It's all right if America's Most Nutso gets out, just so you get your good to the last drop in! How long does it take you to pour coffee, Wade? Half an hour? Forty minutes?"

"Maybe it was frozen and they were having a coffee-sicle," said Hip-Hop.

Paul turned on him. "And you. You're the chief of security, aren't you? Do you think maybe you could explain to me where Steiger got a code card to the front gate? Call me a nut, but these things interest me." He looked at the three guards, all of who had apparently found something very interesting on the floor in front of them. "Any answers?" he continued. "Other than just sheer and obvious stupidity? No?"

Hip-Hop finally looked up again. "Dr. Wiseman, I *am* the chief of security. And I resent your accusations, as well as your stepping on my authority."

"Meaning what?" asked Paul. He couldn't believe that Hip-Hop was actually going to have a pissing contest with him right here and now, in front of the others after a blatant screw-up of these proportions.

"Meaning if anybody's gonna do any ass-chewing on Wade and Sandy, it ought to be me! And if *I'm* gonna get ass-chewed, it sure as hell ain't gonna be by you!"

"And *I* am the chief of staff," Paul responded coldly. "So like it or not, *everything* that happens to the prisoners or staff is my responsibility. And that means I'm in charge," he said. "Whether you like it or not."

MEETING

Jacky waited in the hallway, pacing nervously back and forth, waiting for Hip-Hop to come out and wondering exactly what he had gotten himself into here. The money had sounded great, and though he had spoken to several people about The Loon prior to arriving here, nothing had given him a hint of what a powder keg this place was.

Between politics and prisoners, he thought, I'll be lucky to get out of this place alive.

Below the argument, there was another noise: the low whine of the wind as it whipped over and around the walls of The Loon. It was a disconcerting sound, like being in an air raid shelter that was located a mile underground: the danger was muffled, but no less real for that fact.

Then a sudden clanking drew his attention to the stairwell that went down to the first floor and beyond.

That's a noisy staircase, he thought, then realized that was probably intentional, too: stairs that made noise were very helpful in making sure you always knew when someone was coming up the stairs...and having time to prepare if the person was an *uninvited* guest.

Jacky felt himself tense. They had just had a prison break, and very nearly a successful one. What was to prevent that from happening again? And any prisoner in this place would be just as likely to come up the stairs as he would be to try and run. That was one of the problems with crazies: they didn't always act in their best interest.

He loosened up a little when he saw a severe-faced older man in a lab coat come out of the stairwell and head straight to Dr. Wiseman's door. The man took out a code card and slid it through the door's card reader, apparently unaware of the full-blown argument that Jacky could hear going on the other side of it.

"Uhh…" Jacky mumbled, "I think Dr. Wiseman's busy right now."

The man looked at Jacky in such a way as to make Jacky feel as if he were a particularly nasty amoeba in a Petri dish. "Do you know who I am?" said the man.

Jacky looked at the man's coat. Unlike most of the people here, this man had no nametag on. "Sorry," said Jacky. "I…that is…no, I don't."

The man looked at Jacky, and even though Jacky stood an inch or two taller than the other man, he got the distinct impression the old fellow was actually looking *down* on him.

"I am Dr. Crane, owner and general director of this institute."

Jacky felt like he was about to wet himself. Perfect, he thought. Just perfect. I'm in the rabbit hole and I've just pissed off the Queen of Hearts.

"I'm sorry, sir," he began. "I didn't know. I was just –"

The man cut him off with an imperious wave. "Think nothing of it."

Then he turned on his heel and entered his code on Dr. Wiseman's door before throwing it open and walking through, leaving Jacky alone to ask himself if one hundred and twenty five thousand a year was worth it.

STATUE

Sandy watched in distress as the argument between the three men in the room raged. They were all talking over one another, Wade, Hip-Hop, and Dr. Wiseman all shrieking almost loud enough to drown out the sound of the nasty blizzard outside. Almost.

"...damn cold up there, and so what if we don't look down because our eyeballs are frozen shut...."

"...so don't you yell at my people unless I *say* you can yell...."

"...are the sorriest excuse for guards that I've ever...."

The three of them were going at it so loudly that no one noticed the door humming and clicking. But conversation slammed to a halt with the suddenness of a lightning strike when it opened and Crane walked in. Only Wade – always Wade, always the one to make things worse, just like he had on the tower by spilling coffee all over Sandy's lap – kept on shouting for a moment.

"...so next time you wanna yell," he was screaming, "why don't you just haul your skinny desk-running ass...." His voice trailed off then as he finally noticed Dr. Crane and fell silent after muttering an embarrassed and worried, "Shit."

Crane looked them all over. Sandy felt those blue eyes on her like a heat lamp, and felt totally in agreement with those who called the man "God."

After a long moment of nothing, Crane smiled. That was never a good sign. Crane smiling, in fact, was probably the only thing that scared Sandy more than Crane *not* smiling.

"Good morning, children," said Crane in a syrupy-sweet voice. "What seems to be the problem?"

All were silent for a moment, and Sandy felt no inclination to be the one to break the quiet. She thought fleetingly of Darryl, and wished that she was with him rather than here. Hell, she would rather be stuck in an *oven* than here.

But then Hip-Hop, Wade, and Dr. Wiseman all started speaking at once, again creating a wall of noise that was as real and intimidating as those that surrounded The Loon. Crane didn't seem to mind at all, though, and listened to everyone scream about everyone else for what seemed like an hour before finally waving at everyone but Dr. Wiseman to be silent.

Dr. Wiseman visibly gathered himself, then began in a much more calm tone: "Sir, we just had a breakout attempt. I tried to find you and let you know. *Steiger* got all the way to the outer court, and I believe it was due to the irresponsible -"

Crane again waved imperiously, and Sandy saw Dr. Wiseman fall silent, visibly fuming. "Did he get out?" asked Crane.

"What?" said Dr. Wiseman.

Crane grew impatient, looking like he was dealing with a neighbor's idiot children. "Steiger. Did...he...get...out?"

"No," said Paul. He looked down at his desk and shuffled some papers a bit nervously.

At that moment, Crane threw a vicious look at Wade. Dr. Wiseman didn't notice it, and Sandy expected that both Wade *and* she were about to get summarily dismissed and chucked out into the snow, but to her surprise, Crane only had eyes for Wade.

She sighed internally, then started as she thought, How does he know what happened? He hasn't really heard anything yet, so why is he mad at Wade?

Dr. Wiseman looked up then, and Crane redirected his stare back at the younger man. "I'll have an official report for you on the state forms by this evening," Dr. Wiseman said. "But the upshot is that I'm recommending we get ourselves a pair of new guards and put someone else in charge of the Institute's security measures."

Sandy felt her knees go wobbly and fought a sudden urge to pass out. She was getting fired.

To her surprise, though, Crane held his hands up in a manner she had never seen from him before.

Good gracious, she thought. Is Crane *placating* Dr. Wiseman?

Crane was many things. He was a scientist, a businessman...even an imperious beast sometimes. But the one thing he definitely was *not* was a peacemaker. And yet, there he was, hands up, saying softly, "I don't think that will be necessary, Dr. Wiseman." Sandy's wobbly knees firmed for a moment, then threatened to betray her once more as Crane turned his gaze on her and Wade. This time he did not look placating. He was angry.

But again, she thought he mostly looked angry at Wade. "I will deal with these three," said Crane.

"Sir," began Dr. Wiseman, "I really think that –"

"My office," interrupted Crane, and turned and left without a sound.

Wade, true to form, tried to throw a nasty look over his shoulder at Dr. Wiseman before leaving. The effect was marred, however, by the fact that he was clearly terrified of whatever awaited them in Crane's office.

Hip-Hop just left.

Sandy followed him, and she, too, looked over her shoulder. But not to throw a nasty look. She was just curious. Darryl had her somewhat infatuated, she knew, but Paul was also an interesting man. Not romantically, he was far from her type. But he had an air of melancholy around him that she found intriguing. Not a wimpy, please-pity-date-me kind of melancholy, but a genuine air of sadness that she suspected came from some horrific event in his past. But what that event might be, she couldn't even guess at. Jorge might know, she suspected; the two of them were friends, had even gone to some of the high school ball games together. But other than Jorge....

So she looked back. Curious.

Paul was looking at something: a picture on his desk. It was of a boy, she knew, but when she had asked about it once, about who the boy was, Paul had quickly changed the subject and ushered her out.

Now he was holding it. Not moving. He might as well have been a statue.

A crying statue.

SURVIVOR

Rachel had time to scream, but not much else. And in the time-dilating effect of panic, when the world slowed down around her as she leadenly tried to swerve the car so as to avoid hitting the massive snow bank that had drifted out onto the road – the bank that she was now about to hit dead-on due to her carelessness and fatigue – she noticed with a twinge of fear that Becky was *not* screaming. But she should have been. She was a little girl, her mommy was screaming, and now they were spinning around, a flat spin that made Rachel woozy.

But not a sound from her daughter.

She whipped the wheel back and forth, trying vainly to regain control of the car, praying to *la Virgen y los santos* that she would be able to stop the car before it hit.

The car was still spinning.

Becky was not making a sound.

It was all wrong, all wrong.

The car spun again, and she caught a glimpse of the snow bank, closer now.

She hit her brakes, trying to pump them, trying anything that might save her and her daughter's lives.

Still spinning.

No noise from her daughter.

All wrong.

Then the car slowed.

Spinning slower now.

But the bank was closer, too. She couldn't tell if they were going to hit it.

Another revolution.

And then….

The car stopped.

Rachel looked out her side window. The snow bank was literally only inches away from the glass. She had almost killed them. And even if she hadn't killed them, if the car had been stopped by impact, or immobilized in any way, she and Becky would certainly have frozen to death before reaching the Crane Institute; before reaching Jorge.

Becky.

She looked back at her daughter. The little girl was white and pinched-looking, the only color in her face fever-like highlights on her cheeks. She had her mouth tightly clenched, her hands clutching each other. But no sound.

No noise.

"Becky?" said Rachel. "You okay, *mi hija*?"

Becky did not respond. Did not move.

"Becky?" Rachel felt fear grip her, even more tightly than it had a moment ago, when death had loomed. To die with her daughter would be horrific, but to see her daughter go catatonic because of today's events…that would almost be worse.

To her relief, a moment later Becky slowly looked at her. The gaze was distant, but there was no doubt that Becky was *there*, though certainly scarred.

Children are survivors, thought Rachel. Look at me.

Then she cursed herself for putting her daughter into a situation where she would have to *be* a survivor.

She put the car into second gear, then tried to ease the car around the snow bank. Becky wasn't speaking, but Rachel couldn't deal with that right now.

They had to get to Jorge before the blizzard worsened. Because with every passing second, dying out here became less of a possibility and more of a probability.

HOOKS

Crane watched Hip-Hop and Wade from under heavy-lidded eyes. He didn't speak, letting his minions fidget in discomfort, making them wait on his pleasure. It was only right that they should feel his disappointment, his *disgust* at what had happened. Or rather, at what had *not* happened. Then he swiveled to look at Sandy, who was standing slightly behind the two men. Less at fault then either of them, Crane knew, but her general mediocrity was a constant affront to him. He would have fired her long ago had he not needed her for her...*usefulness* in fulfilling his plans – the *real* reason behind the existence of the Crane Institute.

Finally, he said, very slowly and quietly – he knew his silence pierced people more than any tirade could, "Who would like to tell me what happened?"

Hip-Hop and Wade glanced at each other. Sandy looked at the floor.

"Sandy?" he asked. She shook her head.

He sighed. "Very well, then. You may wait outside while I see if either of the gentlemen wish to answer."

Sandy looked up with what seemed an almost hysterically-relieved look. Crane knew she was thinking that she had been let off the hook. But it wasn't that. She just couldn't feel it. Like a master fisherman, Crane knew the best hook was one that was set so subtly that the fish was not aware of it until too late, but so deeply that no amount of struggle would get it off.

Sandy was a fish, swimming with a hook in her mouth. Soon he would reel it in. Soon it would be her turn.

As soon as Sandy departed, Crane turned to Wade and Hip-Hop. The two men had straightened their shoulders a bit when Sandy exited, as though they felt that with her gone, they could all be pals. But Crane knew they, too, were deeply set on his hooks, though theirs were of a different nature. So he was not surprised to see their shoulders slump again when he asked, "Why didn't Steiger make a successful getaway?"

Wade finally said, "I'm sorry, sir. I dumped an entire Thermos of coffee in her lap. Thought I distracted her for long enough for Steiger to get farther along. I didn't count on him burying himself like he did. I guess I blew it."

Crane focused a wrathful gaze on Wade. The man seemed to visibly wither under its power, which almost – *almost* – made Crane smile. All the planning that went into each jail break, all the effort. And now this one was wasted. The code key that Wade had slipped unnoticed into Steiger's cell had been retrieved, and though Crane had used his account privileges to loop video playback from that morning and to destroy any record of the card from the computers, so there was no way it could lead back to him, Hip-Hop, or Wade, still it was a tiresome chore. And now it would have to be repeated at some point.

"Sandy is such a sweet girl," mused Crane aloud. Wisely, neither Wade nor Hip-Hop – Crane loathed the name – spoke up; good dogs knew their places. "She's very useful," he continued, "for providing corroborating stories which lay the blame on something other than the Institute. Nevertheless, the fact remains that Steiger was supposed to escape and did not."

Crane turned to his computer. He brought up one of the cameras from outside. It was getting much darker, the snow creating a curtain of white that all but completely obscured visibility at times. And it was just getting started.

Perfect.

He turned back to the two cowering men. "Steiger is going to escape again. Tonight."

"How?" said Hip-Hop.

Crane sighed. This was the problem attendant to working with dogs: no capability for their own thought. He supposed that was fine, in the long run, since any house could only afford one master. But it was tedious at times. "Arrange it so that Steiger gets one of the guards alone in his cell," he said, his voice oozing patronizing tones. "Arrange it so the guard has enough time alone in there so that Steiger can...*convince* him to give up his access card and its accompanying code."

"But," said Wade, "Steiger'll kill anyone he gets in his cell."

"Yes," said Crane. A calculated risk, but Hip-Hop had been through this before, and Wade...he could see that Wade even now was realizing he was in too deep to get out. It would be done as Crane required. "Who will it be?"

Wade furrowed his brow, and Crane was sure whatever hamster that ran the wheel that passed for a brain with Wade was probably sprinting for all it was worth. "What about the new guy?" Wade finally said.

Crane smiled, thinking of the way that the new guard had spoken to him when he was entering Dr. Wiseman's office. "Fine," he said. "I don't much care for him."

FROZEN

Rachel drove, thankful that finally the road had straightened out.

She risked a glance in the rear-view mirror. "You okay, baby?"

Still no answer, and she still couldn't stop or even take her eyes off the road for more than a fraction of a second. The road was straight, but still slick and dangerous. It could still kill them.

The storm was much worse now, snow coming down harder than ever. She could barely see through the windshield, and knew in her heart of hearts that at this point even getting within walking distance of Jorge's work would be a miracle.

As if in agreement, the car shuddered for a moment as the wheels hit an ice patch and skidded for a few feet.

The storm was worse.

The snow was heavy.

They were going to die.

"Please, God," she said.

MACHINE

Paul took Hales through the sleeping quarters on the second floor. It was Spartan; military. Two lines of bunks, a footlocker for each, and the obligatory first aid kit. The only thing that differentiated it from an army barracks was the color of the sheets – light blue instead of puke green – and the number of pictures on the wall.

Paul pointed at one of the beds. "You can use that one," he said. "Most of them are going to be empty, so we're pretty open here."

Hales flopped down on his bed, clearly tired, then looked at Paul as if to say, "Sorry, was that okay?"

Paul waved him off. "The roads are probably closed. So you're likely going to be here for the next day or two."

Hales was silent, clearly digesting this information. "My machine picked a helluva week to stop working," he finally said.

Paul handed the man a thick book. "Training manual," he said. "Read it."

"What do you want me to do after?"

Paul stared out the window: since the staff sleeping quarters was on the second floor, there was a small window, covered in bars, that allowed a view of the prison courtyard. The wind was pummeling it with gale force, throwing snow at it with a sound like pellets being hurled at the glass. The storm had finally come, but Paul knew that what they were seeing was just the leading edges of it. Things were going to get much, much worse. Bad enough to freeze a person who was out in the weather for more than a few minutes without proper protection.

"The Loon is like a finely tuned engine," Paul said to Hales. "It'll run forever, under the right conditions. But throw a wrench in the works, and all hell breaks loose."

He turned to Hales to see if the man had gotten his message.

Hales cracked a smile, and Paul couldn't help but like the young man, in spite of the inconvenience his presence was causing. "You want me to just sit tight until you say otherwise?" said Hales.

Paul smiled back. He almost felt as though his face might crack; smiling was not something he did often these days. It felt good. He hoped Hales made it and stuck around. The guards that Paul genuinely liked were Jorge, Mitchell, and Daryll – "the beaner and the bears," Jorge always said with his wiseacre grin – and having another friendly face would be a welcome addition. "That would be a good idea," he replied.

Paul exited the room, calling over his shoulder, "Bathrooms are left of the stairs, next to the staff kitchen. Food's in the kitchen if you want to scrounge around. Our boss may be a bit eccentric, but he keeps the place stocked."

In response, he heard Hales murmur something that chilled Paul, as though it were a harbinger of ill tidings: "I don't think I'm very hungry."

The wind whistled.

The storm.

CROOKED

Wade's eyes grew wide. He couldn't believe what he was hearing. He knew he'd have to do something for his money – an extra hundred and fifty grand a year under the table and tax free wasn't piss, so he expected some dirty work. But *this*. "You want me *outside*?" he asked again. "Covering the front exit?" He could hear the weather outside, even through The Loon's thick walls, and wasn't happy at his assignment.

"Correct," said Crane, the snotty look on his face digging into Wade like a jab in the ribs.

"Won't the cameras pick me up?" asked Wade. That was a deal-breaker. One-fifty could buy you a lot of play with Wade Shickler, but no amount of money was enough to buy a jail term for aiding and abetting in a breakout attempt.

Crane folded his fingers together and looked at Wade like he was a booger or some turd hanging off his ass. "With the weather as bad as it will be tonight, the external cameras will be useless, Mr. Shickler. You don't have to worry about being seen."

"But the wind will foul any shot with a tranquilizer pistol," said Wade. He knew he was grasping at straws; knew that he was going to end up doing what Crane told him too, but he couldn't help trying, any more than a drowning man would claw for air even at fifty feet below. "I mean," he continued, "it's not like I *tried* to hit Steiger today; I aimed about forty yards to the side of him, and the stupid wind put me so off course I accidentally bagged the guy."

"I had wondered why you were the one to actually stop Steiger from escaping," said Crane dryly. Then: "In any event, if you are concerned about the accuracy of the pistols, then I suggest you get in the tower and use the high-power trank rifle that is, I believe, there for such eventualities. Hit Steiger as near to the wall as you can, then bring him into the lab."

Wade pointed at Hip-Hop, his voice growing whiny as he said, "Why can't he do it?"

"Because," said Crane with more than a touch of irritation, "he will be arranging the accident in the prison."

Crane turned to Hip-Hop. "I want it done better this time," said the owner of The Loon. "Wade will be on the wall at seven p.m. I expect Steiger to escape by seven fifteen." He turned back to Wade. "Trank him, and bring him back to my lab through the generator shack. Steiger will be found missing a short time later. We will search, but as he is not on the grounds, and was in possession of the unfortunately dead new guard's pass, we shall presume him escaped. Probably dead in the frozen wastes. This shall be a well-organized, perfectly controlled operation. No more errors. Any questions?" he finally asked, his gaze widening to look at both Wade and Hip-Hop. Wade said nothing; neither did Hip-Hop. "Good," said Crane, looking down in a way that Wade knew was a dismissal.

Wade turned to go, followed by Hip-Hop. He was stopped by Crane's voice. "Oh, and Wade," said Crane. Wade turned back around. "It's going to be sixty degrees below out, without wind chill. So wear a coat: I can't afford to take the time to find another crooked security guard."

Wade felt himself grow cold inside, realizing perhaps for the first time how little his life was worth to Crane.

"Wouldn't want to inconvenience you," he said as he left. But he said it very quietly.

People were going to die tonight; probably more would follow in the months and years to come. And Wade did not ever want to find himself on that list.

ROADSIDE

The wipers were frozen to the thick sheet of ice that the windshield had transformed into. They no longer lulled Rachel, for they no longer went *flip-flop, flip-flop*. They were still.

The car sputtered.

"Please, not now," said Rachel. As if in answer, a large gust of wind buffeted the car, rocking it back and forth on its springs. Then the car stuttered again.

Coughed.

Stopped.

Rachel tried turning the car off then on again.

Nothing.

"No, please, no," she was mumbling. "No, no, no...."

"Mommy?" said Becky from the backseat, and even though the car was dead, even though they might – or would *probably* – freeze, Rachel almost laughed. Because Becky was talking again, and so Rachel knew that her daughter was going to survive this day after all.

But then another gust hit the car, actually feeling like it had *moved* them, and the laughter died in her throat, replaced by a cold clutching feeling, as if death were seeping into the car and gripping her now with its icy fingers.

"Yes, baby?" she said, but Becky didn't answer her. Rachel opened the front door and hurried around to the trunk. The snow was already building up around the small vehicle.

Another ten minutes and it would be up to the windows. Ten more and it would be buried on one side.

An hour, and there would be no trace of the car.

No trace of *them*.

She started pawing through magazines, pushing aside the spare tire, searching for something. Pinching back panic.

She saw a glow in the snowy wasteland. Far, but hopefully not *too* far. It was the Crane Institute. What had Jorge called it? The Loon. The place looked like it was less than half a mile off, judging by the light.

Too far, she thought. We'll never make it.

Then she thought, We *have* to make it.

At last, Rachel found what she was looking for. She picked it up, slammed the trunk closed, then went back into the front seat. She pulled the emergency kit apart. She had been the one to get it, because at heart she was still a tropical *mexicana*, and this much snow – or any snow – continued to unnerve her. So the emergency kit was something, one of the few things, that she had stood up to Tommy on.

The thought of Tommy brought back sudden images. A gout of blood. A knife in his hand. The sound of the vase crushing his skull.

She looked at the contents of the car emergency kit. Emergency blanket. Road flares. Band-aids, tooth paste. There was even a needle and thread and a little bar of soap. She dumped it all out, and spoke to her daughter, trying to keep her voice even, trying not to betray the terror she was feeling at the prospect of taking her little girl out into the worst storm she had ever seen.

"Okay, honey. We're stuck, but Uncle Jorge's building is nearby. But let's take this stuff just in case, okay?" Becky didn't answer. "Honey?" said Rachel. Then she said, "Would you like to carry this stuff?" Still nothing. She tried another tack. Sighing in mock relief, she said, "Just as well, because carrying this is definitely a big kid thing. No little kids could do it. Not little like you."

"Not little," said Becky.

"Oh, no?" said Rachel in mock surprise. "How will you prove it, *princesa*?"

Without a word, Becky unlocked her seat belt and leaned forward, grabbing handfuls of the emergency kit's contents and throwing them in her own brightly-colored bag, the bag she had packed when Rachel told her that...

(*I killed your father.*)

...they were going.

Soon everything was packed. Rachel smiled at Becky, hoping to coax a smile in return. But all the little girl offered was a slight upturn of the corners of her mouth.

Better than nothing.

Rachel grabbed her daughter. Hugged her. Hard, like it was their last hug. She resolved that it would not be. They *would* make it.

They had to.

Then she got out. The wind blasted the door out of her hands, tearing at her flesh.

She smiled again at her daughter, encouraging, trying to throw off the clinging vestiges of the nightmare they had just left behind.

And hoping that they were not simply embarking on a new one.

VISITOR

Paul entered the staff room in time to see Jacky stretch, put down his employee manual, and wander over to the window. The wind was howling constantly now, a low whine punctuated every so often by a sharp shriek as gusts passed over The Loon. Paul could see the outer wall, but only just barely. In an hour or so, he knew, even that would be impossible, and a few hours after that you would be able to get lost and die within mere feet of the structure.

We're in it now, he thought. No one in or out until this is over.

As if to echo his thoughts, Hales murmured, "That's creepy."

The wind agreed, wailing a staccato burst of sound.

"You get used to it," Paul said, and couldn't help but laugh as Hales whipped around as though he had been tazered, literally grabbing at his chest, a look of surprise so deep Paul had to apologize.

"It's okay," Hales said, leaning and panting for a moment, his shock at hearing Paul behind him so severe that he was out of breath.

Paul waited for him to calm, then handed him what he had brought up from his office. "It's your card. Keep it on you at all times. I programmed your social security number as the code for now. After the storm we'll give you something a bit less obvious, but right now I want you to be able to remember it." Paul paused for a moment as something occurred to him. "You do know your social by heart, right?"

"Yeah," said Jacky.

"Good. That card will get you into every part of The Loon except the generator shack. Don't lose it. Don't give out the code." Paul sobered, the smile he had worn upon seeing Hales' frightened response to his entry fading. "And do *not* go wandering around alone until you know the ropes. You open the wrong door without announcing yourself and you end up with a dart in your neck and a killer headache…if you're very, very lucky."

The wind whipped up again, as though it were irritated that Paul and the other man were no longer paying attention to it and demanding that the situation be rectified. Paul obliged, looking out the window and watching the snow flail about in manic flurries. Night-time dark out. Everything was either a blur or gone completely.

"Not even four o'clock and it looks like Halloween out there," he said. "It's going to be a long night."

Hales nodded grimly before pocketing his code card. "Thanks," he said.

"Don't mention it." Paul handed him another paper, though still looking out the window. "I got your schedule ready. I'm putting you with Darryl. He's the big guard, kinda looks like he played for the Dallas Cowboys or something."

"*Which* big guy is he?" asked Hales, clearly confusing Darryl and Mitchell, The Loon's resident strong men.

Paul smiled a bit again. He'd had the same problem when he first came here. "Darryl is the one who looks like he played for the Dallas Cowboys. Mitchell is the one who looks like he *eats* Dallas Cowboys." Upon seeing Jacky's confusion, he laughed. "Don't worry, the staff will all differentiate to you soon enough. Especially since there's not going to be much to do for the next..." Paul drifted off, squinting through the window. "What the *hell* is that?" He said suddenly.

A shadowy figure was at the outer gate, barely visible in the maelstrom outside. Paul tensed, thinking irrationally that it must be Steiger again. But no, Steiger was still in his cell; he'd actually just checked on the man before going to program Hales' code card. So who was that? Another breakout attempt?

Then he watched as the very last thing he would have thought possible occurred: the shadowy figure cracked open the door in the outer gate...admitting another person.

"You expecting a visitor?" asked Hales.

PUNISHMENT

Darryl Simons was a Montana boy, through and through. That was why he didn't mind the blizzard that was now raging outside. Montana was as much a part of him as his bones or his blood, so hating it would be like hating himself.

It hadn't always been like that. There had once been a time when Darryl would have given anything to get out of this place. And for a while it had looked like he was on his way. Then a sudden hit by a left tackle who had appeared out of nowhere left Darryl with two popped knees and a burst dream of college football – possibly even a pro career. Darryl had been surprised to find out during his time in the hospital how little it mattered to find out that he would, in fact, be staying in Montana.

His parents had been upset, especially his father. They had raged and railed and carried on about the left tackle, about the failure of Darryl's teammates, about the game of football itself.

Never about Darryl's knees. Never about Darryl. His family loved *him*, he knew, unconditionally and without reservation. But they had wanted him to leave, to get out, to *escape* the icy clutches of the mountains they lived in – to hide from the unyielding stare of the Big Sky State.

Darryl had calmed them. And in so doing, he had discovered that he was calm himself. That he didn't mind the prospect of Montana. That he was even *happy* to find out he would be staying for a while.

Perhaps even forever.

Or until he died. Which since Darryl had every intention of living forever promised to be the same thing.

Not that he *loved* the raging storm outside, any more than he would have loved a sudden and severe case of appendicitis or pneumonia. But he didn't hate it. It was part of Montana. It simply *was*, and Mitchell recognized the futility of hating something that was, ultimately, part of his own makeup as much as it was a part of Montana's ever-changing sky. The storm was not to be hated, simply accepted. And perhaps used as an excuse to find a warm somebody to curl up with.

That thought led inexorably to Sandy.

It wasn't that she was the prettiest person Darryl knew – an ex football star in a small town like Stonetree had his pick of pretty girls. But Darryl wasn't looking for mere outward appearances. His parents had raised him differently than that. He wanted something more, something different.

Something...*good*.

And then Sandy appeared, showing up for her first day at The Loon like a puppy right out of the pet store: anxious to please, quick to learn, fast to smile. The smile alone was a reason to like her, if for no other reason than because it was a smile utterly bereft of the usual traces of jadedness or irony that so typified many people who worked in the corrections industry. Jorge was a good example of that. A good guard, a good man, a good *person*, but even he had a sarcastic streak a mile long that Darryl knew operated primarily to keep the Hispanic guard safe within a protective shell of humor

Sandy had no such protections. She was a candle to the world, and that made her both vulnerable and terribly attractive.

Darryl felt himself drift away from attending to the monitors in the "reception room" of The Loon. Normally he had no trouble paying attention while on monitor duty. The monitors made him feel a bit like God. Not in the strange, even creepy way that he suspected Dr. Crane felt like God. But in the simple, all-seeing way that he imagined God felt. Click, and he could see the bathrooms. Click, he could see the kitchen. Click, the prison. Click, outside. Almost anywhere in The Loon, and he could be there.

But not today. Not with the storm raging and making outside visibility an ever-greater fiction. And not while thinking of Sandy. Luckily, Leann was also on monitor duty, and Darryl trusted the harsh but effective older woman to cover him during any momentary lapse of watchfulness. He rarely allowed himself to daydream on watch at The Loon – it was just too good a way to get hurt or killed – but he was also human, and once in a while the siren effects of Sandy's smile drew his attention even when she wasn't around.

That was why it was such a surprise when one of the two doors behind him – the door leading to the staff facility and not, thankfully, the one leading to Dr. Crane's office and living quarters – suddenly clicked and then slammed open, followed immediately by Paul and the new kid...Hales his name was. Jackson Hales.

Darryl glanced at Leann and saw the older woman jump. Apparently she had been caught unawares by Paul's sudden entrance too, which made him feel a bit better about his indulgent lack of attention.

"Whassup, Paul?" he asked.

"Who's coming in?" asked Paul brusquely.

Darryl glanced at Leann, who cocked an eyebrow. A small move, but it nonetheless eloquently communicated "How the hell should I know?" to Darryl as effectively as a soliloquy.

"What are you talking about?" she said, glancing at the monitors, which was a joke because the storm had gotten bad enough that outside visibility was just short of nil.

"No one that I know," said Darryl at the same time.

Then, as though God were punishing him for thinking he was all-seeing in even a limited way, Darryl heard a buzz on the intercom, followed by Jeff's voice: "It's Jeff. Coming in, so don't trank us."

"Us?" said Paul into the intercom.

"We got visitors," said Jeff.

Darryl lifted an eyebrow himself, but immediately pressed a button. The front door buzzed open, and the last thing he would have expected walked in.

UNCERTAINTY

Paul had seen pictures of her, so he knew who one of them was. But he had never seen Jorge's sister up close, certainly not up close with various bruises and frozen blood on her face. At first he thought the blood must have been caused by an on-the-road accident of some sort, then he saw more clearly that it was the result of some altercation. He had done enough time helping battered women to recognize the signs of domestic violence.

Then he saw under the blood and bruises, under the outside of her, and nearly gasped.

The pictures Jorge displayed so proudly to those who would listen – "*Mi hermanita*," he would say, which Paul knew meant "My little sister" – had not done Rachel de los Santos justice. She was beautiful. No, not just beautiful, *stunning*. And Paul was, indeed, stunned. He felt himself gaping like a halibut, felt his mouth move with no sound coming out. He knew he must look like a fool, but for a wonderful moment he didn't care. Beauty palpably radiated from her gaze, the beauty of someone who has fought for years and years to live in an ugly world, even though she herself was an angel.

Then Rachel de los Santos reached down into her coat, and this time Paul really *did* gasp, for when she opened it he saw another pair of feet, and a little girl – again, someone Paul had seen in Jorge's photos; this one was his niece, Becky – stepped forward. Like her mother, she bore fresh bruises and even a trace of blood on her face, as well as a thin beauty that

Paul sensed might shatter like fine chinaware if pressed too hard.

I won't press you, he thought, I'll protect you.

He had a moment to wonder where that thought had come from, his thoughts turning bleakly to Sammy, when Jeff, sounding almost embarrassed, spoke. "They were at the outer gate," he said, and he sounded more like a kid who had just gotten caught with his fingers in the sugar than like a grown man who had clearly just saved someone's life. Paul glanced at one of the readouts on the monitor board, and saw the temperature outside was ten below zero and falling fast. The two girls wouldn't have lasted long out there.

But where had they *come from*? Paul wondered.

Apparently Leann was having the same thoughts, because she responded to Jeff with a harsh "They *what*?" and Darryl followed up with "Jesus, Mary, and Joseph, what were you ladies doing out there in this kind of weather?"

Neither visitor spoke, and it didn't take a psychiatrist to tell that the bruising was fresh. Paul spoke gently to the mother. "Rachel, right? Rachel...Taylor," he finally said, remembering what Jorge had said his sister's married name was.

A flash of anger sparked in the woman's eyes, but she didn't lash out, merely murmured, "It's de los Santos, not Taylor."

Paul understood. Again, it didn't take a medical degree to see what had happened, and while part of him was glad that the two women had escaped an obviously abusive relationship, another part of him groaned. Not today, he thought. Not with the storm, and with Steiger acting so unusual, and Dr. Crane playing Houdini and disappearing, and...

He could have gone on that way for quite some while, but told himself to shut up.

Then he turned to Leann and said, "Get on the horn and find Jorge." Leann nodded and immediately picked up a phone. Paul leaned down to Becky. He knew who she was, but said, "And what's your name?" He looked at her lip, which was puffy as though she had smashed into something. Probably her father's fist. "What happened?" he asked. "Did you trip out there? Fall and hurt yourself?" He smiled, trying to jolly her into responsiveness.

It didn't work. She merely turned and buried her face in her mother's coat.

"Her name's Becky," said Rachel.

Paul smiled at the girl, hoping she would turn and see him. "Becky," he said. "Pretty name for a pretty girl." But it was no use; the little girl did not turn back to him.

Behind him, Leann hung up. "Jorge's in the prison area and can't leave Marty alone back there." Paul felt Leann, Jeff, Darryl, and even Hales looking at him expectantly. What was he going to do with these uninvited and potentially dangerous guests? Not that they would intentionally harm anyone, Paul could see instantly. But loose cogs were not good in a machine as tightly wound as The Loon.

"Jacky," he said after a moment, not realizing that he had slipped into the familiar form of Hales' name, "you ready for your first assignment?"

"Ready and waiting."

"Would you please escort Rachel and Becky back to my office and have them wait for me there?"

"Sure," said Jacky. He held out his hand to Becky, trying to coax the little girl into taking it. "Come on, cutey."

Paul was unprepared for the violence of Rachel's response. The mother slapped Jacky's hand away from her daughter, nearly screaming, "Don't touch my daughter!" She pulled Becky even closer to her, and as she did her coat slipped down in the back and Paul glimpsed several long, dark bruises that ran down her neck and shoulders.

He felt rather than saw Darryl and Leann both stiffen behind him, and could tell they were feeling the same mix of emotions he had felt: happiness that the woman and her child had made it here and were not dead in some white trash home somewhere, anger at a man that would stoop so low...and nervousness at the new and highly uncertain element that had just been introduced at The Loon.

ASSIGNMENT

Jacky came *this* close to wetting his pants when the woman yelled, "Don't touch my daughter!" He was glad he hadn't, since he suspected spontaneous urination would not endear him to anyone on staff at The Loon – but at the same time he had to wonder again what more could go on that would be out of the ordinary. He knew his presence here was unplanned and, he sensed, unwelcome, and now this woman and her child were here.

At the same time, he also felt pride that he had been given his first assignment. He knew it amounted to little more than a babysitting gig, and that Dr. Wiseman was probably giving him the job as much to keep Jacky out of everyone's hair as anything else, but he still couldn't help but feel flushed with glee as he used his very own card and his very own code to buzz through the door to the staff area, then took Rachel and her daughter, Becky, up the clanking steps to the second floor.

Another buzz and swipe when they got to Dr. Wiseman's office, and Jacky bowed semi-gallantly to the woman and motioned them through. Even with her bruises – and Jacky wished he could be alone in the room with the guy who had done that to her – the woman was a looker. Long legs, curvy but not *too* curvy, she was just the way Jacky liked them. Too bad she was older, and had a kid, and probably a husband, and...

Whoa, he thought. That's one "too bad" too many, and just about enough to stop me dead.

He followed them through the door, pulling out a chair for Rachel and another for Becky. The little girl was wearing a bright backpack, and Jacky was shocked to see what looked like a pair of real road flares sticking out of the pack.

Becky seemed to notice his gaze, because she suddenly shifted her pack and shoved everything deeper inside, then zipped it up solemnly. The words "Emergency Pack" were stenciled in childish scrawl across the pack, and Jacky wondered what kind of shitty life this kid had led to make her have something like that all done up and ready just in case the guy who had obviously been beating her finally snapped.

Jacky gulped, thinking of the abusive fathers he had met. None of them were anything more than pint-sized psychos who would probably fit in just fine at The Loon. That led inexorably to thinking about the kind of people who *were* here: Bloodhound, so vicious even after heavy doping. The strangely silent inmates. Steiger, so cheerful and yet – if Dr. Wiseman was to be believed – the deadliest thing that the world had seen since smallpox.

He gulped again. Come to think of it, if the girl's father was anything like The Loon's inmates, maybe he *didn't* want to be alone with the man after all.

LOCATIONS

Jeff Radstone flushed hot in spite of the cold when Paul turned to him and said, "What the hell were you thinking, Jeff? We're not a babysitting service."

Jeff didn't like being pushed around: it was part of why he was a guard, so he could be the one push*ing*. And yet here he was, backed into the wall by Paul's sudden outburst. He knew that Paul was just worried about the storm and about the woman and her kid. He didn't know the details, but rumor had it that Paul had lost his own son somehow. So Jeff imagined it would be tough for Paul to see Becky, such a beautiful little girl, so terribly bruised and beaten. And since the girl's father wasn't here for Paul to lash out at, apparently Jeff was a handy substitute.

Christ, he thought, I should be a goddam shrink myself.

Out loud, he responded to Paul's verbal onslaught with a loud, "What the hell was I supposed to do? It's cold enough out there to freeze a turd before it's half out your ass."

Paul's lip curled in clear disgust at the image, but Darryl came to Jeff's rescue with a loud guffaw that did wonders for defusing the tension in the air. "That's disgusting, Jeffrey," said Leann.

Jeff did a little mini-bow to the older woman. "Thank you, milady," he said. Then turned to Paul and, seeing that the doctor had himself back under control, he said in a quieter voice, "Was I supposed to just leave them out there?"

Paul pinched the bridge of his nose like he was nursing the mother of all migraines and sighed. "No. Of course not. You did good, Jeff. Sorry I yelled, just...forget it. Anyone else on the wall with you when they came in?"

"Sandy," said Jeff.

"Have her lock the outer door manually and bring her in. If it's that cold," he said with a half-smile, "we can't risk losing her to a turd-sicle."

This time it was *Jeff's* turn to guffaw. Paul was an okay guy. A little high-strung, but Jeff supposed that anyone in charge of this particular loony bin would have to be.

He saw Paul glance at the monitors. The outside ones showed – literally – only snow. The doctor continued, "Looks like you can't see three feet in front of you out there, anyway" Then Paul asked Darryl, "Where's everyone else at?"

The football player checked his monitors. "Marty and Jorge are still on inmate patrol in the prison, Sandy's outside but we'll get her in, we're in here, the new guy's upstairs with our visitors." Darryl clicked rapidly through the monitors' viewpoints until he located the rest of the crew. "Donald, Vincent, Mitchell, Wade, and Hip-Hop are all working on getting dinner ready for the inmates in the downstairs kitchen."

Paul pinched his nose again. "I forgot about dinner. Who's on for delivery tonight?"

"Wade and Hip-Hop were scheduled to do it, but..." Darryl paused. "That's weird."

"What?" said Paul, and Jeff could hear the tension creeping back into the doctor's voice.

"No big deal, Paul," said Darryl reassuringly. "Just looks like Hip-Hop changed the roster to have Jacky go with him to feed the inmates instead of Wade." The big man shrugged. "Probably wanted to show him the procedure."

"When's dinner?" asked Paul.

"About an hour," answered Leann.

"Okay," said Paul. "Call me if anything *else* happens. Tell everyone not on active duty to get plenty of sleep tonight. No slumber parties: we'll all need to stay alert while this storm's on. I'm going up to talk to our new guests." He glanced at Jeff once more. "Sorry again, Jeff. The storm's driving me nuts faster than the inmates. You did good bringing them in." Then the doctor snapped his fingers as a new thought apparently came to him.

"Where's God?" he asked.

"I can't see him on the monitors, so he's probably in his office," said Darryl.

"I wonder if he's even noticed the storm," said Paul.

EYES

It walks.
Change.
Then it slithers.
Change.
Then it crawls.
Change.
Then it flops like a fish-thing.
Change.
Change.
Change....
Something is wrong.

It is shifting more and more. And it is already hungry again. In pain again. Its captor sits in the light and watches it writhe in pain and now its captor is laughing and it wants to kill the thing that has kept him prisoner, to kill it and kill it forever.

It writes in its own acid-drool on the floor. "KiL u fOReVer." Then wipes the drool-sketch out with more acidic secretions.

Its captor is not laughing now. It looks angry.

And with anger comes the light and the burning.

REPLACEMENT

Dr. Crane stood before his creation and watched it shift. Something was different now, the thing was unstable, moving faster and faster from form to form, almost as though it was losing control of itself.

That was not entirely unexpected. Indeed, it was the reason – one of the reasons – that Crane had moved the timetable up on this iteration of his experiment.

He looked at his watch. Only a few more hours and Hip-Hop and Wade would set the plan in motion. Steiger would "get out," only to be caught again unbeknownst to most of the staff and to *all* of the outside world. The Loon was an excellent place to hide the inmates that "escaped": no one expected to find them in a hidden lab in the basement of the very facility from which they had just they appeared to escape.

The creation was hissing, oozing, almost appearing to melt before Crane's eyes.

Unstable, he thought. They are all unstable.

Out loud, he said, "Restless? Can't say I blame you. I wouldn't worry though. Tomorrow morning I'll have your replacement, and you'll be just a bad dream."

OPTIONS

Paul walked into his office and was struck again by the beauty of the woman who now sat with her daughter on her lap, both of them watching Jacky as though they were worried he might erupt out of his seat at any moment and start beating them with a nightstick.

After what Paul supposed they had been through, however, he couldn't say he blamed them.

He glanced away as soon as they looked at him, hoping that neither had noticed how his gaze lingered a moment *too* long on Rachel's lovely face; how it lasted just a smidge too long on Becky's childlike sorrow.

He thought of Sammy again.

And now, here was another child who would, like it or not, depend on him for the next few days. He prayed silently that this time it would work out better than it had the first time.

The little girl again buried her face in her mother's clothes when Paul walked in. He didn't try to jolly her out of it again. She was grieving, perhaps in shock. She needed a bit of peace and quiet.

He looked at Jacky. "Jacky," he said, "Why don't you go downstairs and help the guys in the large kitchen. They're getting dinner ready for the inmates and could use some help. Then Hip-Hop wants you to assist him with the meals themselves."

161

Jacky nodded, then tipped an imaginary cap at Rachel and Becky before leaving the room. Paul turned to face the woman and her daughter. "My name's Dr. Paul Wiseman. I'm Chief of Staff at this facility." He waited a moment, and when no response was forthcoming, asked, "Do you know where this is?"

"The Loon," said Rachel quietly.

The little girl continued looking away; continued to say nothing.

"What were you doing out there in this storm? You knew it was coming, didn't you?" Rachel shook her head. "You didn't? Why were you out?"

He didn't expect an answer; not really. And he got what he expected: evasion. "Where's Jorge?" asked Rachel.

"He's patrolling the prison," said Paul. "We don't have enough people to really go around right now. Bad time to visit."

"I'm sorry," said Rachel. "If you can help me get my car dug out we'll leave."

Paul saw in her eyes that she already knew that was impossible, so he answered her truthfully and quickly: "You can't. You're stuck here with us, I'm afraid."

"How long?" she asked.

"Until the roads clear. Late tomorrow at the earliest. We'll get the county people or the Rangers to dig your car out then."

Rachel paled. Paul could see her going through her options. And when she quietly whispered, "What are we going to do?" he had no answer.

Because he suspected the question was not really for him.

He suspected that whatever these women weren't telling him, it was much worse than what he had originally thought.

SOON

Crane threw a long last look at the creature. It was still shifting, pulsing in the darkness of its prison, which now seemed wet; coated with slime. The thing was almost dissolving, its metabolism going so fast to keep up with its transformations that unless it got something to eat fast – which Crane had no intention of providing it – it would perhaps just literally fall apart.

A hissing sound came.

Crane looked closer.

The thing was writing again. Etching words on the ground. That was disturbing to Crane. Highly disturbing. All the other test subjects had shown great promise for what he wanted, but none of them had shown the least trace of humanity or even awareness.

The writing shouldn't be possible. Not with what had been done to this creature's brain.

For a moment Crane debated letting it live. But only a moment. If it could write, who knew what other surprises – some of them probably much less pleasant – this thing was hiding?

The sizzling stopped.

Crane flashed his ever-present LED light at the creature. It shrieked and pulled away, leaving only the words on the floor:

SoON
soOn SOon
sooN Soon
SOON

MUTE

Becky felt like her blanket had been thrown over her head ever since Daddy had hit her earlier in the day. It hadn't been the first time he had beaten her, but it had been the first time that he had hit her with his fist.

The first time Mamá ever hurt him.

Then she thrust the thought out of her mind. It was hard. So much blood.

Then the blanket fell again around her mind. Making it hard to think, but at the same time cloaking her, shielding her. Protecting her, just like a good blanket should. Blankets were for babies, that's what Daddy said –

So much blood -

Stop. Don't think of that!

She shuddered.

The Nice Man must have seen it, because he said, "Is she okay?"

"She's fine," said Mommy. But she said it too fast. Too fast.

Rachel wanted to talk, but couldn't.

She was not fine.

Nothing was fine.

BLOOD

Paul was getting seriously worried about the little girl, but knew that his mother would not permit him to touch her. So he took them across the hall to the staff sleeping quarters. It looked more like a barracks than ever to his eyes, though he knew he was projecting his version of what Rachel was seeing onto the place. Still, even if it *was* a barracks, it was the safest place to sleep.

"You can sleep here," he said, gesturing at the cots.

"With other people?" asked Rachel.

Paul saw instantly what was coming, and grimaced inwardly. Stupid, he thought of himself. But there was no helping it. "Yes, everybody sleeps here," he said.

"We can't stay," said Rachel.

"Look," began Paul. "The roads are closed, and you can't leave. None of us can lea -"

"No, I mean we can't stay here. Not if everyone is sleeping here. I won't let my daughter...."

Her voice trailed off, and Paul examined her face. Becky was in serious shock, and if he couldn't get her to respond to him soon, he would have to do something about it whether Rachel approved or not. But now was not the time. He could see that the woman was on the verge of breaking.

"Miss, please," he pleaded.

"No," was all she said.

She bit her lip. Hard. Paul thought he could see blood.

DELIVERIES

Hip-Hop was nervous. So much depended on the next few minutes. He was wracking his brain, thinking of the best way to get Jacky alone.

The soon-to-be-dead new kid.

Hip-Hop thrust the thought from his mind. Don't think of him as Jacky, he thought. It's just Hales or the new kid.

But it was hard. The kid had an infectious smile that made people want to like him, to help him.

To not kill him.

Hip-Hop focused on two things: the plan and all the money he was making here.

The new kid was nice.

Money was nicer.

How do I get him alone?

Then, as so often seemed to happen when Crane was planning things, the universe seemed to bend itself to the plan. Hip-Hop was in the main kitchen – the galley, the staff called it – getting a bunch of microwave dinners ready for the inmates. No forks, no spoons, no knives. Never any cutlery for the inmates. Just finger foods and soft plastic cups with water.

Vincent and Donald were there, helping out. Or coming as close to helping as the Mafia wannabe and his split-lipped retard of a pal ever came, which wasn't too close. Mitchell was there, too, the gigantic man as quiet and hard-working as ever, doing the work of both Vincent and Donald as well as his own.

Wade was there, too, Hip-Hop's co-conspirator quietly helping, clearly waiting for Hip-Hop to take the lead on what to do.

And then there was Jacky.

The new kid had picked up on the procedure for laying out the food on the trays quickly, which seemed silly but wasn't when you were dealing with over one hundred people who all needed to be fed and who would gladly use anything you gave them to kill someone with if at all possible.

He'll be a good guard.

Another thought to thrust out of his mind. Hales wasn't going to get a chance to be a good guard. Because Hip-Hop's job was to get him alone with Steiger and let nature take its course. Steiger would get the new kid's card, would get the new kid's code...

Don't think about how he'll get it.

...and would get out. Steiger was too smart not to. Too smart for his own good.

So how do I get him alone? Hip-Hop thought again, and that was when the intercom buzzed. "Guys?" said Wiseman, his voice tinny and filtered through the speaker.

Hip-Hop thumbed the 'com on from their end. "Yeah, Wiseman?"

"Could two of you come upstairs please? I need some help moving stuff."

Hip-Hop rejoiced at how easy this was suddenly going to be, but he gave no sign of it. "Moving stuff?"

"Interior redecorating."

Hip-Hop looked at the wall clock. Six fifty p.m. Things were going to go down soon. He caught Wade's eye, and his fellow planner crooked an eyebrow.

Hip-Hop thumbed the button. "I'll send up Vincent, Donald, and Mitchell. Their shift was going to end soon, they can help you then finish early and bunk down while me and Jacky play waiter."

"Hey!" said Vincent. Even though he had the opportunity to be done early, evidently the little prick didn't like the idea of having to do anything as laborious as lifting something. "Don't I get no say in this?" The idiot switched to the worst De Niro imitation ever. "Are you talkin' to me? Are *you* talkin' to me?"

Hip-Hop ignored him. Apparently Wiseman either did the same or didn't hear him, because the doctor said right over Vincent's bitching: "Sounds good. Send them up to Dr. Bryson's office, please."

"Bryson ain't even here, man," said Vincent.

"And tell Vincent to quit complaining," said Wiseman, and Hip-Hop smiled as Donald and Mitchell laughed and pointed at Vincent, who flipped them off. Wiseman was a goody two shoes – no way would Crane even have *thought* about inviting him to be a part of what was going on below The Loon – but at least he could be funny sometimes.

"Okeydoke," said Hip-Hop into the mic.

"And Hip-Hop," continued Wiseman, "make sure you keep an eye on Jacky when you're doing the deliveries."

Hip-Hop noted that Wiseman was already calling the new kid Jacky. He hoped that no one was *really* attached to the kid. It would make the coming hours just that much harder. Still, a job was a job. He looked at Jacky and smiled.

"I'll take good care of him."

OFFICE

Paul watched half-attentively as Vincent and Donald struggled to get a pair of beds into Dr. Bryson's office without banging into a wall or some other furniture. Like most of the staff, Bryson – the staff physician who was in charge of the inmates' physical health – was waiting out the storm in nearby Stonetree, so it made sense for Paul to have Rachel and Becky sleep in here. They were close to the staff quarters, they were reasonably safe. Plus, Bryson was a neat freak who went a bit overboard on his standards for cleanliness, and Paul had to admit to himself that it would be fun seeing Bryson come back to a changed office.

He glanced out the barred windows. Outside The Loon, Darkness reigned. The kind of weather where you couldn't see anything other than snow and the dim electric lights of The Loon, shining like multiple weak eyes, their lenses filmy with a blizzard cataract.

The weather was now no longer dangerous, it was deadly.

"Hold your end, dammit," said Vincent.

"Hold your own end," murmured Donald in a rare display of gumption.

Paul jumped in before Vincent could start a fight. "Easy guys, it's not quantum physics."

Vincent was unmollified. "Why we gotta do this, anyway?"

"Lady and her daughter don't feel really comfortable spending the night with us," was all Paul said in return. More than that would probably be lost on Vincent anyway.

He watched for another moment to make sure everything was going along as it should, then left the room, leaving the door wedged open behind him. He crossed the hall to the staff sleeping facility. Inside, Mitchell was quietly making up the bed closest to the wall. As always, Paul marveled that the cots would even hold the silent monster of a man.

On another cot, Rachel held Becky tightly on her lap, the little girl's face dreadfully white as both watched Mitchell with clear distrust.

Paul felt a pang of sympathy for the two women, part of it because of their obvious discomfort, part of it because he couldn't help but imagine Sammy when looking at Becky.

He cleared his throat before any tears could work their way to the surface and went to the small sink. He grabbed a pair of disposable cups from a nearby dispenser and filled them with water. "We're almost done with the bed," he said, holding out the water to Rachel and her daughter. Neither of them took a cup. "Sorry, but we won't be able to fit two cots in the other room, so you'll have to double up."

"That's all right," said Rachel.

Paul locked eyes with Rachel at that moment, and felt a surge of electricity thrum through him. He remembered a cool kiss, and remembered that he had known what it felt to be loved once.

That was a long time ago, he thought, and turned to leave.

"Dr. Wiseman?" came Rachel's voice.

He turned back to them. "Paul," he said.

There was a long pause, as though Rachel struggled before she finally managed, "Thank you. Doctor."

A sudden gust hit the walls. Different than the others had been; stronger. Strong enough to rattle not just the windows but the walls themselves.

The wind howled, an almost-human sound of angry gusting.

Then there was a snap as the lights went out.

OFFICIAL

Mitchell O'Hallan felt the lights go out as much as he saw them. He was the largest person on staff – by far – and the largest person in The Loon, but he was also desperately afraid of the dark. Had been ever since his mother had locked him in a closet when he was a kid for stealing brown sugar. He knew he shouldn't have done it, shouldn't have stuck his hands in the bag and felt the delicious stuff crumple as he crushed doughy clods of the stuff between his already-massive fingers and then shoved the sweet grit into his mouth. But it was just too tempting. And when his mother threw open the door to the pantry and saw him there, he was neither surprised nor concerned. Whatever was coming, it had been worth it.

Or so he thought.

But it must have been one of Mother's bad days, for without a word she took Mitchell and threw him into the coat closet, leaving him there for several hours. He had been quiet at first, then panic had set in and he had attempted to get out. She had put something heavy in front of the door, though, and Mitchell was stuck. Stuck and at her mercy...the mercy of a woman who was generally a good and caring person but who occasionally did not even know her own children's names.

So now whenever he was in the dark, he could feel it. Heavy, like the coats that had rested on his shoulders like wraiths ready to eat his soul on that day so long ago. The dark was real to Mitchell, and it was not a friend.

Still, he had managed if not to conquer his fear over the years then at least to control it. He no longer wet himself when the dark came. And now, as though to prove to himself that he could still function in the nightmarish world of black in which he found himself, he said in as calm a voice as he could muster, "It's official."

Near him, the woman and her daughter gasped as the lights went out. "What's going on?" said the woman. She sounded on the verge of panic.

"Don't worry," said Paul. Mitchell knew Paul was a good man; knew that if the woman had needed or wanted it, Paul would have held out a hand for her to hold.

Sometimes it stank being the size of a small whale. No one ever offered to hold *Mitchell's* hand.

"It'll just take a second," Paul continued, "and then the generator should kick in."

Mitchell hated that Paul had used the word "should" instead of "will." "Should" implied that the generator might *not* kick in.

And what would happen *then*?

Part Three: The Dark

Of thought and fear and loneliness. Window glass
Feels icy to my touch, double panes
Against my wrists as cold as graveyard brass,
Bringing yet more chill into my veins
To dissipate what little warming hope remains.

- *The Little That it Takes*

But inside...inside, where dark
Shadows roam in rooms
Abandoned to waiting, stark
Emptiness, shapes loom -
Unfocused, horror's birthmarks...

- *In the House Beyond the Field*

FLASHES

The galley. Dark. Hip-Hop, Jacky, and Wade were frozen in the positions they had been in when the darkness fell. Two conspirators, one planned victim...and all were silent. No sound but the wind outside, rushing past the walls.
***

Dr. Bryson's office. Vincent and Donald had still been struggling to get the cot set up in the cramped space when the darkness fell. They had been arguing.

They were not arguing now.
***

The door to the prison area. The electromagnetic seal unlocked for a moment, a soft sigh as a vacuum was released.
***

The prison. Marty and Jorge both jumped violently as the lights went out, the area transforming suddenly into a medieval dungeon, full of hiding places and terror. Even through the soundproofed walls of the cells, the inmates could be heard.

Screaming.
***

Crane's living quarters. The scientist had several flashlights on, making the place reasonably bright. Nevertheless, sweat beaded on his brow. Afraid.
***

The place where it is tortured, hurt, harmed.
The place becomes dark.

The thing is relieved. Light is pain.
How long will the darkness last?
It moves. It extrudes a tendril and slides it between the bars
to its prison.
And for the first time ever...nothing stops it.
***

The generator shack. Even over the howling wind, an audible click could be heard.

Then a humming as something inside began to work.
***

The Loon. All over the complex, lights went on and electromagnetic doors reactivated.

They had been loose for less than five seconds.

STUDYING

There is a click and a snap, and it screams. Pain racks its body as the lights come back on.

They are not as strong as they were. Not as intense. But strong enough. Intense enough. Wherever the light touches, the thing feels itself sizzling.

It screams.

Then something registers over the pain.

Its cage.

It is outside *its cage. For the first time, it is outside.*

The pain is still there; still real. But the thing fights through it. It flows over itself, its form wet and ever-changing as it constantly shifts.

Feet.

Tendrils.

Hands.

Unnamed things from genetic memory, from a time when everything lived in a primordial ocean.

The thing moves to the computers. To the monster's computers, to Crane's *computers.*

The computers are in shadow. The beast shudders as the light-pain subsides. But it is only afforded a moment's relief before a new pain grips it.

The hunger.

It is dying. Faster and faster, it can feel itself disappearing.

The computers have information, the thing knows that.

It extrudes a pseudopod, a tendril that dances across the keys of the computer, slick snakelike flesh wriggling and crawling and somehow managing to input the information it needs in order to find what it wants.

It has lived with the monster for its whole life. It has watched the monster. It knows the keys to press.

The computer screen blinks. The beast coughs and a thick bubble bursts open on its wet skin, exposing a dozen newly born eyes, blinking fleshily at the computer screen, looking at files.

Studying blueprints.

SCARED

Donald let out the breath he had been holding for what seemed like forever.

He and Vince were still in Dr. Bryson's office. Nothing had changed. Everyone had expected the lights to go out, and that's what had happened. Nothing to worry about.

So why did he feel so scared all of a sudden?

He almost asked Vince if he felt...*different.* Then decided that was a stupid question and, as he had since he was very young and the other kids had teased him about his cleft lip, Donald clamped his mouth shut and decided silence was the best course. Even so, Vince must have seen something in his gaze. The younger man's lip curled in scorn. "Gutless wonder," said Vince. "Scared of the dark."

Donald did not deny it.

LIE

Paul looked at Rachel and Becky as the lights came back on. Neither had moved, but he could see the tension in their features. Nor were they alone. Mitchell had his bedding clenched in his hands so tightly that if it had been a person, Paul would have been worrying about how to treat shattered ribs.

Paul grinned lopsidedly in what he knew was a hopeless attempt to lighten the situation. "That was fun, wasn't it?"

"Mommy," said Becky, and Paul's heart soared. She was speaking. Not that she was saying anything good: "The lights," said the little girl.

Rachel looked at Paul. "Why aren't they coming back on all the way?" asked the girl's mother.

Paul tried to smile again, but he was positive that his look did nothing to help their moods. "We're on emergency power," he answered. "It takes a while to cycle up, but it won't light up all the way in here. Full power goes to the security systems, the doors, and the computers." He shrugged apologetically. "This is the best we're going to get, I'm afraid. "

"There's no way to turn them up?" asked Rachel.

"Sorry," said Paul. "Not without stealing power from somewhere else. And believe me, you'd rather have the doors all working." He tried to raise everyone's spirits one more time. Directing his gaze at Becky, he said, "Besides, this way you're spared looking at all us ugly folks, kiddo."

Becky just stared at him wordlessly, never taking her eyes from Paul's face, and he felt curiously as though the little girl were measuring him.

He also realized with a chill that he had called her "kiddo."

He had called Sammy that, once upon a time.

And Paul shuddered. Because Sammy was gone, and for a moment he felt as he had that day when he had cut a perfect slice across his son's name on the birthday cake.

No, he said to himself. Nothing will happen to Becky.

But he felt – he *knew* – that was a lie.

TIME

Hip-Hop put the final touches on the inmates' meals, then nodded at Wade. To his immense relief, the incredibly stupid guard actually understood Hip-Hop's meaning. Either that or he was just acting naturally, and that worked, too.

"Have fun, boys," said Wade with a yawn. "I'm goin' to bed."

"That's right, brag, you prick," said Hip-Hop with a laugh that he hoped the newbie would not see as artificial and forced.

Apparently he didn't, for Jacky laughed, not sensing the animal tension that Hip-Hop felt boiling just beneath his skin. Hip-Hop started pushing a massive cart full of meals, and nodded to Jacky to do the same. A moment later he and the newbie were walking toward the door to the prison tunnel. Wade turned the other way, toward the lobby, and Hip-Hop saw the man looking at his watch and standing motionless before the doorway.

Waiting.

He didn't need Jacky asking questions, so he said loudly, "Come on, Fresh Meat, we don't got all day."

Jacky hustled after him, and Hip-Hop laughed like they were going to be best friends. And that might even be true...for another half hour or so.

After that, the newbie was on his own.

Speaking of time...Hip-Hop glanced at his watch.

6:58. Only a few minutes before things started to pop.

UNMANNED

Sandy was proud of herself. She had managed to go maybe ten minutes without thinking of Darryl. That was probably nine minutes longer than she'd ever managed to do before. It was nigh unto a Herculean feat, especially considering that he was sitting right next to her, watching the monitors with that signal intensity that was just one more thing she found so amazing about him.

The intercom buzzed. Crane's voice hissed out, the tinny sound the speaker imparted doing nothing to dull the imperious power in his words. "Sandy?" he barked.

She thumbed the 'com. "Yes, sir?" she answered.

"Who's at the monitoring station with you?" Crane asked.

"Me, Darryl, Jeff, and Leann."

"I want to see the four of you."

Sandy gawked at the intercom; saw Darryl doing the same.

"*All* of us?" she asked. That would leave the front desk completely unmanned. Not usual protocol. In fact, she could not remember that ever happening before.

Crane ignored the implied question and instead chose to address her breach of conduct. "I am not accustomed to having my orders questioned. All of you in my office, *now*," he said.

Sandy glanced at Darryl, who just shrugged his head and stood, leading the way to Crane's door.

She followed.

So the front was unmanned for a minute. What could happen?

SHOOTING

Wade heard the door to Crane's office close just as he stepped into the lobby.

That had been close. Crane liked to time things to the second.

He rushed to the front door, passing his keycard through the reader, then entering his code.

The door buzzed and he opened it. A flurry of snow burst through the egress almost instantly, and a gust of wind actually swatted him backward before he braced himself properly.

He pushed out into the snow, closing the door to the prison staff area behind him. The foul weather tore at him, ripping through his thin clothes, but he knew that there were parkas in the tower.

He just had to get there and be ready for Steiger when the lunatic got out.

Wade smiled. Things were going as planned.

And, he had to admit, even though he was out in the shithole of all snow storms, he was looking forward to shooting Steiger.

ALONE

The walk through the tunnel that linked prison to staff area seemed much longer than Jacky had remembered it being only a few hours earlier. Maybe that was because he was pushing a huge cart loaded with enough food for fifty wackos. Maybe it was because he was tired. But most likely it was because the blood-red lights in the tunnel were even dimmer than they had been the first time.

He was afraid. Afraid, and he wasn't even doing anything.

Still, he had thought he would feel better when getting into the prison. After all, at least the prison had full lighting, from what he understood. So he was surprised when Hip-Hop pushed the door open and they stepped in and Jacky felt the dread he was nurturing grow a foot or two within him. Fear was becoming a living, breathing being, and he knew that if he didn't push it down it would swallow him whole.

He thought about his mother. She always made him feel better. Her warm smile, her infectious laugh, the "Hug candy" she kept for neighborhood children who came by for a licorice whip in exchange for a quick hug with the kind-hearted woman.

It worked. It always did. He felt himself relax.

Then he jumped as a voice speared out at him: "Hey, man, we thought you maybe forgot about us or something," said Jorge, the thin and sarcastic man who Jacky understood was Rachel's brother.

"Seriously," echoed Marty, the other guard on duty, as taciturn-seeming as before.

"Relax, Wonder Twins," said Hip-Hop with a chuckle.

"Hey, man," said Jorge instantly, "I resent that. I ain't related to that," he pointed at Marty, "piece of *pendejo* white trash from the wrong side of the trailer park."

Jacky looked at Marty, a bit nervous. But Marty didn't say a word. Apparently this kind of ribbing was normal.

"Any problems when the lights went out?" asked Hip-Hop.

"Not after Jorge changed his underoos," mumbled Marty.

Jorge laughed, but even to Jacky it sounded forced. Nervous laughter, tinged with fear.

Hip-Hop sighed beside Jacky. "Get out of here you two," he said to Jorge and Marty. "Me and Newbie'll take first guard tonight."

"Diving right into it, eh?" said Marty to Jacky, but Jacky got the impression there was a strong undercurrent of "Good luck – you'll need it" beneath the actual spoken words.

"Glad it ain't me, man," said Jorge.

"Don't spook him," said Hip-Hop with a grin. Then his smile faded. "Jorge, you know your sister's here, right?"

Jacky saw the normally feisty guard get an unusually strained look on his face. The fun went out of him as he nodded, said, "Yeah," and then he and Marty stood to go.

They swiped through the door without a word.

Jacky and Hip-Hop were alone in the prison.

Jacky looked around. All the cells. All the crazy people in them, just waiting for their chance to....

He shuddered, unwilling to finish the thought.

Thank goodness for Hip-Hop, he thought.

COFFEE

Wade pulled the parka on, almost moaning in relief as the wind stopped cutting at him quite so mercilessly. He pulled a face mask from the pocket of the parka, put it on as well, then pulled up the fur-lined hood and pulled it tight.

Much better.

He grabbed the trank rifle from its storage space. It was a special military model, not your usual zoo-type dart gun. It could fire up to eight darts at the equivalent of semi-automatic, unlike the usual single shot guns that most places had. It was also much higher powered than any other dart rifle. This was imperative because in this wind, Wade knew it would take every shred of push the rifle had to get it to hit Steiger.

He walked out onto the guard tower parapet, looking over.

No Steiger. But soon, he knew.

He glanced over, and saw something odd on the ground nearby: a brown stain that glinted oddly. With a start, he realized it was the coffee that he had spilled on Sandy earlier to distract her from Steiger's previous escape attempt.

The coffee was frozen solid, grafted to the floor by the wind and hail.

Jesus, he thought. Come on, Steiger, get out here so I can blow your ass to sleep.

He settled down to wait.

Not long now.

PLOT

Hip-Hop stood outside the bars of the first cell, careful not to touch them. Touching them would not be good.

He took one of the paper food trays from the cart: it was thin, designed to go between the bars of the outer cell to each inmate's personal prison room. Using a plastic loid, Hip-Hop pushed the food through the outer cell, then flicked open a small slot on the inner cell door with the same long instrument. Then he used the loid to push the plastic plate through the slot, flicked it closed, and withdrew his tool.

A small light next to the food slot glowed green the entire time. Green was good.

He turned to Jacky.

Not Jacky, just the new guy. Don't think of him as Jacky.

The new guy was watching intently, but Hip-Hop knew from experience he'd have to explain the whole process.

"One hundred twenty six to go," said Hip-Hop. "That's it. Easy. First thing to remember is never touch the bars."

"Electrified?" asked the newbie.

Hip-Hop nodded. "Won't kill you, but you'll wake up with a helluva headache. Only way to turn off the bars is with the cell key. You'll need this," he added, handing Jacky a thick set of keys. "Keys to the outer cells, the inner cells, and the lift." Hip-Hop pointed to a skeletal one-man elevator in a nearby corner as he said this. "I'm going up to the ones on the third level," he said. You start on this level and work your way up. We meet in the middle."

"What about the little green light next to the food slot?" asked the newbie.

Hip-Hop nodded approvingly. Kid had a decent brain in his head. "Security measure," he answered. "You always, always, *always* check that light before coming near the outer cell. If the light's green, the inner door is locked. If it's red, the inner door is unlocked and you don't get anywhere near the bars?"

"Why not?"

Hip-Hop shrugged. "'Cause some psycho's liable to pop out from his cell and grab you and pull your face off with his teeth."

Hip-Hop left the newbie to think on that, pushing his food cart to the lift and riding it to the third floor. He could see Jacky below him, barely visible in the perpetual twilight of the storm lights. He saw the new guy turn to do his first cell, then disappear from view.

Hip-Hop got off at the third floor, pushing his cart over to a cell, then left it there.

He removed his shoes so they wouldn't clank on the metal decking of the prison walkways, then hurried to a nearby stairwell and walked quietly back down to the level below. On the second level he looked down and saw the new guy, already on his third or fourth cell, ass in the air as he carefully pushed trays into the occupied cells.

Hip-Hop drifted quietly over to cell two twenty three.

Steiger's cell.

KEY

Steiger lay on his small bunk, hands folded loosely across his chest.

A snick sounded. He knew it was the food. He had been getting hungry and his internal clock – which was as perfectly calibrated as the rest of him – told him it was time for dinner. That dinner was late, in fact.

Then he heard something different. No soft swish of paper sliding across concrete.

No, there was a metallic scraping as something slid into his cell.

Steiger smiled. As usual, the universe was bending itself to help him in his quest to bring disorder; he knew what the sound was without even looking.

It was the sound of a key sliding into his cell.

SMARTY

Vincent was disgusted. Who did that woman think she was? He stomped across the hall to the staff sleeping quarters, which were wide open. Another problem caused by that woman. Wiseman had decreed from on high that the staff quarters should stay propped open so that woman and her demon kid would be able to get back and forth without having to be accompanied by someone with security clearance.

What? he thought. She shows up unannounced and so now we should all be at risk because *she's* an idiot?

He threw himself onto a cot, Donald close behind him as always. "That woman could give mean lessons to Don Corleone," he muttered.

Paul was in there waiting for him. Mitchell was in one of the beds, snoring snores appropriate for someone who could eat mountains for breakfast – that was a good one, he'd have to remember that and tell it to Donald later – and Marty was stripping down for the night. Marty was as big a prick as Wiseman was. He was a complete downer, a no-show in the party of life.

"Room all set up for them?" asked Wiseman.

"Yeah. The bed's where she wants it. No thanks, no tip, but she's happy with the freakin' bed."

"Hey, man," said Marty, his expression even more sour than usual. "You wanna keep it down and shut your mouth? Tryin' to sleep over here."

"Shut it for me, Marty. Where's your beaner friend?"

Wiseman left the room, probably so his delicate shell-like ears wouldn't be assaulted by someone who didn't use the word "tinkle" when they had to take a leak.

Marty was talking, but Vincent hardly heard him. All he was aware of for that moment was how much he hated Wiseman. How much he wished he could knock the smarts right out of the guy.

And for some reason, he had a feeling like he'd get the chance to do just that. And soon.

PROMISE

Jorge listened in horror to his sister as she detailed what had happened. He remembered the day she had married Tommy, and how much Jorge had hoped that she would at last find peace; that she would at last have found someone who would treat her as she deserved. It had seemed his wish was granted at first, but then something had changed. Tommy had lost his job, yes, but more than that it was as though something that had always lived within the man had crawled out of the dark places it had been hiding, and slowly consumed him.

Jorge had known Tommy had grown cruel. He had not known how bad it had gotten, however. Not until now. Rachel was too damn self-contained for her own good. And now...

"I think," Rachel said, "I think...Tommy, I think that I might have..."

Her voice was high and strangled sounding, as though her husband was reaching out from hell with icy hands that could hurt her even in death.

Jorge kissed Rachel on the cheek, glancing at Becky pointedly. No matter what had happened, now was not the time to talk about it. Not in front of his niece. She was sitting on the bed beside her mother, holding her Emergency Pack tightly in her hands, looking at nothing. Both of them had faraway stares, reminding Jorge of a tableau from a Holocaust picture, shock and fear the only visible emotions.

"Don't worry," he said. "We'll fix things. We'll be okay."

Rachel shook her head, and Jorge knew his sister would have said more, but at that moment there was a knock at the door, which had paper towels mashed against the doorframe to keep it from closing.

"Yes?" Rachel said automatically. Paul stuck his head in. Jorge liked Paul; even loved him like a brother. But right now he wanted to knock his friend's head off for interrupting.

"Everything all right?" said Paul.

Rachel shrugged noncommittally.

"We're fine," said Jorge. To his sister, in Spanish, he said, "Do you want me to stay?" She shook her head minutely, and he knew better than to argue with his stubborn sibling, so he said in English, "Listen, I've got to get some rest. Not many folks here, and I've got to take care of a lot of stuff. But I'm right down the hall. You or the kid need anything – *anything* – you come and get me, 'kay?" Rachel nodded. "And when this storm is over, we'll figure everything out, I promise."

He waited for a response.

None came.

He felt as though perhaps it was because she didn't believe his promises of happy endings. He couldn't blame her.

Because neither did he.

BEAR

Paul watched as Jorge hugged Rachel, then kissed the top of Becky's head. The little girl was still almost catatonic, and Paul knew that something had to be done about her mental state or permanent damage would cease to be likely and become inevitable.

Jorge left, and gave Paul a pleading look as he did, which Paul interpreted as a request for help. Either that or a request for Paul to leave, but Paul was a psychiatrist, and he couldn't leave this situation alone. It was one of the reasons he had gotten into the field of psychiatry in the first place: it just wasn't in him to *not* help someone who was hurting inside.

"You okay, sport?" he asked the little girl once Jorge had left.

She stared at him.

Paul moved to his desk. The little girl's eyes didn't exactly follow him, but he got the sense she *was* watching. To make sure he didn't try anything harmful, if nothing else.

"'Cause I was thinking," he continued, "if I was in a new place with a bunch of weird folks I didn't even know, I'd need a friend. So...." Paul opened his desk and removed something from a locked drawer. He felt something tugging at his heart.

This was Sammy's. Is Sammy's.
Sammy doesn't need it anymore.

"So I talked to someone I know," he continued. "This guy named Mr. Huggles. And he also needs a friend, coincidentally, and asked me if I knew anyone."

With that, Paul pulled out Sammy's old bear. The guardian who had rested for a moment too long. He had kept the bear in that desk since the day he began work here, and this was the first time he had ever touched it: to touch it more than to move it when absolutely necessary had seemed almost a violation of his son's memory. But now....

"Yeah," he continued, swallowing as though trying to rid himself of a particularly bitter pill. "So I said, 'Well, Mr. Huggles, I know this one girl, but she's tough as nails, and she doesn't look like she needs a friend,' and he says to me," and Paul switched to a funny voice, the silly-bear voice he had always used with Sammy, "'Tough as nails?' 'Yup,' I said. 'Well,' said Mr. Huggles, 'maybe *she'll* protect *me*.'"

Paul paused. The little girl's star was still far away, but perhaps not *as* far away. Her stare was not as blank, and he thought he could see the tiniest hint of a smile tugging at her lips.

He hesitated a moment, not sure he really wanted to do this, not sure he really wanted to offer up a piece of his past like this, then held out the bear. "How about it?" he said. "Would you mind watching out for my friend?"

A long moment passed; long enough that Paul's arm started to feel tired. Then Becky reached over the desk and took the bear. Paul glanced at the little girl's mother, who was staring at him with wonder, and felt a kind of surprised delight flit across his face in a way that it had not done since the day Sammy died.

Since the day you killed him.

The thought tore away whatever joy he might have been feeling. Tore it away and changed it to anger, to fear.

Paul rose and walked out without more than a small smile at Becky.

He almost jumped out of his skin when a hand grabbed him from behind.

It was Jorge. *"Gracias, amigo,"* said his friend. "I know what that bear meant."

"It's okay," said Paul. And in that instant it was. "What's her story?" he asked, though he suspected he already knew the broad outlines.

Jorge's lip curled in a combination of disgust and fear. "She married a scumball. More than that, I can't say. Not now."

Paul looked at his friend, a moment of silent understanding passing between them. Because he had been in there alone with the girl and her mother, he could claim that he had counseled them on an emergency basis, and that would protect their conversations from others in a cloak of psychiatric privilege. But even with that protection, there were certain things a psychiatrist was legally bound to report.

Paul suspected that Jorge was not telling him more because he didn't want Paul to have to call the police.

Paul nodded at Jorge. "They're safe," he tried to communicate.

Jorge nodded back, but Paul got the distinct impression that his friend knew that Paul was not telling the truth.

The walls shook minutely with the force of the storm outside.

No one here was safe.

DISAPPEARED

Hip-Hop watched silently from his vantage point on the third floor, a spot that was well-concealed in shadows, yet that allowed a view of the second floor. Jacky was making his way along the catwalk, cell by cell, moving ever-closer to Steiger's cell. The kid was doing good, being careful. Checking each inner cell to make sure its light was green before putting the food on the ground and sliding it between the electrified bars of the outer cell.

Easy peezy, thought Hip-Hop.

Two twenty one. Two twenty two.

Two twenty three. Steiger's cell.

Hip-Hop crept closer to the edge of the catwalk. The light on the side of Steiger's cell was green as Jacky put the food on the ground, then used the loid to push it into the cell.

What happened next was so fast that Hip-Hop, who was waiting for it to happen, almost missed it.

The food was halfway to the food slot on the inner cell door when the light suddenly turned red. Steiger must have had the key in the lock, just waiting for the right moment to pounce. The madman erupted out of his cell a nanosecond after the light turned red, the explosive movement catching Jacky utterly by surprise. With frightening precision, Steiger darted a hand between the electrified bars, grabbed Jacky by the lapel, and yanked the young man into the bars, letting go of him a moment before Jacky made contact with the iron.

Momentum drove Jacky into the bars, and the young guard shrieked when he touched the electrified metal and twitched like a dying fish for a moment before going limp.

Hip-Hop moved away from the edge of the catwalk as Steiger carefully maneuvered Jacky's body away from the bars, touching only the guard's belt and other non-conducting parts of his uniform. Then he turned Jacky to maneuver him around until the guard's key ring was within easy grasp.

Hip-Hop felt himself holding his breath as Steiger opened the outer door one level below. The madman looked around; apparently didn't see Hip-Hop. He dragged Jacky into the cell, closing the outer and inner doors behind them.

Hip-Hop shuddered as Jacky disappeared from view, pulled like a fly into a trapdoor spider's lair. Only a fly would have had more chance of surviving.

CARROT

Jacky blinked, his vision strange and blurry. He had no recollection of what had happened at first, but then he had a flash of Steiger....

Steiger!

He jerked upright, his head pounding. Where was he?

Before he could do more than simply register the white walls, a pleasant voice said, "Oh, you're awake!"

Jacky looked over and saw Steiger. The Hacker was sitting on his bed, playing with Jacky's keyring. He scooted closer to Jacky, who cringed away, terrified. How long before they notice I'm gone? he thought. How long until they come looking?

Steiger either didn't notice or didn't care that Jacky was trying to push himself through the wall in a vain attempt to get away. His expression never changed from one Jacky would more expect to see on the face of a friendly neighborhood grocer or the family doctor: helpful, nurturing, and genuinely happy to see you. Indeed, even as Jacky thought this, Steiger reached out his powerful hands and firmly but gently helped him into a sitting position.

"I was so worried," said Steiger, "what with the way you collapsed and all. How are you feeling, by the way?"

"Uh, fine," said Jacky. He had never been so terrified. He felt vomit rising at the back of his throat, the taste of fear thick in his mouth.

"Oh, thank God," said Steiger. "Can I get you anything?" He laughed lightly, as though this were a friendly chat over the fence with a good neighbor. "I'm afraid I don't have much, but what's mine is yours."

"No," said Jacky. He let his hand drop to his belt and realized his weapons – trank gun, nightstick, mace spray, everything – were all gone. Again, if Steiger saw what he was doing he paid it no heed. "No thanks. I'm fine."

"Let me help you up," said the madman, and again Jacky felt himself in the vise-grip of those too-strong hands, this time helping him into a standing position.

"Actually," said Steiger once Jacky was on his feet, "before we waste too much time, there is something I wanted to talk to you about." Steiger let go of Jacky with one hand and produced something.

A code card.

"I found this in your pocket," he said. "I know from sad experience that it won't work without the code, and I wondered..." and here the madman grinned slyly, and with the expression Jacky could see for the first time tell-tale traces of madness etching their way across Steiger's face. "...would you mind giving me your code?"

Jacky just stared at Steiger, utterly transfixed by terror, completely unable to move or make a sound. Steiger apparently misunderstood the silence as stubbornness, though, for he said, "Oh dear. There are two ways we can go about this: I can be nice, or I can be mean. The carrot or the stick."

Steiger moved suddenly, his motion too fast to be seen, and suddenly Jacky felt a searing pain in his leg. He shrieked and dropped to the floor, cradling his leg and seeing that several of the keys on his key ring had embedded themselves as if by magic right above his knee.

Steiger smiled again, that same genuinely caring smile, but Jacky could also see the insanity behind it. Steiger laughed as he took hold of one of the keys and turned it, slowly, creating new waves of agony that splashed through Jacky's body. Jacky screamed again, this time as much a call for help as a scream of pain.

"Knock, knock," said Steiger, still twisting the key. "Open up, Mr. Hales." He laughed as Jacky screamed again. "Doesn't do any good, you know." He motioned at the walls around them. "Soundproof." He paused a moment, then said, "By the way, that was me being nice. Should I show you what 'mean' means?" Without waiting for an answer, Steiger giggled, his voice growing higher as though he were nervous...or aroused. "'Mean means,'" he said with a giggle. "How funny. Didn't even mean to, and I made a joke. 'Mean means.'"

He laughed again, and reached for Jacky.

Jacky saw the hand coming toward him, and knew he was going to die.

SLIP

Wade looked at his watch. He had to wipe a coat of frost off the crystal to see anything, and even then the heavy buffets of snow made the numbers blurry, but he could make out that it was around 7:10. He didn't have any idea how Steiger would make it past the guards at the front desk, but had no concerns about it. He just kept counting money in his head. His father had been an alcoholic who pissed away a decent job and an even better savings, leaving Wade an orphan with no money and no prospects at the age of sixteen. Wade had lived in foster care for two years, and during that depressing period where he was shuffled from one lackadaisical foster family to another he had decided that no matter what, he would never be poor again.

In spite of that decision, however, no magic doors had opened up for him. He had eked out a subsistence living until finally scoring the job at The Loon. He had immediately begun stockpiling money. Not in a bank; they were part of the system that he deeply distrusted. No, every penny was in a hidden safe under fake floorboards in his bedroom. He had almost one million dollars stashed in there, between his regular pay and the "bonuses" he got for little bits of work like this.

Still, even though he could feel his steel piggy bank growing with every moment, he wished Steiger would get the hell out here so he could do his job and get back inside. Inside was going to be hectic soon, what with the breakout and the probable death and/or maiming Steiger was likely to be involved in on his way out, but at least Wade would be inside for that. Inside and warm.

He looked at The Loon, which was now barely visible in the storm. Indeed, the wind was blowing snow so furiously that Wade had to hold onto the rail or risk being shoved about like a toy doll. The wind died down a bit, and Wade let go to check the heavy trank rifle he held one more time. *Can't be too careful with Stei –*

The thought ended abruptly as another gust hit him, this one with the force of a small car. Wade swayed, fighting for a moment before the wind pushed his rear foot back. His foot came down on a patch of something. Something slippery.

Wade had a millisecond to look down. A brown patch of ice.

The coffee, he thought. The damn coffee I spilled on Sandy.

The stuff had frozen solid, an icy patch that sent Wade careening backward after he slipped on its slick surface. He dropped the trank rifle, his arms spinning in wide circles as he attempted to regain his balance. But as though it were a sentient predator sensing the perfect moment to strike, another crosswind hit Wade, this time from *behind*. Again his arms rotated like twin propellers, again he tried to right himself.

It was no use.

Wade fell forward, pushed inexorably. Over the edge.

Falling.

Falling.

Then he felt his shoulder jerk as he grabbed onto the guardrail that surrounded the tower, his feet dangling over the generator shack that was thirty feet below him in the courtyard area. Heat spread out from his shoulder and he knew he had dislocated it.

He called for help, but knew that no one could hear him. Nor would anyone at the monitor stations be able to see him through the falling snow.

He called again.

"Help!" he shrieked, hysterical terror marring his voice and rendering it high and terrible. "Help me!"

The wind caught his voice and drowned it out only feet away.

He was alone.

The wind howled, mocking him.

He tried to pull himself up, but even without a dislocated shoulder he didn't know if he could have done a pull-up.

He screamed again. "HELP!"

The wind just laughed.

GOOD

Sandy felt warm inside. She was sitting at the monitor station, chatting with Darryl! And it was as though the storm outside had given her strength, because she felt herself being interested and interesting at the same time: listening for just the right times, making perfectly appropriate sounds, laughing at just the right pitch whenever Darryl made a joke.

She glanced at the monitors. The inside ones were fine, but the outside ones showed only snow.

She looked back at Darryl, feeling herself flush as he leaned in close to whisper a joke in her ear. Leann and Jeff were both at the monitoring station, too, but even with them there it felt as though she and Darryl were finally on a date. Not alone, but he clearly had eyes only for her.

No doubt about it: tonight was going to be a *very* good night.

DAISIES

Steiger moved quickly; it was now or never.

The guard station, which he knew from long years' experience was usually manned by no fewer than two guards, was devoid of life.

Steiger smiled. Things were coming up daisies.

He moved to the heavy steel door that led from the prison to the umbilical-like tunnel to the staff area.

He pulled out the guard's card, wiping some blood from it before sliding it through the card reader. A moment later, he entered a code – probably the guard's social security number, from the length of it – and was satisfied to hear the beep-click of the door opening.

Daisies all over.

BLACK

Wade hung on for dear life, feeling his hands freezing to the guard rail bar as they went slick with terrified perspiration, then froze to the cold gray metal beneath them.

He tried to pull himself up, but each time he did his dislocated shoulder screamed at him, and each time he ended up with a slightly looser grip on the guard rail than he had had before.

Finally, he resorted to something he had not done in years: he prayed. His lips moved with the fervency of his wishes as he prayed to God to let him live. Wade promised everything, promised money, promised work, promised time, if only God would just reverse gravity in this place, just for a fraction of a second, just long enough to push Wade up.

But God wasn't listening, it seemed, or was otherwise occupied elsewhere in the universe. Because gravity kept pulling inexorably at Wade.

Finally, with a ripping of flesh his hands tore free from their frozen spots on the guard rails.

Wade fell, twisting as he did, and managed to see the heavy spires on top of the generator shack rushing toward him before he hit headfirst...and then all was black.

TAKEN

Rachel watched her daughter sleep in her arms, Mr. Huggles the teddy bear clutched tightly to her. She felt a moment of peace there, watching the gentle rise and fall of Becky's chest, and knew that as long as her daughter was all right, the world could be dealt with. It was all about Becky, now. Nothing else mattered.

She was content.

Then her contentment turned instantly to horror as the lights in the office suddenly went out, plunging her into darkness. Becky woke instantly, a small cry on her tiny lips.

"Shh, shh, baby," said Rachel. "It's all right."

But even as she said it, she knew it was a lie.

Then it was Rachel's turn to cry out as the door flew open with a bang. Two eyes stared at her in the darkness, and a dark form crowded the doorframe. She almost cried out again before the form said, "It's me. Just me, Paul. Just wanted to make sure you were all right."

Gradually, Rachel's eyes adjusted to the murky darkness that now held them all in its cloying grasp, enough to make out pinlights that glowed feebly at the corners of the room and every few feet in the hall behind Paul. They were almost useless, but she could see enough of Paul's face to know that whatever was happening, it was definitely *not* normal.

"What's going on? What's with the lights?" she asked.

Paul looked around. "Battery-powered," he said. "They only go on if the generator goes out...and that's as bright as they get."

With that, the contentment that Rachel had been feeling died in her breast. Terror was there again, the sole inhabitant of the prison of her heart.

The dark had taken them.

LIGHTS

Crane switched on his flashlight, then pushed the refrigerator until it was flush against the secret door. It would have slowed down any normal pursuer...even any *human* pursuer.

But Crane knew – even as he pushed a heavy desk over in front of the refrigerator he *knew* – that he was making a useless gesture. A *human* might have been slowed down, but not what was coming.

Still, he put his flashlight on the desk, so it was pointed at the refrigerator. Perhaps the light would slow it down, if mere weight would not.

Crane then grabbed another flashlight – the heaviest one he had – from nearby.

Switched it on.

The light was his only hope.

Even though it wasn't really much hope at all.

FIX

Sandy felt her perfect evening – alone in a crowded room with Darryl paying more attention to her than he ever had – shatter as the lights went off. She and Darryl touched hands as they both reached under the desk for the emergency flashlights that sheltered there, but even the normally electric spark of Darryl's touch failed to lift her spirits. The night was dark. And darkness was not something you wanted to find in The Loon.

"What the hell did you do? What the hell happened?" asked Leann, the tough older woman's voice cracking ever so slightly. That in itself almost scared Sandy more than the fact that the lights had gone out: both the darkness and Leann's fear were things for which there was no contingency plan; neither was ever supposed to happen.

Sandy felt terror unfurl within her like the wings of some great bat.

"I don't know what happened," Darryl snapped to Leann. "Why you asking *me*?"

"'Cause you were sitting closest," retorted Leann.

"What, you think I hit the 'everything off' button with my elbow?" said Darryl.

Leann opened her mouth to reply but was cut off by the sudden emergence of Dr. Crane from his office.

The man's face scared Sandy more than anything else could have. The man – so completely unflappable that she had more than once harbored the idea that he was probably a Vulcan or something equally alien – was utterly panic-stricken. No, more than that, he was *terrified*.

"Darryl, Sandy," he said without preamble, his words almost falling over themselves in a fearful jumble, "come with me."

"Where?" said Sandy almost unthinkingly. She never would have questioned Dr. Crane like that normally, but his face had shocked her into a base state of unconscious action.

And normally, she knew Dr. Crane would have rebuked her – even suspended her – for such an insubordinate query...but this time he merely answered.

"We have to go outside."

"Outside?" said Darryl in disbelief.

Again, Dr. Crane failed to respond with anger. Merely fear. "Something's wrong with the generator," said the older man. "We have to fix it." Then he repeated the words, and the way he did made it sound less as though he were telling them of a job that needed doing, and more as though he were prophesying their doom.

"We need to fix it now." And then he added the words that Sandy had heard below his words. "We need to fix it or we're all going to die."

DARKNESS

Hip-Hop looked into the darkness of the tunnel that led to the staff area, and wondered what to do.

He had seen Steiger go into the tunnel. He hadn't bothered checking on Jacky's situation: didn't want to leave any clues of his presence in there before others "discovered" what had happened. Instead, he had gone to the tunnel, to the door that should have been closed automatically...but apparently when the generator went out, the electromagnetic door seals unclamped.

Hip-Hop felt a pit in the center of his stomach. The prison cells were on their own separate backup relay, and he knew they had enough battery power to keep them closed. But all the other doors in The Loon would now be hanging open.

And who knew where Steiger would be?

Hip-Hop didn't know what to do.

He didn't want to go in the tunnel; what if Steiger was still in there?

But nor did he just want to wait in the open darkness of the prison area, just a sitting duck in the no-man's land of catwalks and iron.

What to do? he thought.

Then his radio crackled. Darryl's voice rang out, harsh and jagged in the utter silence of the prison: "Paul," said the wrestler.

Hip-Hop moved quickly, hitting the off button so hard he jammed his thumb.

But the damage was already done: Steiger's black form lunged out of the darkness of the tunnel.

Hip-Hop didn't even have time to scream.

BONUSES

Paul pulled out the walkie-talkie that he always carried in one pocket or another and spoke into it: "Yeah?" he responded to Darryl. He glanced at Rachel and Becky, smiling in what he hoped was a reassuring manner.

"Dr. Crane thinks there's a problem with the generator," said Darryl. "Probably just a loose wire or something, but you might want to go down and make sure that the tunnel doors are manually locked." Darryl paused for a moment at the other end of the walkie-talkie connection, and Paul could hear fear in the man's usually good-natured voice. "Just in case."

Paul, however, almost didn't hear anything after the word "generator." The prospect of total power loss at The Loon rocked him, knocking into him as hard as a cannonball.

Becky shifted, getting something out of her "Emergency" bag, and suddenly a Mickey Mouse flashlight turned on. A child's toy, meant to glow reassuringly in the night, the circumstances around them turned the cute mouse face into a glowing death's head.

"Okay," Paul finally managed to say, hoping that Rachel and Becky didn't hear the unspoken "Oh, shit," he himself heard clearly in the tones of his voice.

The door opened, and Paul almost yelped before he realized it was Jorge. The normally smiling and sarcastic expression Jorge usually wore had abandoned him, replaced by a look that Paul felt worried was also echoed on his own face: barely controlled fear.

Jorge went directly to his sister and niece. "You two okay?" he asked.

"Never better," said Rachel, glancing meaningfully at her daughter. "A little dark never hurt anyone, right?"

Becky shifted her light to one hand; with the other she clamped hard on Mr. Huggles. Jorge nodded, then looked at Paul. "*You* okay? You look like crap."

"I've got to go to the prison," said Paul in a low voice.

Jorge immediately hugged Rachel. "You two will be fine here," he said.

Paul, sensing Jorge's intent, said, "Jorge, I think you should stay with them."

"Hell no, man! I'm not letting you go down there with me at your back. Who's gonna protect you, *amigo*?"

He grinned, and Paul smiled back at him nodded, more grateful than he wanted to let show. Jorge smiled back and added, "Just remember this when you sign for Christmas bonuses this year."

ORDERS

Crane wrenched the walkie-talkie out of Darryl's hands. The idiot was talking to Paul, wasting time, wasting *life*, for God's sake.

"Hey, Doc -" began Darryl.

Crane didn't let him finish. "We don't have time for that!" he shouted, then threw the walkie-talkie down and went to the front door. The electromagnetic locks were no longer functional, so he just manually flipped the lock and opened the door. The elements blasted in, immediately outlining his body in a halo-like pattern of swirling snow.

Behind him, no one had moved. Crane felt panic rising, bit it back, bit it down as hard as he could. Can't lose it, he thought. Not now. Everything was so close, can't lose it.

Out loud, he said, "If we don't get the lights back on, we're dead. We're all dead." Looking at Sandy and Darryl, who were staring at each other like a pair of dumb teen lovers whose parents had found them feeling each other up in the car, he said, "Come on, come *on*." And as soon as the two threw on a pair of the "Crane Institute" parkas that hung behind them on the wall, he spoke to Jeff and Leann: "You stay here. If something – *anything* – comes through the door from my office, shoot it."

He saw the four guards exchange a glance, saw Leann mouthing "Anything?" but didn't care. Sandy threw her flashlight to Jeff, who caught it, and then she and Darryl –

Darryl still holding the other flashlight, thank God – walked rapidly to Crane.

He turned on his heel and pushed out into the storm.

He hoped they weren't too late.

But he feared...and shuddered. What he feared was simply to horrifying to put into words.

POSITIONS

Paul and Jorge headed for the door leading from Dr. Bryson's office to the second floor hallway. "Let's get Marty to help us," said Paul. Then he turned back to where Rachel and Becky sat, the ominous Mickey Mouse flashlight still looking more like a skull than anything else. Paul resisted an urge to shiver. Instead, he said, "I'm gonna get Mitchell, the big huge guy who snores, to stay with you two." Rachel nodded and Paul turned his gaze to Becky. "Mr. Huggles is a little afraid of the dark, so you might have to hold him real tight if he gets hysterical on you, okay?"

The little girl nodded seriously, her hand curling tighter around the bear's midsection.

Paul smiled, and hoped the little girl couldn't see on his face how scared he felt.

He and Jorge went across the hall, manually opening the now-unlocked door to the staff sleeping facility. Mitchell, Vincent, Donald, and Marty were all sitting up when Jorge entered, Marty holding a flashlight.

"Marty," Paul said to the morose guard, "I need you dressed in five seconds. Mitchell," he then said, addressing The Loon's resident grizzly-bear-in-a-guard's-outfit, "would you go and stay with the little girl and her mom?"

Marty fairly jumped into his clothing, something in Paul's tone clearly communicating to him that this was not a time to linger or joke around.

"What do you want me to do with them?" asked Mitchell as the big man lumbered off his mattress.

"Tell them stories or something," answered Paul. "Just keep them calm," he continued, biting back the urge to add "and safe" to the admonition.

"Okay," said Mitchell.

"And put some pants on first," said Paul. Mitchell smiled grimly as he put on his pants then moved – always surprising lithe for such a big man – to the door and disappeared into the hall.

"What's going on?" asked Marty, still dressing himself.

"Don't know," said Paul. "But we're going down to manually lock the tunnel just in case." He looked at Marty's flashlight. "Where'd you get that?" he asked.

"Emergency kit in the corner."

"Any more?" asked Jorge, beating Paul to the question.

Marty and Donald both shook their heads, looking like a pair of twin depressed bobble-heads on a string.

"Figures," said Paul.

"What about us?" said Vincent, gesturing to Donald.

"Stay here," said Paul. "Stay dressed. Just in case."

"In case what?" asked Vincent, clearly covering fear with attitude. His usual – perhaps only – defense system.

"Hell if I know," answered Paul.

And he turned to go down to a door where God only knew what might be waiting for them.

PROMISE

The room is dark. It loves the dark. Eats it. Becomes one with it. Takes it in and grows until it fills up the entirety of the underground room where it has spent its whole second life.

It has found what it needed in the computers.

Knowledge is power. Words from its first life, but still true now.

It moves, rippling toward the stairs, toward the way up to the monster's lair.

It had promised to kill the monster. And again, from its first life it has a dim recollection: you should always keep your promises.

The monster must pay.

OBSCENITY

Darryl didn't understand what was happening. The lights had gone out. That wasn't supposed to happen; wasn't even supposed to be *possible.*

And then Crane showed up, *frightened.* That was *absolutely* impossible.

Yet the lights were out.

And Crane was most definitely scared.

The snow was beating on Darryl's muscular frame like a battering ram. He moved over, trying to shield Sandy from the worst of the hurricane-like winds that threw snow at them so hard it stung. But he knew it probably wasn't helping her much: the snow was coming from everywhere at once, so shielding her was impossible. He focused on the generator shack that stood before them, close enough to touch. Only another couple feet and they would be against the walls, and hopefully the concrete would provide Sandy with some modicum of protection.

At least they were together.

Normally the thought would have warmed him. He had never gotten up the courage to tell her how much he liked her, but being around her had always felt like coming home. Not tonight, though. Tonight nothing was right. Not even being with her.

It's all wrong, he thought. All wrong.

A tap on his back. It was Sandy. He turned momentarily. She was pointing behind them. At first Darryl didn't understand what she was pointing out. He didn't see anything. Nothing but snow.

Nothing.

Nothing.

"Shit," she said at the same time he realized what had happened, "how are we going to get back?"

The Loon was gone. The storm had eaten it whole. And because the power was out there were no lights to guide them back. It was a miracle they had made it to the generator shack alive, Darryl realized. Forget about finding their way back. The weather had gone from dangerous to deadly in the space of their time outside.

"Maybe Dr. Crane brought a compass!" Darryl hollered over the wind. He was trying to sound light and unworried, but even to his own ears his voice was higher than usual, strain making his vocal cords tense.

Nearby, Crane was at the door to the generator shack. He was fumbling with his keys, trying to jam one into the door lock on the heavy steel door that barred uninvited visitors. Finally, one of the keys went in, and all three of them entered the shack.

A hulking gas-powered machine filled the space. Wind and snow blew in through a hole in the roof.

Wade lay across the machine. Dead. Pierced by machinery and cable junctions in a dozen different places, his body leaking blood that was rapidly freezing, his open eyes half covered under a layer of snow.

"Oh, no," said Darryl, at the same moment that he heard Sandy whisper the dead man's name in something that sounded like a prayer.

Before Darryl had more than a moment to take the horrific scene in, Crane went to the body and started yanking at it. Horrific crackling sounds issued from Wade's body, and Darryl thought that it was the sounds of bones breaking before he realized that it was really the sound of the body ripping free from the layer of ice-blood that had secured it to what remained of the generator.

"Easy, Doc," said Darryl. Normally he wouldn't have said anything to Crane – rebuking the man or even hinting that he was anything other than omnipotent was not a good way to ensure job security – but the violent yanking of Wade's corpse bordered on the obscene. "Take it easy," he tried again.

"Help me get this thing working, damn you!" shouted Crane.

BANG!

Darryl felt himself jump at the noise, before realizing that it was just the heavy steel door smacking into the frame, propelled by the deadly wind. He turned back to Crane. "Slow down, Doc," he said. "We'll get it up and running again."

Crane threw a disgusted look at Darryl. "You know *nothing*," he almost spat. He turned back to yanking roughly at Wade, pulling the corpse loose with that awful crackling sound. Then: "If we don't get the lights back on, you will think – *we all* will think – that we've died and gone to hell."

TUNNEL

The door was open. In all Paul's time at The Loon, he had never seen the door that connected the staff area to the prison proper simply hanging open that way. It wasn't right – was just plain *wrong*, in fact – and the inky darkness that lay beyond it made shivers crawl up Paul's spine like tiny insects. Even though the electromagnetic seals were off, the door should still be closed.

He heard someone take in a breath behind him. It must have been Marty, because Jorge muttered something in Spanish before starting forward into the darkness, his flashlight beam and a few tiny pinlights the only illumination in the dark space.

"You coming, man?" asked Jorge.

Paul shook his head. "Where's Hip-Hop?" he said. "And Jacky?"

Jorge shrugged, clearly trying for a look of jaded nonchalance and just as clearly failing. Paul looked at Marty, who was still standing slightly behind him, the dour-faced man's own flashlight illuminating the hollows of his cheeks and giving him a cadaverous appearance.

Paul pulled out his walkie-talkie. "Hip-Hop?" he said into the device. "Jacky?" No response to either.

"Could their walkie-talkies be out, man?" asked Jorge.

Paul shook his head. "No. Something's wrong." Then he took a deep breath and added, "We have to check out the prison."

"Wait," said Jorge. "Something's *wrong* and we're going *in there*? Are you nuts, man?"

"Why are *you* worried?" asked Paul. "You've got the guns and the flashlights."

And he stepped into the tunnel.

HUNGRY

It is in a different room now.
The monster's bedroom. Its personal area.
It's angry. Angry and happy and amazed and frightened.
And hungry. Hungry most of all.
Food, it thinks. Food food food foodfoodfoodfood....

HELL

Leann was starting to long for the good old days – when all she had to contend with was the prospect of unchaining Steiger for a romp around the prison area. She knew the man was insane, but also knew he was trying to appear somewhat normal in the hopes that he would be let out. Predictable.

By contrast, this night had been anything *but* predictable. The storm had been expected, sure, but even she had been troubled by its ferocity. Then there was the power outage. Then the *second* power outage – the one that she had never seen before; had been assured was impossible.

And then Crane, the imperturbable force of nature, looking like a kid who has just seen a monster under his bed.

What next? she wondered.

As if in answer, the wind outside – the sound was ever-present, but still she noticed it the same as she noticed her own heartbeat, thumping loudly in her ears – hit the walls like a huge sledge, a muffled thud that hammered through the reception area where she and Jeff "kept watch" with drawn tranks.

Both of them jerked around, pointing their guns at the blank wall beside them.

She felt foolish, even as she did so, but couldn't help herself.

"Wind," muttered Jeff, and chuckled nervously.

Leann allowed herself a tight grin. "Ain't we just a couple of -" she began.

And then hell burst loose from its moorings and came to visit the earth.

The door to Crane's office, the door to what Leann thought – what she *knew* – was an empty office burst open suddenly. The heavy wood that she knew was reinforced with a small sheet of steel shattered like a game of pick-up-stix dropped by an infant, wood and bits of metal almost exploding inward.

She whipped around, training her flashlight at the door, but before she could get a glimpse of what was behind it, something...*spurted*...out at her.

She had a moment.

A single, terrifying moment to see the thing. It looked like a piece of wet steak, raw and dripping, but at the same time it also seemed eerily loose and fluid. The thing shot out and hit her hand, the one that held the flashlight, engulfing it.

Leann felt a hiss and before her brain registered what was happening she smelled charring flesh. She screamed.

The pseudopod retracted just as quickly as it had emerged, pulling back into the black, dank thing she had glimpsed beyond the doorway.

Leann didn't notice. She was cradling her arm. Her arm that a moment ago had ended in a hand with a flashlight, and now ended in a melted and dripping black and red nub.

She inhaled and screamed again, pain coursing through her in waves.

She heard Jeff curse and heard/felt the sound of a dart being shot with a dry *thwip*, and then the thing in Crane's office barked, sounding almost like a dog. Jeff screamed a shout of mindless terror, then drew his nightstick and rushed the thing.

The pinlights cast just enough light left for Leann to glimpse what happened, just enough for her to know that she was no longer in the real world: somehow a nightmare had escaped from some deranged mind and been made flesh, and had drawn her into its surreal and terrifying realm.

She saw Jeff rush forward, sanity clearly gone from him in an instant.

The thing in Crane's office waited, a gelatinous black shape that in spite of its loose outlines reminded her of something familiar.

Jeff ran.

The thing didn't move.

Until Jeff raised his stick.

Then the thing...*broke* was the word her mind coughed up. It split like a Venus flytrap and Jeff ran right into the middle of it, which snapped shut around the guard.

Jeff shrieked.

And so did Leann. She screamed and screamed and screamed and was still screaming when Jeff stopped abruptly, still screaming when the *thing* started moving again, still screaming when it came to her.

And then she stopped.

Forever.

OUT

Marty's and Jorge's flashlights cut the darkness of the prison like electric knives. Right. Left. Right. They illuminated little in the immensity of the prison, however, serving more to highlight the gloom that surrounded them and Paul than to dispel it.

Paul was right behind them, glad that Jorge had moved into point position: it had goaded Marty into following, and Paul had a feeling that they would need the flashlights. Because something was very, very wrong.

The door to the tunnel had been open. So had the door on the other side of the tunnel, the door to the prison. Things were going bad.

Paul had little time to muse on that thought, however, because he suddenly slipped. He cried out, his arms flapping like a hummingbird on speed as he tried to right himself, finally succumbing to gravity and pitching forward...straight into Jorge's arms.

"You okay, man?" said Jorge. "There's better ways to show me you love me, you know."

Paul ignored the man's humor. Something new had just developed. "Shine the flashlight there, will you?" he said, pointing at the dark spot where he had just slipped.

Jorge and Marty both aimed their beams at the spot.

A small pool of dark liquid reflected the light.

"Is that what I think it is?" whispered Jorge.

"It ain't Strawberry Quick, " said Marty. His flashlight whipped back to the other guard's face. "Let's blow, man, let's cheese it."

"What about Hip-Hop and the newbie?" responded Jorge in an almost detached voice, as though he were discussing nothing more than the answer to a surprisingly difficult crossword puzzle. But Paul could see that the guard's hands were shaking, and knew he was going into stress-induced shock.

"I don't think they give a shit, man," said Marty, looking pointedly at the blood.

"Paul?" said Jorge, the single word conveying to Paul a wealth of confusion and fear.

Paul thought for a quick moment. He didn't like the idea of staying in this place.

Unfortunately, he liked the idea of leaving even less. "We stay," he said. "Marty, lock the tunnel door manually." Marty moved to comply, and as he did, Paul said, "We stick together, checking each cell one floor at a time. Someone's out, and I'd rather keep him in here with us."

"Then lock him in, man," said Jorge. "Let's just lock him in here and get the hell out of this place."

"And what if he got into the other building? What if Hip-Hop or Jacky are in here, wounded?" said Paul. He swallowed dryly, then added, "We have to find out."

GENERATOR

Crane was still searching for a way to fix the generator, to turn the thing on.

Sandy looked at Darryl, and shared a look of dubious concern with him. This was not at all the way either of them was accustomed to seeing the doctor act.

"This wasn't supposed to happen," Crane was murmuring. "This wasn't supposed to happen, oh, God, why did this happen?"

Sandy finally stepped forward, spying something that gave her a tingling hope that this night might not end up in the toilet after all; that maybe she and Darryl could go back and continue their conversation, perhaps even – and she flushed to think of it – find a quiet, empty room somewhere and let nature take its course.

"Here," she said, pointing at a circuit breaker that had been flipped off by Wade's foot. "Looks like he fell – I mean, looks like something hit the cutoff."

She flicked the switch. The generator gasped, slowly cycling up.

Crane almost sobbed in relief, and the sound scared Sandy worse than anything else that had occurred on this strangest of nights.

What the hell was the man so afraid of?

POWER

The only thing that kept Mitchell from falling completely apart in the darkness was the fact that Paul – a man whom Mitchell admired and always wanted to impress – had asked him to watch out for the women. That and the fact that Jorge would ride him mercilessly until the end of time if he ever discovered the big man's secret fear of the dark.

So he sat still and kept his mouth shut – as he usually did – until he noticed how tightly the little girl was clutching at her little bear, how both mother and daughter kept eying the closed door nearby as though expecting a monster or worse to jump out at them at any moment.

He wasn't the most frightened person in the room, he realized. So he opened his mouth and did something extremely rare for him: tried to start a conversation.

"What's your name?" he said to the little girl.

Then a low hum interrupted the conversation, killed it completely in a drowning flood of relief as the overhead light came back on.

"Hell yeah," murmured Mitchell, and stared at the light like it was the finger of a just and righteous God come to save them all from this mess.

He was still staring – and so didn't notice – when Rachel took a silver letter-opener off the desk nearby and slid it into her sleeve.

ONLINE

"Screw you, man," said Marty. " I ain't going in there!"

Paul opened his mouth to plead with the man again. He couldn't blame Marty, not really. They were all terrified, he knew. But before Paul could say anything, there was a deep clicking noise that sounded throughout the cavernous prison. The lights went back on.

Marty seemed to gain strength from the light; Paul was reminded of watching old Popeye cartoons

(with Sammy)

as a child, and thought about the cartoon sailor eating his spinach and growing suddenly strong. That was what Marty looked like in the light.

Marty strode into the prison, which was still dim but much less frightening now that the generator was back online. "You guys gonna help, or what?" he said.

NOW

Crane leaned against the generator in relief, barely noticing the snow that was whipping in through the open hole in the roof of the shack. He looked around; saw Sandy looking at him nervously, then saw Darryl standing in front of the open door, and behind him...

Crane sighed as he realized that the outside lights were back on. They could get back to the institute; the night could still be salvaged.

The lights were back on.

"There you go, Doc," said Darryl in a comforting tone – one which Crane would later have to punish him for. "Lights'll be all the way back up in a second. Everything's gonna be just -"

He didn't get to complete his sentence – *something* darted out of the snow, too fast to see any real details, and grabbed the big man from behind. It yanked Darryl easily out the door, and two dark shapes were visible in the storm for an instant before the snow and fury outside swallowed them both whole. A moment later the screaming wind was drowned out by a much more powerful scream of fatal pain.

It cut off suddenly.

And was replaced by a laugh. That horrible, ear-splitting laugh that Crane had heard earlier. The beast.

239

Crane leapt across the tiny room, yanking the door shut. Sandy shrieked. "Where did he – what happened to him?" she demanded.

Crane leaned against the closed door, perspiring, catching his breath. "What was -" began Sandy, but her voice cut off as the door started to open. Crane whipped around, pulling it shut again before the thing outside could get in.

The door pulled open an inch. Crane was resisting as hard as he could. It opened another inch.

"Help!" he shouted.

Sandy ran over to him. She, too, held the door, but even with both of them pulling as they could, the door inched open. They strained, but suddenly *it* was there. A dark strand of flesh, glistening and damp, curled around the edge of the door. Crane cringed away, but the thing bulged, and suddenly an eye opened on the end of the tendril. It blinked moistly, then swiveled to Crane.

He shrieked and shrank as far from it as he could while still pulling at the door. But it was no use. The horrifying thing followed him.

It touched his ear. Crane screamed.

Then the ropy flesh jerked out of the shack, the door slamming shut behind it.

"My ear! My God, my ear!" Crane shouted, feeling at the outside of the appendage and – surprisingly – finding it intact.

"What the hell was that?" demanded Sandy. "What the *hell* was that and *what the hell happened to Darryl?*"

Crane was not inclined to respond, but before he got a chance to ignore her, something knocked wetly on the door.

Crane felt Sandy brace against the feeble-seeming steel door, and felt himself go rigid as well.

Nothing happened.

"Think it gave up?" asked Sandy.

Then there was a hissing noise, just as there had been in the lab earlier that day, and then crude letters appeared on the door, burnt through from the other side:

RuN

"It's playing with us," Crane told Sandy, feeling his stomach drop through the ground below as he said so.

As if to confirm his words, more letters appeared through the steel behind them:

i wiLL KiL aLL of You
nOW

BLOOD

Jorge felt like he was stuck in the world's spookiest haunted house.

Truth be told, the prison area always had and probably always would give him the willies. But now, with the lights dimmer than usual, and with the inmates that were still in their cells gazing out at him, Paul, and Marty as they did a visual check on each cell to make sure no one had gotten out, the place was more than just creepy. It was downright terrifying.

They moved quickly from cell to cell, Jorge in the lead sometimes, sometimes Marty. Paul always stayed in the rear, since he had no trank and no flashlight. But he was the one who had the cell numbers of the residents memorized in that brainy head of his, so it was fair. Someone had to be in charge, and Jorge trusted Paul to do it...even if that meant he got to stay in the back.

And of course, he thought dryly, who says that someone's gonna pop out at us from in *front*?

All three of them stayed within eyesight of each other, never more than ten feet apart, quickly going through the first floor. Everyone present and accounted for.

"Everybody's where they should be on this floor, man," said Jorge. "I don't know if -" but then he cut off with a startled "What the?" as something slick and wet dripped down his forehead.

He touched himself and drew back a hand covered in blood; thought for a panicked moment he must have been cut somehow before he realized it wasn't his.

It was dripping down from the catwalk above.

CELL

Paul was running up the nearby stairs to the second floor almost before Jorge even noticed what was dripping down on him from above. A muffled "*Díos mío*" told him that Jorge and Marty were close behind.

Paul was on the second floor by that time, rushing to a thin line of blood that was coming from one of the cells.

The wrong cell. The absolute worst cell. Channing or Foster or even Bloodhound would have been preferable as escapees.

But no, this was cell two twenty three.

Steiger's cell.

Paul checked the light that indicated whether the cell was locked. Green. He nodded to Marty, who used his keys to unlock the outer cell. Paul stood back and let Marty enter, Jorge covering him with his trank.

Marty looked in the porthole. Gasped. Unlocked the outer door and entered without a word.

Paul darted ahead of Jorge, terrified that Steiger might come flying out of the cell, but more terrified at the thought of letting Marty face the monster alone.

Paul stopped dead in the doorway.

"Steiger's gone," said Marty in a hushed whisper.

"Oh, no," whispered Paul, as the older guard turned away and was violently sick all over the inner wall.

No Steiger, but the place was a horror. Something Paul knew he would remember as long as he lived.

Hip-Hop and Jacky lay almost neatly atop one another. Hip-Hop's throat had been torn out, probably with bare hands, Paul guessed from the state of the wound. Blood – the same blood that had dripped down onto Jorge – trickled lazily out of the wound.

Jacky was worse. Much worse. He had myriad blood dots all over him, and Paul couldn't even guess what had done that to him until his gaze rose high enough to take in Jacky's face.

His mouth was torn apart, ripped open to expose teeth and the interior of the man's mouth and nasal cavity. His cheeks were punctured as well, and the eyes...they were the worst. Both of them had been put out, and a key stood upright in one of the sockets, jammed through into the man's brain. Paul hoped that that had been the first thing to happen to him, but judging from the arterial spray that coated the walls like some modern art – modern art that no doubt would have sold for millions to the most fashionable art houses – it looked more likely that Jacky had been alive for some time before Steiger either put him out of his misery or he simply ran out of blood and died.

"*Madre de Díos*," whispered Jorge from the doorway, crossing himself as he followed that up with a sibilant "*sálvanos.*"

PUNISHMENT

Crane and Sandy were still pulling on the door with knuckles white from the exertion, even though there had been no more movement; apparently the nightmarish incarnation from hell had given up.

Or was, at least, being silent for the moment.

"What was that?" screamed Sandy, hysteria clearly audible in her voice. "What happened to Darryl, what *was that thing*?"

Before Crane could answer – could tell her to shut *up* and let him think – the frightened woman's walkie-talkie activated. Wiseman's voice crackled through: "Sorry to bother everyone," said Wiseman, "but we have a Code Three."

"Shit," murmured Crane. What had happened? What was happening? Things had been going so well, and now he was guessing that Steiger had gotten out, since that had been his orders to Hip-Hop and Wade. Worse, though, infinitely worse, was the evil that was prowling outside the shack.

"Where?" came Mitchell's disembodied voice.

Sandy started laughing, a low, whining laugh that Crane hated. He couldn't think, and right now he needed to think. There was a way out, but he didn't want to let go of the door. What if...*it*...was just waiting for that to happen? Before today he would not have credited his creation with any kind of sentience. But after seeing the words, after being *hunted* like this, Crane knew that at least some of his assumptions had been dangerously incorrect.

Sandy was still whining and laughing at the same time, even as Paul said, "We don't know where." Then, a moment later, he confirmed Crane's thoughts by saying, "It's Steiger. Hip-Hop and Jacky are down."

Finally, Crane arrived at a solution. It had taken him nearly fifteen seconds: desperately slow. He knew that the beast would be hungry, would be needing food. And while it might hate Crane, it would need to have sustenance even more direly. So Crane would provide that, and would use the distraction to get away.

He grabbed the walkie-talkie off of Sandy's belt.

"Wiseman," he said. "This is Crane. We're about to have real problems."

He could hear the amazed expression Wiseman must be wearing clearly in his voice. "Did you hear me? Jacky and Hip-Hop are *dead*."

"I don't give a shit!" screamed Crane, spittle flying madly from his lips. "Bring whoever's left and -"

WHAM!

The door suddenly pulled outward, yanking out of his too-loose grasp. He leapt out the door and pulled it shut again, this time alone as Sandy ran shrieking to the generator, huddling next to Wade's body.

The door jittered, but Crane held it firm as Sandy cried feebly, clearly out of her mind with terror.

"Doc? Doc?" said Wiseman through the walkie-talkie. "You still there?"

Crane punched the send button on the walkie-talkie. He glanced at Sandy, who was still weeping under a steady rain of snow from the hole that Wade had punched in the ceiling. "I'm here," he said. "Now *you* get here. Bring whoever's left and...."

Crane's voice trailed off. Still watching Sandy, he saw the gentle cascade of snow that had been falling down on her cut off suddenly. Crane looked up and saw the thing dropping on her, the beast falling onto the young woman. She dropped her flashlight at the same time, and the light spun into a corner, sending funhouse shadows left and right in a terrifying strobe.

Sandy screamed, a long, wet scream. Then the scream was replaced by the even more terrifying noise of feeding.

Crane watched the dark shadow of the monster that was now before him, transfixed in spite of himself. It covered Sandy's body like a flowing shroud, a deadly tapestry made of mercury that was ever-changing. Then the rational part of Crane's mind took over, goading him into movement.

In the corner of the room was a broom closet. Crane ran for it, sprinting near to his feeding creation in an effort to escape. He threw open the door to the closet, and there it was: the stairway that was built into the bottom of the closet, the stairs that led down to safety, albeit of a temporary kind. This was how Wade was to have brought Steiger back into the institute, had the night gone as planned.

Crane stepped onto the first step, trying to ignore the smacking, guttural sounds of feeding behind him, trying to ignore the sudden absence of sound from Sandy.

Then he turned to look. Just one more time, just as Lot's wife had done when fleeing Sodom. And like Lot's wife, Crane was immediately punished for his curiosity.

For a moment he could dimly see Sandy's outline in the folds of the beast, silent, ululating quietly in the waves of its body. But he felt safe for a moment: his creation was occupied by its food.

But the moment was only that, for in the next instant a tendril spurted from the gross shadow. The thing leapt through the air, striking Crane's forehead, knocking him down. Crane almost pitched down the stairs, but fell forward instead. He felt at his forehead, felt a gout of blood welling out of a circular hole, then his fingers scraped on something hard and unyielding and slightly porous.

My skull, he thought. The thing burned down to my skull.

A part of his mind thought how very extraordinary that was, but in the next second that part of him hid away in the deep recesses of a brain wracked with terror as another tendril came out. This one slithered and skittered across the floor like a sea snake through the depths, twining around Crane's leg.

The thing constricted, and Crane opened his mouth to scream as he felt his leg ripping off just below the knee.

INTERRUPTION

Rachel tried to hide Becky's face in the folds of her jacket, tried to cover her daughter's ears with her hands in a fruitless attempt to block the awful sound of the woman's scream that came out of the walkie-talkie the giant Mitchell was holding like a toy in his hands. But she knew her daughter was hearing it; could tell by the way the little girl was clenched tight as a fist in her arms.

Almost worse than the scream, though, was the other noise. The noise that sounded familiar and yet not. Like laughter, if the person laughing lived in a deep hole, full of echoes and the evil of thousands of lost souls.

Rachel let out a little peep then as the door to the room slammed open. She saw Mitchell spin around and drop into a wrestler's pose, huge hands outstretched like vise grips to protect them. But the big man dropped his hands when he saw that it was the two guards who had helped put the bed away: Vincent and Donald. Two men for whom she had felt little in the way of affection, who were in turn rude and taciturn as they put the bed where she had asked them to put it.

Now, however, neither looked rude or tough or even particularly brave.

A long moment of silence, broken only by the sound of screaming coming from the three men's walkie-talkies. Then Vincent whispered, "What the hell is going on?"

FOREVER

Crane shrieked as another tendril covered his remaining foot, and felt the sizzle and knew what was happening and was powerless to stop it even though he knew what was happening and how could this be happening but it was. The monster's tendril withdrew, and Crane screamed anew as he saw what was left of his foot: a melted stump, fleshy and grotesque.

The monster moved its entire body then, leaving behind the spot where it had enveloped Sandy, nothing left of the woman but an acid-scarred floor. It hunched up, its fluid mass doubling in on itself.

And then it sprung onto Crane.

And Crane screamed. And screamed and screamed and screamed forever, and knew that the monster was keeping its promise.

TRAUMA

Paul, Jorge, and Marty listened for a moment as the horrid screams continued on their radios, then Paul felt himself run instinctively for the tunnel door. Jorge and Marty followed him, hot on his heels as he barreled into the door...and almost broke his shoulder when the steel door failed to yield.

"Shit!" he shouted. "The seals are back on." He should have realized it before running: with the generators back on, all the electromagnetic prison seals had re-engaged. He entered his code and swiped his card in a series of short, static movements.

Crane's screams, so clear and horrifying on the walkie-talkies a moment before, suddenly went dead, replaced by an odd, wet sound. Like a leathery tentacle being scraped across a rough-hewn surface. Paul couldn't place the sound, but it frightened him almost as much as the screams had.

"Dr. Crane?" he shouted into his walkie-talkie. "Dr. Crane? *Crane!*"

No answer.

"What the hell do we do now, man?" asked Jorge.

"We go find him," answered Paul. He led the two other men down the dark tunnel, running to the door that led to the staff facility. As he ran, Paul yelled into the walkie-talkie, "Mitchell, we have a Code Three. Two men down, Crane's situation unknown. Who's with you now?"

Mitchell's voice crackled through the walkie-talkie. "Donald, Vincent, the little girl, and her mom. What about you?"

"I've got Jorge and Marty with me. Stay where you are and don't let anything through that door."

"Gotcha, boss."

"Jeff? Leann?" called Paul into the walkie-talkie. No answer. "Jeff and Leann, do you read?" he said. "Darryl? Sandy?" Nothing. He called the big man again. "Mitchell, we're going to the generator shack. Check in with us every ten. You read?"

"Ten-four," said Mitchell.

"And tell Becky to watch out for Mr. Huggles for me."

"And tell my sister to stay put while we're gone or I'll tell on her," added Jorge, clearly following Paul's lead and trying to keep things light enough that they would hopefully not further traumatize the young mother or her daughter.

But Paul knew, even as he was speaking, even as Jorge spoke, that both of them were failing. He was failing a child again.

Just like Sammy.

SCRATCHES

Vincent couldn't look at that goddam Mickey Mouse light the brat was holding in her hands. Thing looked like a goddam skull with ears, and Vincent couldn't handle looking at the creepy bit of "fun" paraphernalia for even one more instant. Dim emergency lights once more glowed at the corners of the room, but their weak luminescence did nothing to brighten his mood.

He felt something gnawing around the edges of his mind, a dark thing, dredged up from the depths of all that he was and all that he feared he might be.

It was madness.

And then it was no longer gnawing around the edges, but was instead inside him, in his center, devouring him whole.

Vincent started scratching his arm. And scratched it until, unnoticed in the darkness, he began bleeding.

And then he kept scratching.

WADE

Finished for the moment, it turns back to the other body, the one across the machine. The machine hums and coughs. Making sounds it doesn't like. It throws itself across the machine, and batters at it until it dies.

Then turns back to the other corpse. It is wearing a tag that says "Wade" and the thing wonders if it ever knew Wade in its first life.

Then thought disappears as the beast creates within itself the acid it needs to feed. It envelopes the body like a huge single-celled organism.

And eats.

Hunger is gone.

For now.

VERTEBRAE

Marty Furtak did not care for Wiseman. Didn't hate – didn't *loathe* – him the way that Vincent did, but didn't like him. Still, he had to admit that he was glad Wiseman was in charge as he followed him and Jorge down the tunnel. He had kept a level head, hadn't made fun of Marty when he puked his guts out all over the wall of Steiger's cell, and near as Marty could tell now, he was doing everything more or less right.

So he was just as happy to be following Wiseman as anything else right now.

Not that Marty was *happy* at the moment. Just he couldn't think of any place in The Loon that might be better than here. Sounded like Leann, Darryl, Sandy, and Jeff were all gone, which meant that Steiger must have gotten out to the generator shack and creamed them and probably Crane as well. So here was as good a spot as any. As safe a spot as any.

That assessment changed a moment later, when the emergency lights once again went off.

Marty skidded to a halt. "What the f -" he started to say, but Wiseman cut him off with a curt gesture.

"Generator must be down again," he said.

"What could do that, man?" said Jorge.

"Steiger," Wiseman answered simply.

"And we're going *out* there, man?" said Jorge incredulously. "What're you thinking?"

Marty nodded his agreement. But Wiseman just glared and said, "We don't know what's going on. People might be hurt. We have to help them."

Jorge shook his head, then nodded his reluctant assent. Marty followed suit, though he had no intention of following Wiseman out into the misery that no doubt awaited anyone who set foot outside. He would ditch them somehow, the first chance he got.

And soon he had his chance. Wiseman had to manually unlock the far door of the tunnel to get into the staff portion of The Loon. He held it open long enough for Jorge to run through, who in turn held it for Marty.

"Go," said Marty. "I'll lock this thing down and then catch up." He didn't add the second part of his sentence, "Like hell I will," out loud, but he thought it hard enough he felt sure that Jorge or Wiseman must have heard it.

Still, they bought it, nodding curtly and continuing their run through the reception area, hitting the door to the outside at a fast clip, unlocking it and gone before Marty had even turned around.

He noticed what they hadn't: the torn-up door to Crane's office, the lack of any security staff in the room.

"Screw it," he said to himself. Wiseman could figure it all out when – *if* – he came back. That was what they paid smart folks for, anyway: to figure things out.

Marty turned to the door, which he had let go for an instant to survey his surroundings. The door was almost shut now, and he reached forward to grab it.

And it swung open with a vicious displacement of air, catching Marty flat on the nose. He heard his nose break, but felt no pain, only fear, for as he fell down he saw the last person he had expected step through the open door.

Steiger caught him as he fell, caught him around the neck.

A swift jerk, and Marty felt his neck crack in several places. He immediately went numb from the neck down, and then felt himself light-headed and realized that Steiger must have broken his neck high enough that his body was no longer able to breathe.

And that was the last thought he had before the numbness crept up to his head, enveloped him, and he felt himself fall into the inky black of death.

BECKY

Steiger propped Marty's lifeless body up against the wall, searching through it for keys, weapons, anything that might aid him in his escape and in his greater quest to restore balance to the universe. He put the guard's belt on, along with its walkie-talkie and other accoutrements. Then he paused a moment, words that he had heard when Paul, Jorge, and Marty rushed past his hiding spot in the dark tunnel burning into his mind with the radiant heat of possibility.

"Who," he asked the sightless corpse of the ill-mannered guard, "is Becky?"

Becky sounded like a young girl.

Steiger smiled. If he could not go to his victims, it seemed the universe was bringing his victims to him.

BLOOD

Jorge followed Paul as the two men battled through the hellish storm outside. Jorge sank into a snow drift up to his knees, and felt Paul grab him under the armpits and help him extricate himself from the snow that was both soft and strangely unyielding at the same time.

Jorge yelled, "Thanks!" and Paul nodded.

It was then that Jorge noticed....

"Where's Marty?" he shouted.

He saw Paul look around and the other man's face furrow in disgust. Paul leaned in close enough that Jorge felt the doctor's breath on his cheek when he yelled, "Probably forgot to tie his shoe or something equally critical."

Jorge grinned and rolled his eyes.

"Up to us then?"

"Guess so," answered Paul.

"Any idea how we find our way to the shack?"

"Not a clue!" shouted Paul. The wind was so thick with snow and sleet that they could barely see each other. "Walk until we get to a wall, then follow it until we can see the shack."

"How we getting back?"

"Same thing in reverse."

Jorge rolled his eyes again, but followed gamely enough as Paul started walking. Shockingly, they reached the generator shack after only a few minutes of pushing through the storm.

Jorge gasped when he saw it. The outside of it was wrecked. There were dents in the concrete walls, as though a padded wrecking ball had hit it over and over again. The door was torn off its hinges and ripped in half, and there were strange markings on and around it, marks that looked like some kind of etchings or blowtorch burns on the steel door.

"What happened?" yelled Jorge.

Paul shrugged and went inside. Jorge followed, swinging his flashlight right and left. "Oh, man, this just gets better and better."

The place was a mess. The generator looked as though the wrecking ball that had attacked the area outside had removed its pads and gone at the machine full force. It was in pieces all over the interior of the shack, and Jorge, though no engineer and hardly even capable of changing the oil on his car, could immediately tell that the generator was beyond repair.

And the blood. It was everywhere. Bright sprays of it on the walls, small pools on the ground, interspersed with those same strange burn patterns that he had seen on what remained of the door.

"Where are the bodies?" asked Paul.

"What?" said Jorge.

"All this blood. Where did it come from? Or who?"

Jorge had no answer.

GAME

Steiger stepped into the hallway of the staff facility.

Where to begin? he thought. He knew from his long tenure at the facility that the closest door was the kitchen where meals were cooked, with numerous doctor's offices lining the hall. There was the stairway that led to the second floor – a promising possibility, he thought – and at the end of the hall was the door to the lobby, and beyond that the outside world.

Steiger thought briefly about trying to leave. Power was off, he had the advantage of surprise. Now was probably the most sensible time to go.

But he also had to admit that the prospect of staying for some...fun...also held its charms.

He wondered if he might find a knife or two in the kitchen, and opened it using one of the keys on Marty's key ring, which had been considerately marked, "Kitchen." Steiger would have to thank the dead guard for that next time he saw him.

He had just unlatched the door when there was a crackling, ripping, shredding noise behind him. Steiger reacted automatically, throwing the door open and throwing himself into the kitchen. He turned as he did and glimpsed the door to the lobby come crashing off its hinges before he was in the kitchen, door slammed shut behind him. He wondered about his reaction at the same moment – usually a door coming undone would not have unnerved him in the slightest. Steiger was fairly proud of the fact that very little in this confused world of his rattled him. But some animal instinct within him was suddenly fully alert, sniffing the air. It told him that whatever had just broken the door was something unusual. Something new.

Dangerous.

Fun.

Steiger peeked through the mesh-reinforced porthole that was inset in the top half of the kitchen door.

A dark shape moved by the kitchen. Steiger couldn't see much, it was just black in a sea of black. But something about the strange, fluid way it moved through the darkness made him stay silent.

It wouldn't be as much fun if he were dead.

The thing moved toward the door that led through the tunnel and into the prison.

Steiger waited for several minutes, then stepped out.

Whoever – or whatever – it had been, the thing was gone.

Steiger rubbed his hands together contemplatively, feeling for all the world like a child who has been told that it may play whatever game it wishes, and that there would be only one rule: people had to die.

HURT

Paul looked at the generator while Jorge stood, shivering, with his trank gun drawn and pointed out the door.

After no more than a few moments, Paul confirmed what had been clearly evident from the first second he entered the generator shack: the machine was completely destroyed.

"It's trashed," he said.

"Steiger?" asked Jorge, not looking away from the door.

"No," said Paul. "Maybe. I don't know."

The wind howled wildly, a piercing ghost call that made Paul feel as though some kind of evil spirit was beckoning for his soul to follow it to the depths of hell.

"I think we should get outta here," he said.

Then a thump sounded, harsh and hollow in the darkness. Paul almost jumped out of his skin when he heard it, and saw Jorge jerk in fright.

The storage cabinet opened.

Slowly.

Paul tensed. He felt like an eight-year-old, watching a horror movie through splayed fingers, waiting for something to grab him from behind while he watched the show with a terrified gaze.

The door fell open, and Crane pulled himself out. The doctor looked up at Paul with pain-saturated eyes and whispered, "Help," before passing out.

"Dios!" hollered Jorge, and gagged.

Paul couldn't blame him. Crane was a mess. There was a hole on his forehead that trickled blood, bright read on the white, snow-covered floor. His body and face wherever visible were covered in bruises. Blood was all over him.

And his legs...one was gone at the knee, another ended in a stump near the ankle. Paul was shocked at first that the doctor hadn't bled to death already, and started yanking at his belt to make a tourniquet before he realized that the stumps weren't bleeding; that Crane's legs had somehow been cauterized and sealed shut.

"Is he..." began Jorge.

Paul checked Crane's pulse. "Alive," he said. He examined the legs. Cauterized all right, but not by fire. It looked almost like a chemical burn, ashy dead skin flaking off all around the circumference of the charred flesh. "What did this?" said Paul, as much to himself as anything.

There was blood leading down some kind of stairway that was in the back of the storage closet, and suddenly Paul realized why only Crane had the key to this place: it was something secret, something he didn't want anyone else to know about. What that secret could be, Paul had no idea, but he somehow intuited that it was tied in to the mess they all had been suffering through on this horrific night.

Paul hesitated, then said, "Help me with him."

"What're we doing?" asked Jorge.

Paul nodded to the stairwell. "Going down."

"Are you crazy, man?" asked Jorge. "We don't know what's down there."

Paul motioned at the blood on the stairs. "Sandy or Wade or any of the others could be down there. Hurt."

Jorge closed his eyes as though praying, then said, "Fine. But if I die my sister's going to be seriously pissed."

Paul grinned. "I'll try to keep that in mind," he said.

But the words sounded hollow, even to him.

He still didn't know what was going on, but he was gripped by the sudden feeling that neither he nor Jorge would make it through the night alive.

CRYPT

The prison was silent, a vast mausoleum where the corpses didn't know they were dead yet.

Then, the silence was broken by a thud. One of the prisoners crashed against the door of his dark cell. Then another, then another...and now there were thumps and thuds everywhere.

The inmates were panicking, losing whatever tenuous hold on self-control they might have had. Men's faces appeared at the portholes of the inner cells. Wary faces, frightened faces, paranoid faces, manic faces. Mouths open in silent screams.

Some of the prisoners, including one who was named after a president but whom everyone called Bloodhound, starting head butting the porthole window in his cell. Blood smeared as Bloodhound's nose shattered.

He smiled and licked the blood up, nostrils flaring as he did so.

And under it all was the sound: the wind.

The elements were raging. The storm had at last reached full force.

Part Four: The Feeding

It's less than a rustle in my ear -
An instant of black where night should be.
A sensing of something drawing near.

A fragment of heart-beat stilled, then free;
A flicker of shadow behind the moon.
The moment I tense...it's stalking me.

- *Visitor by Starlight*

It's here. I feel it crouching in cold night
Behind my door. It waits its own
Still time to tendril out
And touch my toes.
I shiver and groan...

-                                    *Secret*   *Shadow*

STORM

The sound of Mitchell's walkie-talkie crackling suddenly to life startled Rachel. Paul's voice sounded out. Rachel strained to hear, though: the storm was whistling and wailing constantly now, and almost drowned out the kind doctor's words.

"Mitchell?" said Paul.

Mitchell thumbed the button on his radio and answered, "Yeah, where are you?"

"Good question. We found some sort of a tunnel that goes under the courtyard."

"What?" Mitchell said, and Rachel could see surprise writ large across the huge man's face.

"Who's with you?" said Paul, ignoring the question.

"The ladies, and Donald and Vincent," answered Mitchell.

"And I've got Jorge with me."

Rachel's heart fluttered when she heard Jorge was with Paul. She didn't know all that was going on, but knew that someone had escaped the prison, and that others were hurt, maybe even dead. But not Jorge. Thank God, not Jorge.

"Hey, sis," said her brother over the radio. "How's that big buffoon treating you and the brat?"

Mitchell handed the walkie-talkie to Rachel, quickly pantomiming where to push to send the signal. "He's been fine," she said. "I'm okay."

"And the brat?" asked Jorge. Rachel couldn't help but smile. She handed her daughter the radio. The little girl was hesitant, her movements still sparing, as though she did not want to draw attention to herself. But as she heard her uncle's voice, Rachel saw her daughter's eyes change. She was going to be brave. To survive.

Rachel was both happy and sad at this. Happy that her daughter was going to speak, and had clearly decided to come out of the self-induced trance that had held her in its sway since their arrival. But sad that such a thing should be necessary. No child should have to concentrate on survival like that.

FUN

Steiger held Hip-Hop's walkie-talkie loosely in his hands, listening to the exchange. He had wondered who this Becky might be, and sure enough the universe had once again altered its path to accommodate him. He was standing in front of the lobby door, having decided that, fun as this place might be, it was time to leave. So he pushed at the door, shoving it open to a wind that almost took him off his feet.

Just a short walk to the gate. Then freedom. And more fun. More setting the universe to rights in the way that only he could do.

He pushed out into the storm, taking his first step when the mysterious Becky's voice came across the walkie-talkie he still held.

"I'm okay, Uncle Jorge. I'm with Mommy," said the voice.

Steiger stopped moving. The voice was beautiful. Innocent. It spoke of milk and cookies left out for Saint Nick, of red balls that bounced with a hollow sound off black pavement in a schoolyard, of ice cream on a hot summer day, of cocoa in the frosty winter nights.

The voice spoke to Steiger. She was a little girl. Just a little girl.

Little girls could be so much fun.

So he stepped backward.

Closed the door behind him.

He would stay for a while.

"Come out, come out, wherever you are," he sang quietly, and laughed a little laugh. Just the kind of laugh that a young girl – that Becky – would love. Come play, said the laugh. Come play and laugh and sing until we are ashes and ashes and all fall down.

He would stay after all.

Little girls could be so much fun.

STRESS

Mitchell took his walkie-talkie back from the little girl and winked at her. She didn't wink back, but her eyes no longer held that dull, glazed look that they had for the entire time in the office. That was good, Mitchell thought.

Out loud, he said, "What about Marty and Crane? Sandy?"

"Crane's with us," answered Paul's voice. "Hurt. We're bringing him in."

"And the others?"

There was a long pause, broken only by the sustained screaming of the wind and the ever-so-soft crackle of the walkie-talkie. Finally, Paul said, "Close the door to Bryson's office. Lock it. And keep a gun pointed at it. We'll warn you before knocking."

Mitchell flinched then as someone yanked the walkie-talkie out of his hand. It was Vincent, the wannabe mobster must have forgotten his own radio in his gutless hurry to get over here. "What the hell's going on?" said the weasely twit in a nasal, panic-ridden voice.

Another pause. Then Paul said, "Steiger's out. The generator's trashed. And something else is going on, too."

Vincent looked like he was about an inch away from pitching headfirst into an abyss of insanity. "What does that mean, huh, Wiseman? You wanna tell me what that means?"

Mitchell used one of his huge hands to wrest the walkie-talkie away from Vincent, not taking much care to be gentle. "Shut up," he hissed. "This isn't the time or the place." He glowered at Vincent, rolling his eyes toward Becky to indicate that Vincent shouldn't scare the kid. Vincent went back and sat next to Donald.

Donald put an arm around his friend, squeezing Vincent's shoulder, then went and locked the door. Rachel and Becky watched calmly, and Mitchell was glad that neither of them was acting as terror-stricken as Vincent.

Vincent he could punch if the guy went too bonkers. But Mitchell knew he didn't have it in him to strike a girl. Call him sexist, but that was the way he had been raised.

Paul's voice inserted itself into Mitchell's train of thought. "I don't know what's going on, Vincent. I'll radio you as soon as Jorge and I find out where we are. Until then, keep your guard up and stay safe.

"Out."

DISSOLVED

A door is in the way.

It doesn't matter.

It goes under the door, its body flattening out against the cold concrete floor. Somehow it retains its ability to think, to act, to do, to be, even in its dissolution.

Once on the other side of the door, it re-solidifies.

Eyes appear along one side. They move independently, half a dozen moving in every direction. Though it does not know how it knows, it is aware that it has found its way into the prison.

The silent prison. The prison of its first life.

There is food here.

It will feed.

WARY

Just a tunnel. Nothing less, nothing more. But in spite of that, Paul was wary, walking carefully through the secret passage that led from the generator shack to a place unknown.

Crane was unconscious beside him, being held aloft in an emergency carry position by Paul and Jorge. Jorge was muttering in Spanish, praying from what little Paul knew of the language.

They followed the passage until they reached the end. A door stood before them. They opened it carefully.

Wary of what might be on the other side.

LUCKY

Mitchell tried making shadow figures in the pitiful light of Becky's Mickey Mouse flashlight, but his heart wasn't in it. For one thing, the light wasn't strong enough. For another, his hands were too big. But most of all, it was because he simply could not stop shaking.

He looked around. Donald was guarding the door, the quiet guard covering it with his half-raised gun. Vincent stared out Dr. Bryson's office window, looking like a man at Confession. He spoke a moment later, his voice dreadful and broken: the voice of a man about to shatter.

"When I was a kid, I was in this gang. And it was so great being...part of something. And then I realize one day that I got no family, I got no job, I got no prospects. Nothing. And so I tell Roger – he was the leader, King Shit of Turd Mountain, he called himself – I says, I'm getting out. Gonna make something of myself. And he says, 'My ass, you're getting out.'"

Donald apparently sensed as Mitchell did that Vincent's reminiscing was not going anywhere helpful or healthy, because he whispered, "Vincent, don't."

The room was quiet as a sepulcher at midnight. Then Vincent continued, "But I did, you know. I got out, and I thought, now I'm done and made it out." He inhaled, a deep, shuddering breath. "Then I realize that knocking over corner stores is all I know, and only one place will hire me, so I end up working at this factory as a minimum wage night watchmen. Me, on the legal side of a gun for once. And then I'm in charge of security at the place. And then I land me a nice fat job on the staff of the Crane Institute and I think how lucky I am. Making more honest money than I ever thought I could. How lucky. Lucky...."

His voice trailed off, and a moment later Becky said from her mother's lap, "Mommy, are we going to die?"

Mitchell looked at Rachel and could instantly see that she couldn't answer. Whether it was because she didn't know or simply was too tired to deal with the question, Mitchell couldn't say. But she looked at him pleadingly.

"No, kid," said Mitchell. "We're not going to die."

Becky smiled at him, just the barest hint of a smile actually, but even that little bit was warm and radiant, like the sun had peeked through the storm for one small moment. The sun fled, though, when Vincent said, "We are, though. You can feel it. You can feel -"

Mitchell felt himself leap across the room in an instant, slamming Vincent against the wall, shaking him like a naughty puppy. "What the hell are you trying to do?" he rasped in a low whisper. "Scare the little girl? Huh?"

Vincent threw Mitchell's hands off. "Touch me with your big mitts again and I'll break your -" began Vincent, but before he could finish the thought, there was a knock at the door.

The whole room oriented on the doorway instantly. Mitchell and Vincent each raised their trank guns to point them along with Donald.

A tense moment passed, everyone in the room clearly worrying along with Mitchell about what might be on the other side of the thin piece of wood.

A weak laugh filtered through the doorway, and Mitchell tensed. It wasn't Paul. It wasn't *anyone* good.

He felt himself move toward Vincent, and was dimly aware of Rachel and Becky moving on their cot so as to be closer to the men.

Safety in numbers, thought Mitchell. Herd instinct. We may be civilized, but in an emergency the veneer falls away and we act like the animals we once were.

The door boomed then as something hit it with rocketing power on the other side. Mitchell was so scared he almost pulled the trigger on his gun. But he didn't, managed to control his spasming finger just in time, and instead waited for the sound to repeat.

It didn't.

"What was that, Mommy?" asked Becky.

Rachel looked questioningly at Mitchell.

He had no answer for her.

BASEMENT

Paul felt like the rug had been ripped out from under him yet again.

They were in a lab, clearly, but not one that Paul had ever seen before. He wasn't up on the latest, but it looked like some sort of biotech lab. He saw the cage in the sweep of Jorge's flashlight; gestured to Jorge to point the light there.

Ten feet or so on a side, bars that looked like they were electrified – though probably not now since the entire place was dark – with the same acid etchings that he and Jorge had seen on the door and floor of the generator shack.

"Where the hell are we, man?" said Jorge.

Paul did some mental calculations, trying to figure out what direction they had gone through the secret tunnel near the generator, then said, "Basement, I think."

"No, man, I been there. It ain't nothing like this."

"Next to it, then. The basement I've seen is awfully small for a place as big as The Loon. This would explain why."

And that was when Crane woke up and started shrieking.

CRYING

Becky pulled closer to her mother as a new noise sounded: a soft tap-tapping on the closed door to the room they were in. She remembered Daddy had tapped like that, oh-so-gentle on the door to her room, as though shy. That was before he changed, though. Before he started drinking and started to Turn Bad.

"Maybe it's Wiseman," said one of the guards, the skinny one with dark hair and a bully-look about his eyes. Not that the bully-look was there anymore; he just looked scared.

Becky hoped it *was* Dr. Wiseman: she liked him.

Apparently it wasn't Dr. Wiseman, though. And it wasn't Daddy, either. Not even the bad Daddy who had hit her earlier that day. This was something else. And though she didn't know the details, her young mind could tell from the way everyone was acting that this was something much worse than Daddy.

A voice came through the door. As it did, the big bear-man, Mitchell, quivered and said, "Steiger," under his breath.

"Please," said the voice on the other side of the door. "Please let me in."

The other guard in the room, the short round one, said a Bad Word under his breath.

"Who is it?" said Mommy.

The bear-man motioned for Mommy to be silent.

"Please let me in," said the voice. The tapping continued, and it was like the person out there was tapping on Becky's brain: it almost started to be a physical pain. The voice started to cry. "There's something out here. It's in the prison right now, but I'm afraid it will come back." A sob sounded. "Pleeeease," the voice moaned."

Then everyone jumped, even Mommy, who had been so brave and saved her earlier from Daddy, even Mommy who was never afraid of the monsters in the dark, even she jumped because the door slammed like it was being hit from behind.

Again she was reminded of her father, but now she was reminded of him after he started to Go Bad, after he began to hit Mommy and look at Becky with looks that were ever stranger and more uncomfortable.

The person outside hit the door again. The guards all took a step back, coming closer to Becky and Mommy. The skinny one looked like he wanted to talk, but Mitchell the Bear motioned him to be quiet.

Mommy started to rock her, to coo and coddle, and for some reason that scared Becky most of all.

The slamming stopped. This time the voice on the other side of the door was a whisper. "Becky," it said, and Becky felt her stomach plunge. Who was this man? How did he know her name? Mommy breathed in sharply, and Becky knew that she was thinking the same thing. "You want to open the door for me, don't you, Becky?"

Mommy laid a light finger across Becky's lips. Don't speak, the gesture said.

The slamming started again, punctuating the man's words. "Little girl?" Slam. "Please..." slam "...open..." SLAM "...the..." *SLAM* "DOOR!"

Then silence.

And then the sound of footsteps walking away, followed by clanking down the scary stairs.

Becky didn't cry.

She held her Mickey Mouse light tightly in one hand, her Emergency Pack in the other.

She turned her head into Mommy's chest.

She wondered what was happening.

She was afraid, oh so afraid.

But she didn't cry.

PHOTOS

Jorge was holding onto Crane's legs – what was left of them. He and Paul had immediately lain the convulsing, screaming man on one of the work tables, Paul sweeping aside notes and files with impunity to lay the man down on the flat surface.

Crane's body shook and shivered, bucking at Jorge, making him almost lose his grip. He *did* lose his grip for a moment, in fact, and his hand connected with the moist, charred nub that ended Crane's leg on one side.

Crane screamed.

But the pain must have acted like a slap in the face, or a dash of cold water, because his convulsions stopped suddenly, and his breathing, though far from normal, grew stronger and less strained.

Crane began to cry.

"This wasn't supposed to happen," he moaned. Then passed out again.

"Shit," said Paul. "Look around. Maybe there's something in here we can give him for the pain."

"What am I looking for?" asked Jorge, utterly lost in the hi-tech lab.

"Syringes, ampoules, stuff like that."

Jorge decided against telling Paul he had no damn clue what an ampoule was and started looking for anything that looked like it might have come from a hospital.

A moment later, Paul said, "Jorge, shine the light over here."

Jorge did, and saw that Paul was looking through a group of files.

"What is it?" asked Jorge.

Paul didn't answer, but flipped rapidly through the files, lost inside them. Jorge looked over his shoulder and saw page after page of photos, dimly visible in the flashlight's beam. Something uniquely horrible stared up at him from each face. Some of the forms were recognizable as human. Others were mere pools of rubbery flesh and mucus. All were strange, all terrible. A date was written across each glossy photo.

Paul opened another folder, this one full of papers. Lists, names, what looked like medical charts.

"Oh, God," murmured Paul. He pointed at one of the pages. "Plannings, May nineteen ninety-seven. Nanzer, April nineteen ninety-five. Allred. Leder. Ellison. Recognize them?"

Jorge felt a sinking in the pit of his stomach. He *did* recognize them. "Those are the names of some of the escaped inmates," he said.

Paul compared the lists with the photos he still clutched in his hand. "The ID numbers match," he said. Then, turning to look at Jorge with haunted eyes, he said, "Not *some* of the escapees, *all* of them." Then he looked at the papers again, and shuddered. So did Jorge, though he was not sure why.

"But they weren't escapees," said Paul.

"What, then?" asked Jorge.

Paul sat down at a nearby chair and started reading. He had to thumb through only a few pages to reach an apparent conclusion, and suddenly looked even more scared than he had in the generator shack or when they found Crane.

He grabbed as many of the lists and photos as he could and shoved them all in a large manila envelope.

"What's up?" asked Jorge.

"We are," said Paul. "First course." He closed the envelope and moved back to Crane. "We've got to get back to the others."

"I don't think we could make it back through the storm," said Jorge.

Paul nodded, then motioned for Jorge to point his flashlight at the other side of the room.

Jorge did so, and illuminated a stairwell that led upwards to somewhere unknown on the first floor.

"You got any more lights?" asked Paul suddenly, clearly deep in thought. Jorge shook his head. "Great," said Paul. A moment later, he said, "All right, we're going up the stairs. As soon as we're on the first floor, you turn your light off."

"*What?*" bellowed Jorge. "Why?"

A new voice answered: Crane's voice. The doctor was still on the work table nearby, still obviously in incredible pain, but he sounded coherent once more.

"Because if you keep the light on," said the doctor, "it will kill you."

VENT

Steiger walked down to the first floor and into Crane's office. He had been here, of course, doing a session with Dr. Wiseman in the larger space whenever it was available – whenever, as Wiseman had so nicely explained to him one day – the owner of the institute was away on business, which was fairly often.

That was why Steiger knew exactly what he was looking for.

The vent.

It was right above Crane's desk, several feet to a side. A tight squeeze, but Steiger knew he could get into the ventilation ducts and start *really* having fun.

STAIRWELL

"Just up here," said Crane from Paul's arms. The words were slurred, and Paul knew that Crane was on the verge of passing out again. "My…office," he said.

He got to the top of the stairs a moment later, and saw that whatever had happened to the door of the generator shack had also happened here: the door to the secret lab had been torn out, burn marks evident on its surface.

"What the hell's going on?" asked Jorge.

"Later," said Paul. "Keep quiet until I say otherwise."

Jorge looked like he wanted to argue, but to his credit just nodded.

"Where are we?" Paul asked Crane in a whisper.

"Up the stairs is my living quarters," answered Crane. "My office is through there."

So that's how you disappeared this morning, thought Paul to himself. You must have been working in your little Dr. Frankenstein lab down there. But out loud he only said, "Jorge, turn off your light and make sure you stick close."

Jorge nodded and the place went black.

DUCT

Steiger had made it. It was tight, and he hadn't been able to reattach the vent behind him, but he was now inside The Loon's air conditioning ducts.

Suddenly, he heard voices. He recognized them almost instantly, even though they were whispered. It was Dr. Wiseman and his friend Jorge.

"How long do I gotta keep quiet?" whispered Jorge.

"Long as you want to live," said Wiseman. "Shut up."

Steiger almost turned around; almost dropped down on them to wreak a bit of merry havoc. But he decided against it. For one thing, he couldn't do that without just backing out and jumping blind, and he hardly wanted to be tranquilized and returned to his cell at this stage of the game.

For another, he had far more interesting prey to pursue.

So he waited until he heard Wiseman and Jorge pass through the office, then began crawling.

"Don't worry, Becky," he said quietly, so quietly a mouse would have mistaken the sound for just another noise in the wind. "I'm coming, dearest."

REALIZATION

Jorge followed Paul through the lobby. Paul had him turn on the light once, just briefly, to survey the layout, and both of them had uttered short curses when they saw the destruction: blood, that strange scarring on the floors, the door to Crane's office in shards.

They went through the door to the first floor staff facility hallway, and Paul had Jorge flick the light again. Just quickly, but Jorge had seen Paul glance at the door that led to the prison tunnel. It was just a quick glimpse, but Jorge saw Paul's face change, as though the doctor suddenly understood something. Jorge wanted to ask what Paul was thinking, but before he could Paul said, "Move," and the two of them held Crane between them as they ran up the metal staircase.

PROBLEM

Rachel felt for a moment as though she were sitting in the "Mush Pot" during an old game of Duck, Duck, Goose: Mitchell, Vincent, and Donald were all sitting around her in a protective ring. Though she had to admit she had never heard of a game where the people on the outside all held drawn weapons.

She supposed she should have felt protected, with the men on all sides of her and her daughter. The opposite was true, however: she felt more alone and weak than ever before.

Everyone tensed as a light knock sounded outside the door. "It's me," came a voice, and everyone relaxed. It was Dr. Wiseman, she recognized his kind tones, though his voice was now stretched and strained.

Mitchell leapt to the door, the big man unlocking it and pulling Paul, Jorge – thank God, Jorge was alive and well – as well as the burden they carried between them into the room before closing and re-locking the door once more.

Rachel gasped as she realized that what her brother and Dr. Wiseman were holding was a man. And she gasped again when she saw his legs, horrible stumps that were oozing pus and blood around charred flesh. She covered Becky's eyes with one hand, turning her gently into her chest so she wouldn't see the nightmare.

Paul nodded to Mitchell, who shoved aside the things on Dr. Bryson's desk to make way to put the man he was holding. The man moaned, but appeared to be unconscious. And no wonder, with such horrific wounds.

"What happened?" asked Mitchell.

"Not one hundred percent sure yet," answered Dr. Wiseman – Paul, he had told her to call him.

As soon as the wounded man was on the desk, Jorge practically jumped across the room to engulf Rachel and Becky in a huge hug. "You two all right?" he asked.

Rachel felt herself nod, though inside she was screaming at her little brother for asking such a stupid question: of *course* she wasn't all right. Who could be all right in this situation.

Jorge looked at Mitchell. "Marty ever show up here?" he asked the big man. Mitchell shook his head. Jorge appeared downcast. "Maybe he's still –" be began, but Mitchell cut him off gently.

"If Steiger's out, you can bet Marty's gone."

Then another voice sounded: the man on the desk, whose face was so pale it practically glowed even in the dim light of the flashlights in the room. "Steiger's not the problem," Crane said.

DIFFERENTIATION

Paul spread the papers he had brought up from Crane's secret lab beside the doctor. Mitchell and Vincent watched him while Donald kept the door covered. Rachel and Becky were sitting as far from the door as possible, looking only at Paul or Jorge from time to time, but avoiding everyone else's gaze.

Paul wanted to go to the mother and her child, to comfort them if he could, but he knew that would have to wait. Because survival wouldn't.

Mitchell pointed at the photos of men and not-quite-men and puddles of goo. "What are those?" he asked.

At the same time Vincent picked up one of the photos. "Paxton," he said. "Didn't he get out like a year and a half ago?"

"No," said Paul shortly. "None of them did." He looked at Crane, anger colder than the storm outside welling up within him. "You weren't studying psychopathology here, were you, doctor?"

Crane hesitated a moment, and Paul could see the man weighing his options. Apparently he decided that candor would provide him with a greater chance of self-preservation, because he finally said, "Differentiation."

Everyone was silent. Paul had no desire to break the quiet, he was too angry.

Finally Rachel said quietly, "I don't understand."

"You and me both, lady," said Vincent.

Paul looked at them. "All the cells in our bodies start out from two, originally."

Crane jumped in. "The sperm and egg essentially join to create one new cell. And that cell splits in two. Both the new cells are exactly the same. Those cells split. Now there four, still exactly the same."

"What's the point?" asked Donald quietly from his position in front of the door.

"The point is that eventually they *aren't* the same," said Crane. He must have seen the lost looks on Mitchell's and Vincent's faces, because he continued, "Eventually, the cells change. It's called differentiation. They differentiate into skin cells, hair cells, heart cells, and so on. But originally we all start as one cell, and that cell changes eventually into myriad different types of cells. Hair cells, skin cells, blood cells: every other kind of cell we use in our bodies in fact. But originally, those cells were all the same. So theoretically our cells could change *their* makeup and become something else, if we could just figure out the way to tell them to do it."

"So you…" began Mitchell.

Crane's grimace of pain became a smile of pride. "I figured it out."

"What does this all have to do with us?" asked Rachel.

"What he's saying," answered Paul grimly, "is that we've got something worse than Steiger to worry about. Something that can turn parts of itself…" his voice faded, as he was unsure how to communicate what was happening.

"Into anything it wants," said Crane.

Jorge looked disgusted at the thought of such an aberration. "Why would you do that, man?" he asked.

"Idiots," whispered Crane, and Paul could feel the mood of the room darken even more than it already had. "If we can unlock the secrets we keep in ourselves, everything will change. Imagine a world where if your kidneys stop working, you can just grow a new one. Same with arms or…" he glanced at his burnt stumps, "…or legs. Or fingers or anything else. This is the key to making ourselves perfect."

"Maybe someday," Paul snorted, looking at some of the notes beside Crane. "But right now it means we have an escaped psychopath that you've made into a monster that can change its arm into a mouth, right Dr. Crane?"

Paul's cold anger morphed into icy fear as Crane said, "It's much worse than that, Dr. Wiseman. It can secrete highly concentrated stomach acid in huge quantities…enough to burn a horse into nothing. Or it could flatten out and slide under a locked door."

Paul felt himself and everyone else look at the door, as though it would happen right that moment.

"Shit," said Vincent. "Could that really happen?"

Jorge looked at his sister and niece. "Next year *I* pick the family reunion location, okay?" he said, and in spite of their dire straits Paul felt relief when the little girl actually smiled at the comment.

Then he looked at Crane, who was also smiling, but for a different reason. "You're proud of it, aren't you?" said Paul.

"I'm afraid, first and foremost," said Crane, and his pale face seemed to whiten a bit further for a moment before he continued. "But yes, I am proud of what I have accomplished."

"Why here?" asked Vincent. "Why The Loon?"

"Obvious," answered Crane with a sniff which turned into a gasp when he moved. Paul couldn't understand why the man wasn't screaming: apparently the opportunity to brag in public for the first time about his work was keeping the man focused on the conversation and keeping his mind off the pain. "The inmates here," Crane continued, "they're not people. No one cares if they disappear...as long as they don't reappear, either."

"You bastard," said Paul. Then he asked, "How do we get away from it?"

Crane's eyes closed meditatively. "You don't. This was a final stage experiment. It has to take in tremendous amounts of sustenance. Has to eat every fifteen minutes or so, especially after changing. If it doesn't, it will die. So it's very hungry, and we probably look like a big smorgasbord to him."

"So what, we can't kill it?" asked Vincent.

Crane looked amused. "No, it's killable, Mr. Marcuzzi. Enough fire might do it, or blowing it into small enough pieces. And it's highly photosensitive: enough bright light will kill it."

"You knew that?" Jorge said to Paul.

Paul nodded. "I suspected it, based on the setup of the lab and some of the notes I saw while we were in the basement."

"Then why'd you have me turn off my light, man?"

"Because a little light just hurts it and makes it mad," answered Crane. "It probably wouldn't have come near you if you were pointing it at him, but the second you wavered or turned your back..." and he made a slicing motion across his neck.

"A Jorge-d'oeuvre," said Paul. Then he turned to Crane. "Will the trank guns work on it?" he asked.

The doctor shrugged. "No idea," he said. "Probably not."

Paul looked at Crane's legs. "It attacked you in the shack, didn't it? Why didn't it kill you?"

Crane hesitated. "You remember Luke Rodney?" he said.

"Of course. Escaped a few months ago."

"No," said Crane. "He never left. And right now he's probably coming toward us. Luke never liked me much." Crane drew in a shuddering breath, then continued, "It didn't want me dead. Luke – the thing that Luke has become – wanted me hurting. Dead comes next. For all of us, I suspect."

"What do we do?" asked Vincent in the quivering tones of someone about to dissolve into hysteria.

A moment of silence passed. Then Rachel said, "Food. Water."

"Lady," began Vincent. "This is not the time to –"

"No, she's right," said Paul. "We should check this floor, one room at a time, then close it off and guard the stairs. We need to have access to the staff kitchen, sleeping area, and bathrooms."

"Why?" demanded Vincent in that same high-pitched, fearful voice. "Why don't we just stay here until the storm ends?"

"Because we might get real hungry before that happens, and all our food is in the kitchen," said Jorge. Then he added with a snort, "And I don't feel like crapping in the corner for the next two days, either."

"And I need to look around to see if I can find some meds for Dr. Crane," added Paul. Everyone looked darkly at the institute owner at that, but no one challenged him.

Mitchell nodded. "We have everything we need to hold out up here," he agreed.

"So we check the floor, then decide what to do next," said Paul.

The others nodded slowly, then Crane spoke up. "I know what we do next," he said, his voice slurring as he began to lose consciousness once again. Everyone looked at him.

He spoke two more words before his eyes closed and he was silent: two words and nothing more. But the words were enough to chill Paul to his core.

"We   die."

HALL

Mitchell moved slowly, carefully. He felt like he was opening a lion's mouth and preparing to stick his head in it, rather than opening a door and looking out. Paul had wanted to be the one to open the door, but Mitchell argued successfully that it should be him. After all, he had reasoned, he was the most physically formidable, so he should go first.

For the first time ever, though, Mitchell wished he had been born a weakling.

He looked out of Dr. Bryson's office. Shone a flashlight down the hall toward the staircase. Nothing. He swung the beam the other way: Paul's office. Door closed. Nothing in the hall.

The door to the staff sleeping quarters was directly in front of him, and on either side of that door stood the doors to the bathrooms, like silent sentinels keeping watch. And beside him was the staff kitchen door. All closed.

"Nothing," he whispered behind him, and crept into the hall. Paul stood behind him a half-second later, followed by Donald who was holding the Mickey Mouse flashlight in one hand and his trank in the other. Vincent followed last.

"Okay," said Paul. "Mitchell and I will check my office. Donald, you aim Mickey at the stairs. Anything comes up and you shoot it. Vincent, you watch the door to the barracks to make sure nothing jumps out at us."

For once, surprisingly, neither Vincent nor Donald complained. They just nodded quietly, though Mitchell could see the strain around Vincent's eyes, and it worried him.

No time to ponder that, though, as Paul walked quietly to his office and Mitchell had to follow to give cover. When Paul unlocked the door, the noise sounded like a hammer blow to Mitchell, who couldn't help but look around to see if any predators had been summoned by the rasp of the door lock.

After Paul unlocked the door, he stood there for a long time before moving. Mitchell couldn't blame him: planning to throw open the door to a room that might or might not have a lunatic – or something worse – waiting inside was a hard idea.

Mitchell saw Paul tense, and steeled himself for movement. Mitchell nodded encouragement, his own trank gun out and ready.

Paul   opened   the   door.

RATS

Rachel sat as close as she could to her little brother, marveling and luxuriating in the confidence that he threw out. She knew it was an act – it had to be, no one could be as mindlessly optimistic as he appeared in a time like this – but she appreciated it nonetheless.

Nearby, Crane moaned, still unconscious. She envied him his nightmares: they couldn't possibly be as bad as what they were all going through.

With that thought came another, accompanied by a pang of guilt: *People are dead because of me.*

Murderess.

"Jorge, I'm..." she faltered, searching for some way to communicate the depth of her feelings. She failed, however, settling for, "I'm sorry."

"Don't worry," responded her little brother, her *hermanito*. "Paul's the smartest guy around. He'll get us out of this."

There was a clinking noise above them, and Rachel felt Becky's neck snap upward, the little girl searching for the source of the noise in the frightening darkness.

"Just rats," said Jorge. "They crawl around in the vents. It's the warmest spot in The Loon."

Rachel looked around in the dark. Crane moaned in his unconsciousness, and Rachel moved toward the man.

"Sis, don't," said Jorge, but he had misunderstood her intent. She didn't want to touch the doctor, but rather started feeling around in the desk. "What are you doing?" he asked.

She didn't answer, but a moment later she pulled the letter opener out of her sleeve where she had kept it hidden and used it to pry at one of the seams on the desk, opening it until there was a gap big enough to slip her pinky into.

Then, satisfied, she replaced the letter opener in her sleeve and returned to Becky and Jorge.

He was staring at her like she had gone mad. Perhaps he was right. "Sis?" he said with a query in his gaze.

"Just in case," she responded.

Jorge waited for more, but she had expended her small talk for the moment. Her brother looked at Becky and said, "Your mom is crazy, you know?"

Becky nodded.

BEDS

Paul motioned for Mitchell to shine his flashlight beneath his desk.

Empty. Nothing there.

Paul exhaled in relief, then nodded to Mitchell. "So far, so good," he said.

"Famous last words," replied Mitchell with a lukewarm smile.

Paul led Mitchell back into the hallway, going to where Donald and Vincent were still standing guard at the door to the office where Rachel, Becky, and Crane were ensconced.

"It's clean," Paul whispered.

Vincent motioned toward the staff barracks. "Who goes in there?" he asked, clearly hoping for an answer that didn't involve him.

"Need more people on this one," said Paul. "So you, me, and Mitchell." To Donald he said, "Donald, you keep watching the stairs. Anything comes up, you shoot and then yell, got it?"

"I don't wanna go in there," said Vincent. "I got no light."

"Me either," said Paul. "At least you have a gun."

The ploy worked: Vincent was a coward and a bully, but he wasn't about to be shamed in front of what was left of his posse.

Paul sidled over to the door to the barracks and opened it. He tried not to weep when he saw the place. Though he had spent many nights there, and had been in it thousands of times over the years, he had never before looked at it as a potential hiding spot. As such, it was terrifying. Only about six million places to hide, the space under each bed a potential deathtrap waiting to be sprung.

He took a deep breath and went to the first bed. Looked under it. Nothing. Vincent and Mitchell watched him as   Paul   moved   to   the   next   bed.

DESK

Rachel pushed a door near to the doorjamb, close enough that it could be wedged under the handle if need be.

Then, groaning under the weight, she moved the desk with Crane on it so that the gap she had opened was facing the doorway.

Jorge watched her, clearly wondering what she was doing.

She didn't tell him; couldn't tell him that she had turned into the kind of person who could calmly plan to maim someone this way.

She finished her work, then returned to her daughter.

ARRANGEMENTS

An hour later, Paul thought they were as ready as they ever would be. Several dismantled beds from the barracks created a misshapen barrier between the bathroom doors and the stairway. Mitchell stood behind it, vigilant, watching the stairs. He had a flashlight aimed at the top of the stairs, his expression as dark as the space around him.

Donald was in the barracks, standing protectively over Vincent. The mafia kid had taken a turn for the worse over the last hour, growing more and more sullen. Finally he refused to speak altogether and was now curled up on one of the beds in the barracks, mumbling incoherently to himself.

Dr. Crane was on another one of the beds, insensible. Paul had found some medication in Bryson's desk – some codeine the doctor had needed after a squash injury last year – and gave it to Crane when the man had woken. He was asleep again, shock keeping unconscious more often than not.

Becky had also found a small toolbox somewhere in Bryson's office, and that had supplied the tools necessary for them to dismantle the beds. Paul liked the kid. She was tough and though quiet she struck him as very smart. He had tried to tousle her hair when she had brought the toolbox to him, but she ducked under his hand and avoided the movement. Still, it was as close as he had gotten to touching her, so he counted it as an improvement.

Now, Paul pushed the last of the extra beds into one corner of the barracks, leaving seven in the back of the room. One of them held Crane's unconscious form, the other six were for them.

Rachel and Becky were watching him. When he finished, Rachel said. "Six beds? There are eight of us."

"I didn't know if you and Becky would want to stay in Dr. Bryson's office or not. I hoped you would stay here, but...." He shrugged. "Didn't want to force you to stay with us."

Rachel looked as though she were about to agree with his assessment, then an expression of gratitude flashed over her face. "We'll stay here. With you and Jorge," she said, and the expression dazzled Paul, even in the dark room. He smiled at her, and though she didn't exactly smile back, the corners of her mouth *did* seem to tilt up ever-so-slightly.

Rachel went to the pile of extra beds and pulled one next to the others. "We'll sleep on this one."

"Okay," said Paul, and was amazed to find that he was already planning on taking the bed next to Rachel and Becky.

What about Sammy? he thought momentarily. It was still the date of his son's birth, and the anniversary of his son's death, and Paul suddenly felt ashamed, as though the attraction he felt to this woman and the protective urge he had toward her daughter were shameful and to be buried deep down.

Then he thought of Sammy's smile and wondered if his son would have *wanted* Paul to watch over these girls.

The thought made him smile, the first smile he had had in connection with his son since that day in the park.

Vincent's voice, muffled since the man had his face turned away from them, staring at a blank wall, said, "So that's it?"

"I can't think of anything else to do," said Paul.

"We just sit here?" Vincent sat up and stared at Paul, a glare on his face. "Why don't we make it easier for Steiger and whatever else is running around out there? Maybe we could blindfold ourselves and sit naked in one of the cells."

"If that's what you want to do, be my guest," said Paul coldly.

Surprisingly, Donald spoke up. "Vincent, put a sock in it," said the man.

"Yeah, man," added Jorge from the doorway. "*Cállate.*"

"No way," said Vincent. "I wanna know what the brilliant doctor has in mind. We don't even know what's out there. Maybe Steiger's not even here anymore. Maybe he left."

"No," said Jorge decisively. "He didn't, and you know it."

FILES

Mitchell looked at the barricade.   When Paul had inspected it a few minutes back, he had left the file of documents and photos he'd lifted from Dr. Crane's secret lab, and Mitchell was burning with curiosity.

He opened the file.

Began   to   read.

SYMPHONY

Inside the prison area, the mad thumps still resounded as more and more of the inmates shook off the last dregs of their medication and began throwing themselves bodily against their walls.

Some of them had managed to pry open the food slots that were inset in the base of each door and were holding them open with bloody fingers. They screamed.

The screams echoed in the darkness. Music of a terrifying symphony, a symphony of madness that answered to no conductor, but only to the urge to rip, to kill, to rend and destroy.

The screams went on and on. Never stopping, never letting up.

They would scream until the end of time.

VIOLENCE

Paul tore some clean cloths he had found into strips, examining Crane's legs as he did so. Rachel was standing nearby, holding Becky to her, covering the girl's eyes so she couldn't see the charred stumps that were all that was left of Crane's legs.

"He gonna be all right, man?" asked Jorge from nearby.

"Don't know," said Paul. "At least he's not bleeding. His little pet cauterizes as it goes. But he's in a coma, so all we can do right now is leave him alone, try and keep him comfortable."

The wind rattled the window, moving the double-paned glass so much it seemed like it would hit the bars that covered it from outside and shatter into a million pieces.

Vincent, still on his bed nearby, shuddered. "Are you sure Steiger's not gone? Maybe he took off and croaked out there."

Paul shook his head. "I doubt it. Steiger wants to escape, not kill himself. That means he's in here, and his only chance is to kill us and wait until the storm rides itself out tomorrow or the next day." He tied one of the makeshift bandages onto Crane's left leg. The doctor groaned but did not wake. Just as well. "After the storm's over he's got a good chance of going overland and getting away. So our best bet right now is just sitting tight and as soon as the storm clears we can call out for help."

Vincent snapped his fingers. "That's it!" he shouted.

"What?" asked Donald. Paul kept working.

"I got my truck out front," said Vincent. "We could take it and pile in and get out of this place."

"We wouldn't make it a mile," said Jorge. "Stop talking stupid."

"We would, though," insisted Vincent. "We'd make it."

Paul started work on Crane's other leg, speaking quietly. "Vincent, your truck could only hold three or four people, max. Anyone in back would freeze."

Vincent looked at everyone in the room. Paul could practically hear the gears spinning as the kid did the math. Eight people total. Too many. But instead of that, Vincent said matter-of-factly, "Who's staying then?"

The room erupted around Paul in a sort of controlled pandemonium as everyone tried to talk at once. Only Rachel and Becky remained silent.

"Hold it," shouted Paul. "Shut up!" Everyone grew silent. "That's better." He turned to Vincent. "We can't go. One, your truck won't make it. Two, we aren't leaving anyone behind. Anyone. You got me?"

"Then we're dead, boss."

Paul grew angry. "Don't talk like that," he whispered, motioning toward Becky with his eyes.

Vincent saw him and grinned. "Why?" he said, his smile now a white slash across a bloodless face. "Kid ought to know who killed her."

Paul moved before he knew what he was doing. He leapt up and yanked Vincent to his feet, throwing him across the room. Vincent seemed to weigh less than a book, his arms flapping madly as he careened into a wall and bounced off. Paul grabbed him again, fist cocked, ready to pummel him into nonexistence for saying he had killed...

(*Sammy*)

...the little girl.

Donald and Jorge piled into him, driving him to the floor before he could mash Vincent's stupid face into the wall. They were both yelling at him to stop, think what he was doing, *stop it stop it!*

"It ain't worth it for this Italian piece of shit, man," said Jorge.

Paul slowly stood. He pushed Vincent away from him, then saw something horrible.

Rachel and Becky. They were staring at him with fear. Paul felt himself deflate, all the anger leaving him in a millisecond. How would they have viewed his outburst? he wondered. These two abused women, how would they have seen him? As another violent man, another source of danger.

It all came crashing down on him then: Sammy's birthday, trying to talk to his ex-wife who still hated him for killing their son, Steiger's escape, the storm, the *thing* that was somewhere in The Loon, everything. Tears welled out of his eyes, and he walked out of the barracks as fast as he could.

In the hallway, Mitchell looked up from the papers he was reading, as imperturbable as ever. "What was all the noise about?" he asked, as though sounds of a scuffle in a dark lunatic asylum were something he experienced every day and twice a day on weekends.

"Little disagreement," said Paul.

He walked toward his office. He couldn't be around other people right now. Not him.

Not a murderer like him.

SAMMY

Jorge watched Paul leave, then shut the door quietly behind him.

He returned to Vincent, helped him up...and then buried his fist as far in Vincent's gut as he could. He heard a satisfying "oof" as the air burst out of Vincent's lungs, and the man keeled over. Jorge jerked him back up again, held the twit nose to nose, and said, "You ever say something like that again, man, and I'll kill you."

He slapped Vincent right across the mouth to drive in the seriousness of what he was saying.

To his surprise, Vincent began to cry. "What?" said the wise guy, whose bravura had utterly deserted him. "What'd I say?" he asked.

"What did you say?" repeated Jorge incredulously. He relaxed his grip, and now it was his turn to look surprised. "You didn't know?" he said.

"Know what?" asked Vincent.

Jorge paused, wondering whether to share this or not, but decided that Vincent needed to know. That way he could stay away from the subject in the future...and if he didn't Jorge would pound him. Simple.

"Paul was married once," said Jorge. "Had a beautiful wife, and the cutest little boy I've ever seen. One day the kid was playing, and he ran into the street after a toy. Paul saw the car coming, and he ran out and knocked Sammy out of the way. The car – truck actually – hit Paul, and he was in full traction and a body cast for six months."

"What about the kid?" asked Donald.

Jorge gulped. "Hit his head on the curb when Paul pushed him. Died the next morning of a fractured skull. So Paul wakes up three days later, and there's his wife, telling him he killed their kid."

"Jesus," whispered Donald, and Rachel crossed herself nearby.

"That was the last time he ever saw her, outside of court. She raked him over the coals, and he let her."

Vincent looked almost remorseful for a full second, then his expression hardened once again.

"Well, it's not my fault," he said. "Can't expect me to know all that."

Jorge clenched his teeth and said, "You know now. And I meant what I said."

"What are you talking about?" said Vincent.

"Bring up Sammy ever again, Vincent, and I don't care how tough you think you are. I'll kill you."

FATHER

Paul sat in his dark office, holding the picture of his boy, his beautiful boy who would never smile like that again, and felt the tears dripping down his cheeks.

Then the door opened and Rachel and Becky entered. Both of them – especially the little girl – looked shy and nervous as girls about to go on their first date.

Paul wiped the tears from his cheeks as best he could.

"Hi," he said to Rachel.

"Becky wanted to talk to you," responded the young mother. Then she let go of her daughter's hand and stood just outside Paul's office. He was surprised at the amount of trust she was implicitly extending to him.

"Why are you crying?" asked Becky, moving slowly toward him.

He thought a moment about how best to answer the question. "It's my son's birthday," he finally said, "but he's not here and I can't celebrate with him."

"Where'd he go?" she said.

"Away," he replied.

"He's dead," said the girl. It wasn't a question. Paul nodded. "Are we going to die, too?" she asked.

Paul was struck momentarily dumb by the question, especially given as it was in such a matter-of-fact tone. He held out his hands to her. And, slowly, she reached out and held them. He embraced her, hugged her tight and for that moment felt as though he had his family back again. Then he put her on his lap and said, "No, honey. We're not going to die."

"Honey," said Rachel from the doorway. Implicit trust only went so far, it seemed, because she said, "Come back to the room with the others. Dr. Wiseman has things to do."

Mitchell entered at that moment, the big man squeezing in next to Rachel. "Yeah," he said. "Like answer a question I've got."

Rachel jumped; Mitchell's entrance had been as silent as a plague. She gathered her daughter to her and both were gone in an instant. Paul watched them go, aching for the feel of the little girl in his arms. God, he missed being a dad.

Finally he looked at Mitchell. "Who's guarding the stairs?" he asked.

"Jorge's on it. Donald and Vince are sulking in the barracks."

"What's the problem?"

Mitchell waved the paper he was holding. "This thing's diet is the problem."

"Eats every fifteen minutes," said Paul. "Crane already told us that."

"Yeah," nodded Mitchell. "But *what's* it been eating?

Paul thought a long moment. Then: "I'd imagine that's what happened to Wade, Sandy, Jeff, and Leann. It would explain the burns all over the place where they should have been."

Mitchell nodded. "Sounds about right."

"So what's your question?" asked Paul.

"That happened almost four hours ago," said the big man. "What's it been eating since then?"

SCREAMS

It heard the screams when it first came to this place. Loud screams, soft screams. Screams like the wind outside, airy and light; screams like the shrieks of a dying dog, heavy and wet.

Now other screams abounded. Short, harsh cries that burst out and then were gone.

It was eating.

It finished its last meal, a person that had seemed familiar to it, perhaps someone from its first life, the life before it had become...what it is.

It pushes against the sealed door the person had been behind, willing itself to thin out, to lengthen, to flatten. There is a slot at the bottom of the door, and soon it is thin enough to get through. The effort tires it, but there is no other way.

It must have food.

Food.

It stays in its quasi-solid state, pushing through the bars that surround each cell, reforming enough on the other side to grow feet and hands, disgusting appendages it uses to walk/slide/slither/pull its way to the next cell.

Empty. It can tell. It has many noses, all of them excellent, and it cannot smell the sweat/anger/fear of a man in the cell.

It moves to the next cell, and reverses its shift, pushing back through the bars, then pressing itself into the food slot in the inner cell door.

It reforms slowly on the other side, taking its time. The cell's occupant barely even notices it has company, and the beast makes no sound until it is ready.

Then it feeds.

Another scream joins those around it.

Another scream rises to the ceiling.

Then another scream ends.

Dies.

The beast feeds.

QUESTIONS

Paul held the door open for Rachel and Becky, then followed them into the barracks. He looked at Donald and Vincent, who were quiet and sullen. Jorge stood behind him in the hall, Mitchell guarding the stairwell once again.

"We have a problem," he said.

"That's the understatement of the century," said Vincent.

"Stow it, Vince," said Jorge. Vincent glared at the man, but remained silent.

"Remember I said that that thing needs to eat every ten or fifteen minutes? And that it could go under doors?" Everyone, even Jorge and the two girls, who had already heard this, nodded. "It's been four hours," said Paul. "What's it eating?"

Surprisingly, it was Donald who answered. "Oh, no. The other prisoners."

RESCUE

Paul stood at the top of the stairs and tried not to feel doomed. He and Mitchell were looking at the meager supplies and weapons they had: a pair of trank guns, and a few improvised Molotov cocktails they had made from some cleaning fluid, rags, and a few empty beer bottles they had found in the barracks under the sink. Hardly the kind of thing you wanted to go visit an army of psychotics with, not to mention the thing that was now somewhere in The Loon.

Paul held one of the few flashlights they had, Mitchell held the other, and though they both had their game faces on, Paul suspected they both wore the same strained expressions. They were scared.

"I need a lighter; matches," said Paul, suddenly realizing he had no way to light the Molotovs if necessary.

Jorge, who was going to take over guarding the stairs for Mitchell, pitched him a lighter.

Rachel and Becky were standing in the door to the barracks, and Becky's little girl voice whispered, "You *smoke*, Uncle Jorge?"

Jorge looked embarrassed. "No, I think I just quit, honey."

Vincent and Donald also stood nearby. Vincent had been pestering them for the last half hour while they got ready, insisting that this was a very bad idea. "You're nuts," he said from nearby.

"There are one hundred twenty-six people still in the prison," said Paul yet again. "They might be in trouble." To Jorge, he said, "Stay here. You've got seniority, you take care of things. We'll have to go down without walkie-talkies: Steiger's somewhere, and if he hears us talking on them we're gone. So cover the stairwell, and shoot anything that comes up without calling first."

"So what are you going to do?" asked Vincent. "Let them all out? They're *crazy*. That means they're not going to be good and just make a deal They're just a bunch of psychos."

"And they're still *people!*" said Paul as loudly as he dared. "I don't know what I'll do, but I have to see. Maybe I'll, I don't know, unlock their cells and we can barricade them in the prison."

"What?" shrieked Vincent, not bothering to speak quietly.

"Paul," said Jorge. "As much as I hate to agree with Don Wimpione here, I don't think that's a good idea."

"Are you kidding?" said Paul. "It's a *terrible* idea." He flicked his flashlight on and off, making sure it worked. Stalling, he knew, but he was terrified. "I don't know what we'll do. I have to see," he added again.

He turned to go down the stairwell, Mitchell and his trank gun right behind.

"What'll you do if you find…*it*?" asked Jorge.

Paul flicked the lighter, holding one of the bottles in a throwing grip. "I'm gonna douse the thing and torch it."

"And Steiger?" said Jorge. "What if you run into him?"

Mitchell answered, holding up his trank and a tazer. "Call me old-fashioned," he said.

NICE

Becky watched as Paul and Mitchell slowly descended the gaunt stairwell.

"They're going away," she said.

"They'll be back," said Mommy.

Becky curled her hand in her mother's. "I hope so," she said, then added, "Paul's nice."

"Yeah," said Rachel, and Becky felt her mother's hand grow slick with sweat.

PLAN

Paul and Mitchell stood before the tunnel that led to the prison. Both were panting, not from exhaustion but from the physical exertion of maintaining complete stealth in the gloom of the prison. Terror had left Paul feeling sluggish and fatigued, and he could tell from Mitchell's eyes that the big man felt the same.

They looked at the closed door to the tunnel.

"So what's the plan?" said Mitchell. "We let those guys loose one at a time and we're dead before we've done two of them. And no offense, but that is not an okay plan for me."

Paul's brow furrowed in thought, then he said, "The master door circuit. It's on its own battery."

"*What?*" said Mitchell in a whisper loud enough to be heard in the next state over.

Paul nodded. "It's the only way. I go inside each outer cell, I unlock the inner cell, real quiet, then leave and lock the outer door behind me. Then when they're all done we go down and hit the master release button twice. The inner doors will open, and we make some noise, draw the guys out of the inner cells. Then when they all know they're loose, we hit the button three times, the outer doors unlock, and we run."

"And we hope we're faster out the tunnel than the nuts who are nearest to the door."

Paul nodded. "We get here, we lock this door from the outside. That way they're still contained, but at least they're not just sitting ducks waiting to get…*dissolved* or however that thing eats."

"I hate this idea," said Mitchell.

"Me, too," agreed Paul. "You let me know if you think of anything better, okay?"

"What's to stop them from just popping out at you after you've unlocked the inner door but are still in the outer cell?"

"You," said Paul. "You'll be covering me."

"I was afraid you were going to say that," said Mitchell with a sigh.

"Would you rather have my job?" asked Paul.

CRAWL

Steiger moved at a slow crawl through the air duct. He didn't know where he was exactly, but knew he was on the second floor somewhere: he had climbed a vertical shaft with a small ladder inset in it that connected the two floors. But beyond that, he had no clue.

That was fine. He could go with the flow. Things always worked out when you went with the flow.

He heard a noise. Looked ahead.

There was a dim light in front of him. Coming from a vent in the floor of the duct. A ceiling vent to one of the second floor rooms, he guessed.

Light meant people.

And people meant fun.

He grinned.

ESCAPE

Vincent sat on his bed, dangling the keys to his truck before his eyes.

His thoughts were confused; jumbled. He felt like he couldn't put things together right. But he knew one thing: he was getting the hell out of Dodge, whether he went alone or not.

He finally looked over at the little girl, still so quiet, still sitting on her mother's lap, and Vincent Marcuzzi came to a decision.

He looked at Donald, who nodded as though reading his mind. Then Vincent stood and, in one single fluid motion, grabbed Becky by the arm. The little girl screamed as he pulled on her, and said, "Come on, kid."

Rachel was on her feet instantaneously, battering at Vincent's arm ineffectually. "You let go of her," she screamed.

Vince had to wrestle with her for a quick moment before Donald stepped in and grabbed the young mother from behind. "It's okay, lady," said Donald. "We're getting out of here."

"What?" said Rachel quietly. "How?"

Becky pulled out of Vincent's grasp and went to Rachel.

Vincent sighed. "Lady," he said, "I got the baddest four wheel drive in three counties. It'll get us to Dayton or Stonetree."

"Dr. Wiseman said it wouldn't make it," said Rachel.

"He's wrong."

"He said it wouldn't fit everybody," she replied.

"And he's not here, is he?" asked Vincent pointedly. "So I'm not suggesting we take him with us."

"You mean, you want to...to...."

"Come on, lady," said Vincent. "You want to get your daughter out of here, right?" He dangled the keys before her, and said, "This is the way home."

A hand darted out of nowhere, snatching the keys out of Vincent's hand.

"Shame on you, man," said Jorge.

Vincent clenched his fist and turned to strike. Who the hell does this beaner think he is? he thought, but the movement to lash out stopped dead as he came face to muzzle with Jorge's trank gun.

"I imagine a dart in the eye would really hurt, Vince. So calm down." Jorge waited a moment, then slowly lowered his gun. "This is a real bad time to be at each others' throats, man."

Vincent deflated. It just isn't fair, he thought. I should be at home right now, watching TV or maybe even getting laid or something if I'm lucky. Not here, not now, not like this.

Jorge put the keys in his pocket and headed back into the hallway. Rachel grabbed her daughter's hand and followed instantly.

"Where you going?" he said to Rachel. "The nutcase is out there."

"I feel safer out there than I do with someone who would abandon his friends and leave them to die," said Rachel.

FRENZY

The beast moves into another cell.

A moment, then there is a thud and a muffled wail.

It's moving faster now, tendrils and pseudopodia rippling out of it randomly as it slakes its hunger with blood and flesh.

Hungry, it thinks, and then feeds.

It is frenzied, the blood lust from its first life rising to join with the desperate need to feed of its second life.

Food.

Everything here is food.

INSIDE

Paul and Mitchell entered the prison, Mitchell swinging his light left and right in a sweep pattern that mostly caused more shadows to leap out of the darkness, illusions of movement that drew Paul's gaze to them like magnets drew iron slivers from sand.

"See anything?" whispered Paul. Mitchell shook his head. "Cover the light," Paul said. "If they see us doing this, we're screwed."

The light died, only a red glow through Mitchell's fingers now as Paul crept to the nearest cell. He took a deep breath. This was it.

He went to the cell and realized both hands were full, so he put one of the Molotovs next to the outer cell, holding the other in his free hand. Then he carefully – quietly – unlocked the outer cell and stepped in. Mitchell covered him, flashlight now pointed at his leg so that there was a small glow of light while leaving his free hand available to hold the trank.

Paul wished that the trank gun made him feel safe.

But it didn't.

He moved to the inner cell. The tension in his body felt like thick air, cloying at him, clawing at him, slowing him down. He couldn't peek in to see if the inmate – a deeply disturbed man named Eves – was waiting to jump out at him:

the very act of doing that might alert the man that he could get out of the cell. Paul had to go in blind and hoping for the best.

He reached out slowly, carefully with the key.

Inserted it as quietly as he could, but still heard the rasp like thunder in his ears, even louder than the sound of the ever-present wind outside. How could Eves not hear that? he thought, but nothing emerged from the cell. Paul quickly retraced his steps backwards and locked the prison cell behind him.

He looked at Mitchell. "One hundred twenty-five to go," he said.

SCRATCHING

Steiger lay silently, looking down through a vent that led to the sleeping area. Cobwebs drifted lazily across his face, but he did not move. The touch was like a gentle caress to him, reminding him that all life must end a withered husk, the juices sucked out of it and as dry as a spider's prey after feeding time.

He had caught glimpses of two guards – Vincent and Donald – in the room. He could also barely see that the door to the hallway was closed.

"I hate that shit-eating beaner," said Vincent below him.

Steiger smiled. He began scratching lightly at the vent.

"What's that?" said Vincent.

Steiger moved back as someone shone a flashlight on the vent.

"Rats," said Donald.

Steiger moved back into position and smiled. This promised to be very fun.

THIRD

Paul and Mitchell finished the last cell on the second floor and moved quickly, silently, up the stairs to the third floor. Nothing had jumped out at them, nothing had even moved outside the cells. But Paul had the disquieting feeling that some of the cells he had opened were already empty. As though whoever was in them had been...he hesitated even in his own mind to use the word "eaten," but nothing else was coming   to   him.

FALLING

Vincent shone his light on Crane's unconscious face. He felt like he was breaking inside, cracking like a vase that had been thrown to the ground and stomped on.

"Your fault, old man," he whispered. "This is all your fault."

Without realizing it, he began beating the man's still form, bringing down his flashlight like a hammer on ribs, arms, face. Crane moaned but did not wake.

Donald threw himself on him. Vincent punched the other man, feeling his hand sink deep into his fat gut. The cracks in his mind were fissures now, great chasms that led down, down, down into a pit of insanity.

Vincent was falling. Falling, and couldn't stop.

ATTACK

Steiger carefully popped out the vent. It made a small noise, but neither of the men in the room noticed him. They were too busy fighting with one another. Once again the universe had provided Steiger with a way to see his plans and dreams come true.

He saw Vincent hit Donald over the head with a flashlight, and Donald went down, poleaxed and insensible for the time being. Vincent turned toward something...it was *Crane*. Steiger licked his lips and thought, for some reason, of the song *Itsy Bitsy Spider*. He even hummed a bar under his breath as he closed in on Vincent and Crane. This was going to be so much *fun*.

Vincent had his arm raised, ready to smash his heavy light down on Crane's face. Steiger had a moment of indecision. What to do, what to do? he thought.

Then Vincent's hand dropped, and Steiger felt his own arm reaching it, his own hand arresting the downward motion of the flashlight.

Vincent spun around to face him, mouth curled, spittle flying from a wildly open mouth.

His face drained of all blood as soon as he saw Steiger, grinning cheerfully at him. Steiger really didn't know why so many people had that reaction to him. He tried so hard to be pleasant.

"Please," he said. "If someone's going to kill the good doctor, I really think it should be me."

And with a vicious motion, he swung his hands up and broke   Vincent's   neck.

WAITING

Rachel stood by Jorge at the barricade near the stairs, adding her vigilance to that of her brother. Becky was between them, as though they could possibly shield her from the nightmare in which they had found themselves.

"Would they have left you and Mitchell and Pau – and *Dr. Wiseman* – behind?" she asked.

Jorge shrugged. "Who can say. They're not going to leave us now. In fact," he said, pulling Vincent's keys out of his pocket and holding them out to Becky. "Who do you think should hold onto these? 'Cause it's kind of an important job, you know?"

"Mom can hold them," said the little girl seriously. Jorge smiled and handed the keys to Rachel.

She took them solemnly, but she mouthed "thanks" to her brother. He nodded back, his eyes saying, "you're welcome," and then they both looked back down the hall, waiting for Paul to come back up the stairs.

Fearing that he would not.

PENS

Donald opened his eyes woozily, and realized that even though he wasn't dead, he had somehow fallen into hell.

Steiger was there. Steiger was there and Vince was dead on the floor next to him, his head bent at an impossible angle, neck bent so far back it was almost a pillow on which his friend's corpse could rest.

Steiger was standing over Crane's body, holding Vincent's flashlight. Donald watched, utterly transfixed, as Steiger opened Crane's mouth with one hand, then plunged the flashlight downward into the doctor's mouth. Donald heard a crack as Crane's jaw broke into pieces, and teeth flew across the room.

The pain must have woken the doctor up, for he screamed a muffled scream around the base of the flashlight that was still in his ruined mouth.

"Afraid?" said Steiger as Donald heard the awful retching/gasping/vomiting sound of Crane drowning on his own blood. "Worried what I'll do? Now you know what it feels like to have your destiny in someone else's hands." The madman yanked the flashlight loose, muffling the accompanying scream with a wide hand. "And now you're about to know what it feels like to be dead."

And with a whip-quick motion, Steiger grabbed a pair of pens from beside Crane on the desk. In a single motion he plunged them down and buried them in Crane's eyes. Crane gave a single, awful jerk, then was silent.

Donald cried out in spite of himself, and felt his pants grow damp as he lost control of his bowels.

Steiger must have heard the noise, for he turned to Donald.

And grinned.

SCARS

Paul was inside the outer cell, about to unlock the inner door, when he noticed something. He leaned down, motioning for Mitchell to aim his flashlight where Paul was.

The floor was covered in acid streaks, like ugly scars on the concrete.

He looked through the porthole to the inmate's cell, momentarily heedless of the danger he was in. The cell was empty.

"Shit," he whispered.

He was too late.

The beast was near.

ANSWER

Jorge heard it first: a low thud from inside the barracks.

"What was that?" he said. Rachel, still holding Becky's hand, shook her head: no idea. Then a second thump sounded, this time louder, and all three of them jumped.

Jorge pointed his trank gun at the closed barracks door, then moved close to it. He whispered through the door loudly, "Donald? Vince?" A moment later he followed that with, "Dr. Crane?"

There was no answer.

ABOVE

Mitchell covered Paul as he moved from cell to cell, no longer being careful and quiet, instead moving quickly as possible. The flashlight covered him with light from behind, but was insufficient to rend through the gloom in the prison and the matching dread that had settled on Mitchell's heart.

Each cell was worse than the last. Acid-etchings on the floor, the walls, the bars. No sign of life.

He felt like someone was watching him.

He swung the flashlight around suddenly, as though he might catch whoever it was sneaking up on him.

Nothing.

Or rather, not nothing. He became aware that the inmates on the second and first levels – the levels where Paul had opened the inner doors – had come out of their soundproofed cells. But strangely, they made no sound. They simply pressed their foreheads into the bars, silent as an army of specters, waiting. Watching.

"What's going on?" asked Paul from the darkness. Mitchell turned back to him, to tell him that the crazies were out. But the instant that he turned, he forgot what he was going to say.

Drip. *Hissss....*

Mitchell glanced to his right and saw something sizzling next to him on the gangplank.

Drip. *Hissss....*

Again it happened.

Mitchell felt himself grow loose, his knees wobbling as he looked up, aimed the flashlight up, and then *screamed* as something dropped from above to the catwalk. He had an instant to see Paul's startled face. Then the thing, whatever it was, stood tall, taller even than Mitchell, massive and wet and frightening, and Paul was blocked from his view.

They had found the beast.

BARRICADE

There was still no sound coming from within the barracks. Jorge aimed his light at the doorway and gently pushed Rachel and Becky behind him.

"What is it?" whispered his sister.

"Don't know," he said. "Move back."

He walked backward, backing away from the barracks door, trying to keep his trank and his flashlight aimed at it.

He forgot about the makeshift barricade, though. The disassembled cots that had been piled in the hall near the stairwell. So did Rachel and Becky, it seemed, for none of them made a sound to warn how close the barricade was until after all three had backed into it.

They tumbled to the ground as one, falling in a tangle of limbs and clothing, Jorge trying to get out from under Rachel and Becky.

And that was when Steiger exploded through the door to the barracks and attacked them.

MITCHELL

Paul leapt toward Mitchell as the thing dropped down, cutting off Mitchell's flashlight beam with its massive shape.

"Oh, God," said the big man, his voice seeming muffled and faraway.

"Mitchell!" screamed Paul.

The beast was near.

INNOCENCE

Steiger jumped at the small group of people, practically salivating at them. There was Jorge, a guard who was clearly one of those people who believed in such outdated concepts as honor and values and morality, a guard with whom Steiger had much in common.

Tangled up with Jorge was a woman, mid- to late-twenties, perhaps. Beautiful. Flaring nostrils and fright-dilated pupils that only added to her appearance.

And the little girl. More beautiful even than her mother, more fragile-seeming than fine porcelain. A darling, *innocent* little girl.

Innocence was Steiger's favorite trait. There was nothing quite like ripping it out of the beating heart of a child.

He jumped at the small group, ripping a bed support from the tangle of cots that they were struggling to extricate themselves from. He lashed out with it, sending it careening toward the woman, toward her face, her tender, beautiful face that he wanted to mash and destroy.

THUCK. The support hit and shattered bone and was accompanied by a satisfying shriek. But it wasn't the woman it had impacted: Jorge had blocked with his arm at the last second, probably sacrificing its use forever. He screamed again, but stood, cradling his shattered arm as he shoved Steiger momentarily away and then stood between him and the girls.

"Go!" shouted Jorge.

"No!" screamed the woman.

"*Go!*" shouted Jorge again, and charged at Steiger.

Steiger smiled, still holding the bed support. He swung it, but Jorge ducked out of the way at the last second.

The guard looked behind him; saw that the woman and her daughter, though they were standing, had not yet moved away. "Go now!" screamed Jorge.

The guard went to grab his trank, but Steiger had used the moment to his advantage. In the split-second that Jorge looked away, he struck again with the bed support. This time Jorge screamed louder as the support hit his clavicle with a crack and the deliciously peculiar sound of breaking bone and shredding meat. Now both the guard's arms were limp and useless.

Jorge threw himself on Steiger, undaunted, and the two of them went down in a heap.

At last the woman and her child moved, running past Jorge and Steiger to Dr. Wiseman's office.

"Not that way!" screamed Jorge. "It's a dead end."

But the girls had already run into the room and slammed the door shut.

Again Steiger seized on the split attention of his opponent. Again he swung his makeshift club. This time it found a more permanent mark: it cracked wickedly into the side of Jorge's head, and Steiger both saw and felt the club sink deep into the man's skull, rendering it concave where once it had been convex.

Jorge's dead eyes rolled up in his head and he dropped, nerveless, insensible, the last breath rushing from his body in a whoosh as he fell, a lifeless corpse.

Steiger laughed.

Then he turned to the door to Dr. Wiseman's office. Innocence was calling him.

BLIND

Paul watched, horrified, as the monster hit Mitchell like a wet wrecking ball. Mitchell screamed as the monster enveloped him, the scream whistling and gurgling. Paul reacted automatically, running into the horrific melding of the two bodies and slamming into it as though he were playing hockey with the thing. The beast went down, trapping Mitchell beneath it.

One of Mitchell's hands could be seen, grasping at air, trying to pull him out from under the nightmare above him.

Paul grabbed onto the hand and pulled, yanking as hard as he could, screaming.

The inmates in the cells below started to hoot and shriek as one. A mindless cacophony of horror.

Paul pulled and pulled, then fell over on his butt. He couldn't think what had happened, until he saw Mitchell's disembodied hand, still clenched tightly in his, and realized that about five feet away Mitchell was no longer screaming. All that could be heard was the horrific sizzle and slurp of the beast feeding.

Paul screamed and threw the hand away from himself, then ran blindly for the stairs.

TRAP

Rachel couldn't believe this was happening. First Tommy, then the storm, now she had lost Jorge.

No time, she thought. No time for such thoughts. Have to save Becky. Have to stay alive.

She grabbed the chair she had placed nearby earlier and shoved it under the door handle an instant before something hit it from the other side. WHAM! Becky whimpered behind her, clutching at Mr. Huggles with white hands.

Another slam as Steiger hit the door from the other side. He was laughing.

The door and the chair both held, but she didn't know how long they would.

She looked around. Couldn't go out the windows. Couldn't go out the door. Trapped.

Then Becky, apparently sensing Rachel's thoughts, pointed up.

The vent!

Another thump from outside. Faster together now as Steiger hit the door harder and harder, screaming Becky's name over and over and laughing hideously all the while.

Rachel helped Becky up onto the desk, then stood on it herself. She grabbed the letter opener from where she had kept it in her sleeve and wedged it into the crack she had earlier pried loose in the desk.

Now the letter opener was where she wanted. She hoped her little trap worked.

She jumped up on the desk beside her daughter and started pulling at the catches around the vent. She bloodied most of her fingers in her haste, the dull throb of her pulse in her torn digits serving as a grim counterpoint to the door's shaking and shuddering.

Slam!

One catch loose.

Slam!

Another.

Slam-slam. And now the wood around the door was beginning to sliver, the chair wedged under the doorway beginning to shake.

Another catch. One left to go.

Whump!

The door handle shook, the door was about to explode into pieces.

Last catch, and she pulled the vent free, lifting Rachel up into the dark crawlspace.

CRUNCH!

The unmistakable sound of breaking wood. One more shot and Steiger would be inside.

She lifted herself up, straining to pull herself into the vent crawlspace, feeling Becky's little fingers pulling at hers.

SMASH! The door crumpled and Steiger, pushed forward by his own momentum, fell over the kindling that had once been a chair and a door. Rachel glanced down and saw as if in slow motion as Steiger tripped, almost fell. Righted himself.

Tripped again.

And shrieked as he stumbled full speed into the desk...and impaled his thigh on the letter opener that had been sticking out and pointed at the door.

He looked up at Rachel. They locked eyes, and then she looked away and pulled herself up with a surge of adrenalized energy.

Behind her, Steiger laughed again, and she heard the metallic clack of the letter-opener falling to the desk.

"I'll kill you for that, bitch," said Steiger cheerfully.

TENDRILS

Paul rushed across the third floor catwalk, not daring to look back, hearing all too clearly the sounds of the beast behind, hot on his heels. Paul looked around for something, anything to use. Nothing. The monster was right behind him. He glanced back in time to see a pseudopod shoot out at him, a viscous tendril that ended in sharp-edged, snapping teeth that reminded Paul of a piranha.

He darted to the side, and the pseudopod barely missed him.

The inmates were screaming, cheering, yelling, as though they were at a football game and the monster on the third floor were their mascot.

Paul saw that the creature was gaining on him; that he would never make it to the stairs.

He threw himself reflexively to one side, again narrowly missing a bite by an external mouth that didn't grow from the beast's body so much as burst forth from it in a whiplike motion. Breath rasping, heart pounding, he threw himself through one of the open cell doors, too panicked to think much about the fact that the iron bars had failed to protect the cell's previous resident. He was acting instinctively.

Still on autopilot, Paul pulled the cell door shut behind him. The monster hit the bars with a splat. Paul instantly jumped as far back as he could and narrowly avoided another toothed tendril ripping his throat out. He fled to the rear of the cell, the tendril snaking after him, feeling the smooth door of the inner cell behind him. Nowhere to go, no time to open the inner cell door. He closed his eyes and waited for the beast to spear him like a bug on a collector's display.

But it didn't happen. He opened his eyes, and saw a tendril mere inches away, tiny teeth snapping hungrily. The tendril was joined by another, and then another, but all of them came up just short. Apparently the beast couldn't extend itself out more than a few feet.

Paul sighed in relief.

The relief was short-lived. Panic returned as the monster pressed itself against the bars, pushing through them like butter around a hot knife.

Paul had only one way to go: he ran into the inner cell and shut the door behind him.

But he knew the beast would get in.

SUBTERFUGE

Rachel felt the tips of Steiger's fingers touch her leg as she pulled herself into the shaft. But apparently his wounded leg wasn't able to jump up quickly enough to catch her, for he didn't try again, giving Rachel the precious seconds she needed to scramble into the tight ventilation duct.

Becky was still there, waiting for her mother. "What do we do, Mommy?" asked the little girl. She had somehow managed to keep her Emergency Pack on her back and Mr. Snuggles in one hand through the whole escapade, and now had her cheek practically buried in the bear's soft fur.

"Crawl," said Rachel, and pushed her daughter ahead of her, crawling through the darkness of the duct. Moving by feel, she soon found herself in a T-intersection, with a branch to the right and one to the left. Rachel pulled off one of Becky's shoes and threw it into the left side, then turned right with her daughter.

She hoped the subterfuge was enough; that it would fool Steiger if he came after them. *When* he came.

SPIDER

Steiger pulled himself up and into the duct, ignoring the pain in his leg.

This was turning out to be far more fun than he had anticipated. He could practically feel the beautiful girl in his hands, could almost hear her whispering love to him, for he knew that all people secretly loved him, desired him, wanted to be with him forever, even if the only way to stay with him forever was to die at his hands. It was a kind of immortality, he realized with a start, for where else would each of his victims been able to live for so long if not in the hallowed recesses of his own mind?

He could tell which way the two girls had gone by the sounds above him when he was pulling himself up the second time, and used the flashlight he had taken from one of the dead guards to illuminate his path.

Soon he came to a T-intersection. He looked to the right and saw nothing. Then to the left. There! His beam illuminated a child's shoe, clearly lost in a mad rush to escape destiny. But destiny could not be escaped.

He turned left, crawling happily toward Rachel. Toward Becky.

A moment later, however, he stopped as another cobweb draped coldly across his face. He savored it for a moment, then crawled a few more steps, then stopped once more.

How could there be a cobweb across this space? he wondered. If Becky and her mother came through here, wouldn't they already have dislodged and destroyed the web?

He realized that he had been duped, but was not angry. Far from it. "Clever girls," he said. "Clever, clever girls, almost fooled me." He smiled as he spoke, enjoying this game of cat and mouse intensely.

He couldn't turn around – the duct was too narrow – but he backed up until he reached the T-intersection, then turned until he could take the right branch. He felt his pants grow wet as he crawled over his own blood which was still leaking from the deep wound in his leg.

Still smiling, he began to hum.

The itsy bitsy spider went up the waterspout.

This was turning into such a fine game of hide and seek. Such clever, clever girls. They deserved to be rewarded for their excellent playing. And he intended to see they got their reward at his hands.

FLAME

Paul moved away from the door as something pushed through the crack. It moved like an oil slick, rippling and folding in on itself. Paul watched in horror, facing his own doom, then suddenly realized that in his panic he had utterly forgotten something:

The Molotov cocktail.

One of them was still down on the first floor, near the guard station. The other, however, he still held in his hand. Indeed, as soon as he realized this he also felt the severe cramp that came with holding onto something too long and too hard, and realized also that he had had the weapon the whole time, and never thought once to use it.

He pulled out Jorge's cigarette lighter and flicked it, lighting the strip of cloth that was jammed into the end of the beer bottle.

The beast was entirely inside now, and starting to rise, its boneless mass nevertheless cohesive enough to provide a similitude of upright posture. As soon as Paul lit the Molotov, a bloodless split – a mouth with razor teeth – burst open in the beast's side, and the thing screamed in pain. The light was hurting it, just as Crane said it would. And just as Crane had predicted, the thing was now looking decidedly angry.

Now or never, thought Paul, and threw the Molotov. Fire skittered across the beast's skin as the chemicals in the bottle lit and set fire to the thing. It went crazy, screaming and thrashing around the cell, Paul barely managing to avoid it in the cramped space.

The monster's pained movements took it to the back of the cell. Paul rushed to the door. Unlocked it and flew out, leaving the monster in a room of fire. As he closed the door he could see the thing moving slower, more sluggishly, as though...perhaps...it were dying.

He closed the door to the outer cell. Locked it. Then he ran.

PRETENDING

Becky pushed ahead as fast as she could. She was scared – terrified, even – but she knew Mommy was relying on her to be strong and brave, so she just clamped her mouth shut like she did when Daddy was Being Bad and kept moving. They passed lots of tunnels, but didn't turn down any of them, just crawling straight ahead for a while.

Then she felt something soft and furry scuttle over her hand and realized that a mouse or a rat was in here. She opened her mouth and automatically screamed. Not even screamed, really, just a little yip like a dog would make, but she felt Mommy get tense behind her and knew that she had made a mistake. The bad man was following them, she knew. Now he could hear where they had gone.

He would be closer now.

Mommy pushed her on, and soon she came to a dead end. In front of her was only empty space, and she couldn't help screaming a little again as she put a hand down into nothing but air.

"Shhhh," whispered Mommy. "What is it?"

"There's nothing, no floor," whispered Becky.

"What?" Mommy maneuvered her way past Becky, then said, "Honey, there's a ladder here that goes up and down. I know you can't see it, but we have to get on it."

Becky nodded and tried to be brave. She knew she wasn't brave like Mr. Huggles or Uncle Jorge or Mommy or Paul. But she could pretend.

Sometimes pretending was all you could do.

BEAST

The inmates' screaming and ranting on the second level was almost deafening, and their grasping arms reached for him as Paul ran past, trying to grab him, to get him, to kill him. He jerked away from one viselike set of hands when an inhuman wail sounded through the prison, so loud that even the manic prisoners quieted for a brief moment.

Paul looked up and saw a dark shape, black on black in the darkness of the prison, falling from the third. It landed – no longer covered in flame but smoking and sizzling with traces of the Molotov cocktail still burning on its skin – on the second floor gangplank in front of Paul. It hissed from a half dozen mouths that opened up on the side of its body, then the beast threw itself at Paul. He dodged, and the beast slammed into the cell behind him.

The cell's inmate, Bloodhound, grabbed the beast and started biting its flesh. Paul was awestruck at the sheer lunacy of the picture, but only for a moment. Then the beast suddenly *shifted*, and the part of its body that Bloodhound had been biting opened like a tote bag, peeling back and then flapping up again to envelope Bloodhound's head.

Paul screamed then as the thing pulled away with a crack and left Bloodhound's decapitated body behind. Paul shrieked again, backing away from the beast as fast as he could, when he slipped on something – blood, or perhaps the acid from the beast's earlier feedings. Whatever it was, Paul hit the railing with the small of his back, felt his world go topsy-turvy as he tipped back and then, so slowly it didn't seem real, fell over the edge of the gangplank.

He landed in a heap on the first floor, screaming as his ankle twisted below him. But he was up in a flash anyway, limping quickly over to the first cell he had opened and scooping up the second Molotov cocktail from the floor where he had stupidly left it. He headed to the tunnel...

And the beast landed in front of him. Snarling.

Even in the almost-dark of the prison, Paul could see the thing, *really see* it for the first time, and felt a kind of terror he had never experienced before. The thing was opaque, shifting, flowing, its semi-transparent skin allowing a view of alien organs within its body. Body parts from recent feedings – Bloodhound's head among them – could be seen in various stages of digestion within its now huge mass.

Paul stopped, his escape cut off. The beast laughed, a terrible, horrifying laugh, and the inmates were abruptly silent.

There was something in here that was even worse than them.

DOWN

Rachel reached out in the dark and grabbed hold of Becky, helping the little girl climb blindly out onto the ladder. "Okay, honey, we'll go down the ladder and get out of here, and we'll find Dr. Wiseman, okay?"

She felt rather than saw Becky's nod, and the little girl shifted carefully over to the ladder.

Then it happened.

A light flared, and Steiger was suddenly on top of her, grappling with her on the ladder.

Below her, Becky screamed.

"Go!" screamed Rachel. "Get away, Becky!"

"Yes," shouted Steiger, and laughed his strange, hyena laugh. "It's so much more fun when I get to chase you!"

DRENCHED

Paul watched death approach, and it was a hideous thing. The monster was still burning, pale blue flames dancing along it in ever shallower tides, then disappearing.

The Molotov hadn't killed it; had only made it angry. Paul felt despair take hold of him as the monster reared back to and then began its final rush.

Then, without thinking, Paul suddenly ripped the rag from the beer bottle...and poured the flammable liquid inside all over *himself*. He flicked Jorge's lighter, holding the flame out in front of his hands, which dripped with cleaning solution.

The monster stopped only inches away from him.

Standoff.

PUNCHED

Becky climbed down the ladder as fast as she could, small hands and feet moving unsurely in the dark, trying not to think of her mommy above her, struggling with the maniac.

She heard something, a strange "whoosh" and looked up to see the bad man - Steiger - punch her mother in the stomach. Her mother doubled over and made a throw-up sound, then Steiger shoved her away, back into the ventilation shaft, and began crawling down.

After Becky.

TORCH

Paul watched the cigarette lighter's tiny flame, careful not to set himself on fire, then slowly started backing toward the nearby monitor station.

The beast sprouted a dozen eyes of varying sizes and colors, watching Paul carefully, and stepping forward – or slithering forward, it didn't seem to have any legs – as Paul stepped back.

"Yeah," said Paul, hoping that the thing understood him, that enough of the inmate it had once been was there to render his speech comprehensible to it. "I know what you're thinking. You survived one fire already. But it hurt. Would you survive a human torch in your stomach?"

GRAVITY

Rachel felt the wind blast out of her; felt Steiger cast her away like a broken toy, and for a terrible moment was sure he had broken something inside her.

Then she heard Becky scream. "Mommy!"

The sound caused courage to well up within her, and new strength possessed her. She rocketed down the ladder after Steiger, a tigress protecting her cub. She didn't try anything fancy: there was too little space in the vertical shaft. She just dropped onto him as hard as she could.

One of the lunatic's hands popped off the ladder and now it was his turn to have the wind knocked out of him.

The hand falling away from the ladder gave her an idea. Rachel looked down and saw Becky. And below that...nothing. She couldn't see the bottom of the shaft. It went down to the first level, and below.

All the way to the basement, she thought.

"Go, Becky, go as fast as you can," she screamed, then locked her legs around Steiger's waist in a macabre parody of love-making. Then she grabbed the arm Steiger was still holding onto the ladder with. She bounced up and down, trying to loosen his grip. She felt a lurch, knew that what she was doing was working, and knocked into him again, crying at the same time, "Lean to the side, Becky, lean away!"

And then she felt a lurch as Steiger lost his grip and fell, fell, fell, and she was falling, too, and praying to God and the Holy Virgin and the saints that they wouldn't hit Becky, that she would have moved to the side and they would miss hitting her, hitting her poor little girl.

Her prayer worked. She felt herself fly past Becky, who was crying, and then felt something even better as she and Steiger twisted as they fell, still locked together in her dangerous embrace. Steiger was falling headfirst now, and she felt his head thud-thump on several of the rungs, then he went suddenly rigid and then loose and she knew he was unconscious.

Then his leg must have caught on something, because she heard a sharp, brittle crack. Suddenly Steiger was hanging upside down from something – the ladder most likely – and gravity yanked Rachel out of his grasp and she left him behind.

And kept falling.

ANTS

The inmates were still watching in silence as Paul continued the standoff. Either the beast heard him and understood, or it was too afraid of fire to move.

Then there *was* movement: a tiny tendril emerged from the beast. Paul tensed as it came close, remembering the drilled hole in Crane's forehead and the toothy mouths he had seen sprouting from the beast.

But there were no teeth this time, just a round tube, open and hollow.

Like a straw, Paul realized suddenly. But it was too late to pull back.

With a "whfff," a puff of air, dingy and fetid, emerged from the beast's improvised blow-hole.

It blew out the lighter.

"Shit," said Paul.

The beast charged.

He had no time to relight. No time to do anything other than act on instinct.

Paul dropped the lighter.

He threw himself backward over the monitoring station desk.

In midair, he reached out and flicked back the cover that protected the blue emergency release button.

He hit the button.

Once....

Twice....

Three times.

A klaxon sounded. And every door in the prison swung open.

The inmates charged, surrounding the monster as a prime target, apparently either forgetting about or uninterested in Paul for the moment. They surrounded the beast, like ants disregarding a lesser intrusion to fight off the main threat to their sick hive.

The monster swooped into action as well, growing toothy mouths, barbed tendrils that it lashed about like flails.

Now the maniacs were on the beast, gripping it, biting it, wounding it with hands and nails and mouths. The beast was wounded, but continually reformed, re-healed itself. It was a war, a war between two armies who would not surrender, not retreat. The men were attacking each other as well, their bloodlust venting on one another.

The place was a bloodbath, and Paul knew that, even though this was the only way any of the men could hope to survive, he would still carry the burden of so many deaths forever.

But at least this wasn't like Sammy. At least Paul hadn't pushed them to death. He had released them, and given them a chance. Not much of a chance, but at least they would die fighting, not locked in their cells like individually wrapped meals for the monster.

The thought was strangely comforting.

Now he just had to get away.

He stayed partially ducked under the monitoring desk, waiting for his moment, waiting until he thought no one was looking.

Now.

He ran, heading for the tunnel as fast as he could. He heard a shriek behind him, then several smaller shrieks. Paul dared a look back, and saw the monster swaying after him, several inmates holding to it and being dragged along in its deadly embrace. Inmate after inmate disappeared, trampled by the mass or killed by the monster or maimed by their own kind. It was a binge of death on all sides, and Paul was hard-pressed to run fast enough to stay ahead of it.

He looked back and to his horror and dismay saw that there were only perhaps two dozen men left alive; the others had all already been put down by the monster in their midst or by one another.

The beast reached for him, and Paul felt a tendril touch the back of his neck, felt agony as one of the tiny toothed mouths burrowed into him. Then there was another shriek as the beast was brought down from behind, brought down like a giant brought down by ants, inmates swarming over it and hacking at it, pulling at it.

But Paul knew the battle was already lost. The beast was going to win.

And it would come for him.

Paul ran, then slammed through the prison tunnel door.

He locked it behind him.

Then slid to the floor and wept.

CLIMBING

Becky could see her mother, lying crookedly twenty feet below.

She could also see her breathing. That was good.

The *reason* she could see her mother was bad: Steiger was between them, hanging upside down from the ladder in the shaft, a flashlight caught in his pants pocket and shining directly down on the still form of Becky's mom.

Becky would have to crawl over him to get to her mother.

She climbed down, slowly.

No movement from the man. He might be dead. She *hoped* he was dead, though she was ashamed of that hope and knew it was not a good thing to hope for. But she couldn't help herself.

She stopped right above his still form. Blood dripped off his head in a steady stream.

He could be dead.

What if he's not?

She decided to test him. She took off her Emergency Pack and dropped it. It hit Steiger's legs with a thunk, then fell the rest of the way down, landing by her mother's still form.

Steiger didn't move. Neither did her mother.

She crawled down closer and kicked him.

Still no movement.

She hitched in a deep breath, buried Mr. Huggles in her shirt where he would be safe, and then started to crawl over Steiger.

DEAD

Paul ran up the stairs to the second floor. He stopped, felt himself go weak when he saw Jorge's clear, sightless eyes, his head a mass of blood. For a moment Paul wondered if the man had been taken by the monster somehow. But no. No burn marks, and the monster didn't leave victims behind.

This had to be Steiger's work.

Paul clutched at himself, aching for the loss of his friend, but there was no time for grief. Only survival.

He grabbed Jorge's trank gun out of the guard's holster, then checked the barracks. Donald, Vincent, and Crane. All dead.

Things just kept getting better and better.

The girls, he thought, and began to run.

ETERNITY

Becky gritted her teeth and crawled over Steiger. She had to hold onto his clothes as much as she held onto the ladder. There was little room to do otherwise.

The moment in time where she had to touch him seemed to stretch out in her mind, like a hallway that went forever in both directions. Though only a short moment, she was crawling in eternity. A hellish infinity of terrified movement over a man that wanted her dead, and she sensed wanted her *worse* than dead, though she could not comprehend what that worse thing might be.

The moment stretched out. Agonized.

Steiger moved. It was just a twitch, but Becky screamed, then bit her lip so hard that blood flowed, an eerie analog of the blood that now flowed from Steiger's scalp.

Finally the infinite moment ended.

She was past Steiger.

But now she had to continue downward, into the depths of the building, and see if she could rouse her mother.

DOWNSTAIRS

Paul ran through the door to his office. Nothing.

Abandoning stealth, he started yelling as he ran through the door to Dr. Bryson's office.

"Rachel! Becky!"

Nothing.

He ran downstairs to search.

SCREWS

Something was slapping Rachel.

Steiger!

She woke with a start, instinctively holding her hands over her head, and almost hit her daughter. At the same time, a searing pain ran through her left arm and she realized it must be broken.

She looked up and saw Steiger's still form, hanging from above them. Unmoving. She began to cry, and cradled Becky in her good arm. She prayed, thanking every saint she could think of for delivering her daughter up to her.

When she opened her eyes, she realized there was a vent nearby. Probably to the basement. She crawled to it, pulling Becky with her as quickly as she could while moving on one ruined arm.

The vent was covered. And unlike the other vents, this one didn't have latches, it was stuck fast, probably screwed on.

Rachel bit back the hot, salty vinegar of tears that wanted to explode from her. She didn't want to scare her child. But it was hard. She hammered at the vent as hard as she could, the sound ringing through her concussed skull like hammer blows on an anvil, but to no avail.

The vent remained unmoving.

Then, suddenly, it pulled off. Rachel *did* scream this time, a frightened yelp as something tore the thing from its hinges.

The scream died on her lips as she saw who it was.

Paul.

"Thank God," he said, and reached out a hand to help them out.

SMART

Paul had heard the banging in the basement and gone to check on it. Lucky thing he had. Now he helped Rachel and Becky out of the air conditioning duct.

"How did you –" he began, but was interrupted.

"We need to go. Now," said Rachel. "Steiger's in there," she said.

"Alive?" asked Paul.

"I don't think so, but I'd rather not stick around to find out." Then, apparently noticing Paul's appearance, she said, "What happened to you?"

"I ran into…whatever it was. Crane's toy." Paul paused, trying to find the words. "I found Jorge. He's…*everyone* is…." The words petered out, unspoken.

Rachel nodded as though she had known that everyone else was gone already, and touched his arm softly.

"We're still alive," she whispered, as if that had to be enough.

And strangely, it *was* enough. Enough for now, at any rate. Grieving would come later, perhaps, but for now Paul was satisfied that Rachel and Becky were alive and relatively whole. The next job was to keep them that way.

Paul looked around. There was no dearth of makeshift weaponry in the basement, but he doubted very much that any of the tools would avail him against Crane's creation.

And when Rachel said, "I don't think I can keep going much longer," Paul's heart dropped. He couldn't fail them, not now.

Tools, cleaning supplies, the bulky heater, some medical kits, a few odds and ends...nothing.

But wait.

Paul felt his pockets. "The lighter. Where's the lighter?"

It was gone, and once again Paul's heart sank.

Then he felt a tapping at his arm. It was Becky, holding a pair of road flares up to him, her Emergency Pack open. "Mommy gave me these. They're like a lighter, right?"

Paul took the flares, then hugged Becky. She didn't shy away.

"Honey," he said, "you are one smart kid."

He smiled at Rachel, and she smiled back in spite of her pain and clearly broken arm.

"What are we going to do?" she asked.

"I don't think we can keep going any longer," answered Paul. "If either Steiger or that thing get loose, they'll get us. So we've got to leave...and make sure they can't follow"

"How?" asked Rachel.

Paul looked at the gas heater. "I'm going to break a gas main and blow this place up."

"What about the other men? The prisoners?"

Paul didn't answer, but felt himself grow weary and sad. Apparently that told Rachel what she needed to know, for she said, "Oh," in a soft voice and didn't ask again. Then her brow furrowed. "If we blow this place up, how will we survive in the storm?" she asked.

"Trust me," he said.

He saw her brow furrow, and could only imagine what she was thinking. *Trust* him? A strange man? Doubtful. But she finally nodded.

Paul felt warm inside for the first time since waking up that morning.

AWAKE

Steiger's eyes opened. He was upside down.

He heard voices. The sound of a man's voice. And the voice of a beautiful woman and a lovely angelic girl's voice.

He loved angels. He would love this one.

He began to move.

REMEMBERING

Paul watched as Becky helped Rachel to the stairs, the little girl serving as a brace to the young mother, who tottered like an bedridden centenarian who was being allowed one last walk.

As soon as they got to the stairwell, Paul took the crowbar he had found and used it to pry loose the gas line leading into the heater. Immediately he heard the hiss of escaping gas.

He put the crowbar down – carefully, didn't want any sparks – and moved to the girls, taking over as Rachel's helper, Becky close behind.

They got to the top of the stairs together. Paul looked at the door to the prison tunnel. It was shut. No movement. He hoped the monster was still in there.

"How long do we have?" asked Rachel.

In answer, Paul lit one of the flares and dropped it on the top step of the stairs. "I was going to just light some trash down in the basement, but this is better. Gives us longer. Gas'll saturate the place and make sure it all goes up."

At that moment a ghastly, inhuman wail echoed through The Loon. The sound of something mad, and lonely, and hungering for flesh.

"It's coming," said Becky.

They walked past the staff break room, and it felt like a million years ago that Paul had first met Jacky Hales, though he knew it had only been twenty hours or so. A lifetime of fear and terror had happened since then. Strangely, though, Paul wasn't as sad as he had thought he would be. Perhaps it was just the fact that he was still alive, maybe it was because of Rachel, warm beside him, her arm around his neck as he helped her. For whatever reason, though, the cold of the storm outside no longer seeped into his bones, no longer made him feel chilled as a corpse.

He felt alive.

He tossed the second flame onto the couch in the break room, watching the couch alight.

"What's that for?" asked Rachel.

"In case Steiger or Crane's pet finds the other flare and puts it out." He took one more look into the break room, now filled with smoke, then said, "Let's go."

They went to the lobby, and Paul grabbed a parka off the rack for each of them, even Becky, who was almost swimming in hers. Then he opened the front door. Wind whistled in. They went through the door.

GRABBED

The wind hit them hard. But Paul felt like it had perhaps lessened a bit; as though the worst of the storm had passed. That was good.

Even so, it was too much for Rachel. She hit the snow, took a single step, and then fell forward with a cry of pain. Paul knelt to help her stand, but she waved him away, despair and agony writ large across her face.

"No time for naps," Paul said, and noticed happily that the wind had died down enough that he didn't have to shout to be heard. "We gotta go!"

Rachel looked like she was about to say something, but there was a sudden shriek, and she and Paul both looked around in time to see Steiger yank Becky inside The Loon.

The door shut behind them.

SNAPPED

Steiger held the suddenly screaming child with one hand while he put a key – which Hip-Hop had helpfully marked "entrance" before his demise – into the lock. He turned it, then snapped the key off.

He didn't want any interruptions for the next little bit.

GIRLS

Paul tried to get the key in the lock, but it wouldn't go.

Beside him, Rachel was frantic. She felt in her own pocket, drawing out a pair of keys. "What about these?" she asked.

Paul looked at the keys then discounted them almost instantly. "No, those are the keys to Vincent's truck," he answered. Then stopped. "Come on," he said, and grabbed Rachel's arm.

"No!" she screamed. "What about Becky?"

"It's okay," he said. "She'll be all right for a little while."

"He'll kill her!"

"Steiger doesn't kill little girls," said Paul, and the cold that had left him earlier was now deep within his bones. "Not right away."

He saw Rachel's face go bleached white. "God, no," she whispered.

DEATH

Steiger wrestled with the struggling little girl. This was almost too much fun.

He threw her bodily into one of the chairs behind the security station, then held her until she stopped screaming. "I'm not going to hurt you!" he shouted. "You're my angel."

Becky kept struggling for another moment, but Steiger felt her grow tired and slowly her muscles stopped shaking. He loosened his grip on her, but didn't let her go. "That's better," he said. "If you'd gone out there, you would have frozen to death. I couldn't have that on my conscience. You believe me, don't you?"

"Yes, sir," mumbled Becky.

Good girl, smart girl, thought Steiger. My angelic little girl.

"Good, good," he said aloud, and stroked her cheek. Gently. Lovingly. "Poor thing," he added. "You need rest. Why don't I take you upstairs and put you to bed?"

Becky nodded meekly, and Steiger smiled at her again, letting her go. He held out his hand. She reached out to take it...then the little bitch kicked him in the mouth and ran for the front door.

Steiger felt a tooth come loose, then turned slowly to where she was scrabbling against the broken door, trying in vain to get out. "I'm afraid not, my precious, my little angel bitch." He chuckled and spit blood on the floor.

"Now, you really ought to be getting to bed."

She kept struggling with the door as Steiger approached her, the little girl so amusing in her feeble attempts to escape. She couldn't escape. The universe was on Steiger's side, and that was too much power for anyone to withstand him long.

At last Becky turned toward him...and shrieked.

Steiger laughed, thinking that the beautiful little girl was screaming because of him, then realized that she wasn't looking *at* him, but *behind* him.

He spun around, and came face to face with the devil itself. A molten mass of motley flesh that spun and whirled, a gigantic fleshy thing that had no head, then two heads, then an arm where a head should be.

Steiger shined his flashlight on the thing, and it shrieked. Steiger smiled. "Hello, playtime," he said, and stood between it and Becky. "You can't have her. This angel is mine."

He threw himself at the devil, letting himself go to a place he rarely indulged: the complete surrender of self to the wave of insanity on which he constantly rode. He grabbed a first aid kit from a nearby wall and used it to batter at the beast. The thing shrieked and wailed, and something...exploded out of it, grabbing the kit like a huge hand and hurling it at a wall, where it exploded into small pieces.

Steiger switched on his flashlight, wielding it like a club, laughing as the beast screamed.

The light, he realized. The devil can't stand the light.

He began shining the light at it, staying away from the thing's reach, from the grasping hands that were there one moment and gone the next, laughing all the while.

The mindless cackle turned to a stunned shriek, though, as a vine-like appendage sprung from the demon's body. It hit the flashlight. Hard.

Steiger felt a strange jarring.

He looked down.

The flashlight had been rammed back. Straight through him. He was reminded of a comic book he had read once, before they stopped letting him have books. A hero named Iron Man, who had a brightly lit nuclear power source embedded in his chest, always alight with a pale blue glow.

Steiger was no Iron Man. The flashlight had impaled him.

"But...the universe is on my side," he said plaintively, and then the darkness took him.

SUPERGIRL

Becky saw the thing somehow punch a hole in Steiger, and ran as far from it as possible. She cringed in the corner of the room, screaming, holding her hands partially over her eyes, too frightened to look at what came next but equally terrified of not seeing what was nearby.

The monster reared up as Steiger fell and roared triumphantly. Becky knew she would never be afraid of someone like her daddy again. Not after this. If she made it through this she would be a Supergirl, not afraid of anything.

But she didn't think she was going to make it through this. No Supergirl. Nothing.

The monster moved toward her. It reached the center of the room.

It roared again....

And then the world exploded.

FLAME

Paul felt Vince's truck pitch sideways as he crashed it through the wall, and caught the briefest glimpse of Crane's pet as the truck hurtled into it and through it, splashing dark ichor and body mass all over the front of the truck before the airbag deployed and he couldn't see anything.

He got out of the truck and heard the other door swing open as Rachel got out of the other side. For a minute outside he had been afraid that the truck wouldn't start, and once it *had* started he had been worried that it wouldn't have enough traction to break free of the snow that held it in an icy grip, but both fears had proven unfounded.

Now he looked at the beast, which was half-splashed across the hood, half pinned between the truck and the wrecked wall that had once led into Crane's office but which had now largely disintegrated. The monster wasn't moving. He hoped it was dead.

"Becky!" cried Rachel from the other side of the truck. Paul ran as fast as he could, leaping over debris to see the young mother straining to lift a piece of wood from off of something.

A small hand.

"No, no, no!" screamed Paul. He had done it again; had killed the child he was trying to save.

He pushed Rachel aside, then threw the detritus off of Becky. He forgot all his medical training for a moment...

(Please don't be dead, don't die, not again Sammy, not again…)

…and lifted her into his arms. "Don't be dead," he whispered. "Don't be dead, don't be. Oh, please, honey, not like Sammy, please." He felt at her neck for a pulse.

"Anything?" asked Rachel, one arm limp and the other reaching for her daughter.

"I can't tell," said Paul. "I can't. Please, honey, please."

Paul felt the enormity of the destruction he had wrought crash down on him like the wall that had crashed down on Becky. He felt himself drowning in a sea of death. Jacky. Darryl. Mitchell. All the guards. All the inmates.

Sammy.

It was too much, too much. He felt himself surrendering to the abyss of death that surrounded his life, then heard as from far away a voice asking, "Please, Dr. Whiteman, please check again," and realized that the girl's mother was pleading for him to save her.

Paul touched Becky's neck…and at that moment the girl coughed and began to cry.

He clung to the sound like a dying man to a life preserver. "Cry, baby," he said joyously, and felt like he was talking to Sammy again, talking to an angel who had never left him alone, not for a second. "Cry, Becky."

All was right. All was good.

They were safe.

And then he saw the beast move.

STAIR

On the top of the stairs that led to the basement, the flare that Paul had dropped sputtered and burned brighter as the first trace molecules of gas made their way up to the first floor.

The flare kissed the gas, and grew brighter for it.

Soon the fire and the gas would join completely and utterly, and The Loon would be but a memory.

GO

Paul watched in abject horror as the beast began to reform, pushing itself like animated Silly Putty over the hood of the truck, then laying in a loose puddle before it began to rise.

Paul thrust Becky into Rachel's one good arm. Rachel moaned in pain, but he couldn't spare a thought for that right now.

"Go," he said. "Get to the generator shack!"

"What about you?" said Rachel fearfully.

"It'll follow you out there if it doesn't have something to keep it busy," he said. And he kissed her. Not the kiss of lovers on a moonlit eve, but the kiss of friends, of partners in terror that would forever lash them together.

As long as forever lasted, which for them might not be very long at all.

"I don't want to leave you!" said Rachel.

"Go!" screamed Paul, and shoved her away just as the beast started to lunge at him.

Rachel ran with Becky into the snow. The monster started lurching after them, but Paul kicked it. "Hey!" he shouted. "Pick on someone your own size!"

It was a lame line, right out of a cartoon or a terrible made for TV movie, but it worked: a dozen seeping eyes erupted like blisters and stared at Paul for an instant, and then the beast lurched after *him*.

PURSUIT

Paul ran into Crane's office.

He heard a snapping noise and a searing pain gripped his right buttock. He looked down and saw a pseudopod there, hungrily gnawing at him with buzzsaw-like teeth. Paul screamed and yanked the thing out of him and then kept running.

He limped through the door to Crane's first floor living area, hearing the ponderous beast – large from its gorging in the prison – lumbering after him, only feet away.

He ran through Crane's makeshift living quarters. Ran to the secret door that he had come through earlier with Jorge.

The door was stuck. The truck must have shifted the walls enough to jam it when it crashed into the lobby.

Paul turned around. The monster was *right there*.

It hissed, and a pair of toothy mouths opened in wide, hungry smiles.

Paul didn't mind dying, he found. But he hoped that the gas would blow before the creature got to him. Otherwise he would have failed to save Rachel and Becky, just as he had failed Sammy.

The monster reared back for its final strike.

And Steiger erupted from behind it. Paul was shocked at the man's appearance, and at the fact that he had a flashlight sticking out of him. The man should be dead, but madness gave him strength.

"I'll kill you, demon," Steiger shouted. "You can't kill me, devil, I serve the universe!" And with that, Steiger knocked into the beast, body-checking it and pushing it over.

Time slowed.

Steiger and the beast fell, the beast below the madman.

As soon as they hit the floor, the beast's shape lost whatever traces of cohesion it might have had. It turned into a loose jelly, a gel that Steiger hit...and sank into. The madman shrieked, then the shriek became a gurgle as he disappeared into the monster's body.

Sizzling. Paul heard sizzling and smelled an acrid, ammonia-like smell.

Silence.

The monster began to reform.

Paul turned and slammed into the door to Crane's secret lab as hard as he could. Panicked strength surged through him, and the door caved in.

He ran down the stairs. Through the lab.

The door in the lab that led to the secret passage to the generator shack had a dead bolt on the outside. Once through, Paul clicked it shut.

He heard the beast screaming, and immediately the door started sizzling; *melting*. And bits of flesh started to push through the cracks around the door. It was still coming at him.

"Can't...you...just...*die!*" he screamed, and ran again.

EXPLOSION

The flare was still burning, crackling over the hiss of escaping gas.

The gas finally crawled up the stairs.

WHOOSH!

Flame shot through the rooms of The Loon like a living thing, a terrible thing that would bring destruction to anything in its path.

SHACK

Rachel got to the wrecked shack, still holding onto Becky, just as a dull WHUMP sounded behind them. She turned and saw flame gouting from the second story windows of The Loon, and felt tears run down her face.

"Paul," she whispered.

FLAME

Paul heard the explosion and ran for all he was worth down the tunnel.

He heard screaming, but did not look back. Not until the screaming grew louder. *Then* he looked back.

And wished he hadn't.

Fire was rushing down the tunnel, straight at him, ready to overtake him in seconds.

And in front of the fire...was the beast. Laughing an insane, wheezing laugh out of many different mouths, sounding like a legion of devils, a chorus of demons as it burned from behind and ran after its prey in front.

Tongues of fire licked at Paul's heels, partially overtaking him as he lurched up the stairs. He went through the door to the generator stairs and ran up, falling on the floor only moments before a gout of flame was vomited forth from the passageway.

The beast erupted from the flames. Still burning. Burning and dying. But not yet dead. And it wanted to take him with it, Paul could tell.

He was tempted to just lay there and let it happen. He was so tired. He missed Sammy. He had done his best.

Then someone yelled, "Paul! Move!"

It was Rachel. The sound made him reach deep into himself to find a strength he had not been aware of. He stood, the beast burning and panting in front of him and gathering itself to make a final lunge that would overtake and engulf him.

Then he spotted something: the gas cans that were used to fuel the generator. One of them was sitting at his feet, knocked over during one of the many struggles that had taken place here during the night.

He grabbed it and swung around, throwing it at the beast.

As it had done with Steiger, the beast did not move or attempt to dodge, but rather just engulfed the object. But it hesitated then, probably not liking the belly full of gasoline inside it. Paul ran at the thing, and said grimly, "Time to die," before launching at it, spinning his feet up in a flying kick that was awkward but nevertheless managed to push the beast back.

It teetered on the edge of the stairs that led down to the secret tunnel, where flames still burned.

Paul raced to the girls, grabbing one of them by each arm and pulling them out into the snow.

He turned his head.

The beast fell.

Another explosion.

And it was gone.

EPILOGUE:
REUNION

This is how the man found a family.

They were together in a snowstorm, a storm that surely would have frozen them alive were it not for the massive flames that surrounded them and kept them warm. State troopers, summoned by the explosion and the brightness of the blaze, came soon, and picked them up in vehicles that took them together to a hospital, where they stayed in one room together and recuperated and told their story to journalists until they were too tired to go on and asked to be alone.

The man lay in a bed, and so did the woman, and every once in a while he would reach out and she would reach out and they would hold hands. The lights in the hospital shone brightly around them, surrounding them with halo-glows. They smiled together. They also cried together over friends lost. But the smiles were more present, and more often apparent.

Outside, a storm still raged, but it was a new storm, and not nearly as bad as the one that had brought them together. It was a perfect winter storm, with lace doily snowflakes and warm linens and warmer herb teas that the nursing staff brought to them regularly while they stayed.

Nearby them, always nearby, a little girl sat and read from various picture books purchased at the hospital gift shop.

Sometimes she would read aloud, and the man would laugh in delight at her beautiful little girl voice and her smile. He loved her. He loved them both, and they loved him back.

How could some people say there is no God? he wondered.

And had no answer.

Acknowledgments

There are far too many people for me to properly thank here. Suffice it to say that if you know me, I probably owe you thanks...for putting up with me if nothing else.

Special recognition, however, must go to my father, Dr. Michael Collings. In addition to being my first and best writing teacher, he also supplied the wonderfully evocative poetry in the beginning of each part of this book.

"Visitor by Starlight," "...Is Death," "'Night's Plutonian Shore,'" and "In the House Beyond the Field" all come from his book of poetry entitled *In the Void: Poems of Science Fiction, Myth and Fantasy, and Horror* (Borgo Press/Wildside Press, 2009); "Secret Shadow (from Aiken's 'Silent Snow, Secret Snow')" comes from *Naked to the Sun: Dark Visions of Apocalypse* (Starmont House, 1985); and "Christmas in Elba" and "The Little That it Takes" are as yet unpublished but I have no doubt they will eventually find homes. As a "plain-ol' poet" (i.e., someone who writes *understandably* as well as "correctly"), my father has always been a source of inspiration to me. I urge you to check out his books, which are available at amazon.com and wildsidepress.com.

ABOUT THE AUTHOR

Michaelbrent Collings is an award-winning screenwriter and novelist. He has written numerous bestselling novels, including *Apparition, The Loon, Billy: Messenger of Powers, Rising Fears,* and the #1 Bestseller *RUN.* Follow him on Facebook or on Twitter @mbcollings.

Made in the USA
Middletown, DE
10 July 2020